Shark Island

Also by Joan Druett

Joan Druett

Shark Island

ST. MARTIN'S MINOTAUR ⚏ NEW YORK

www.minotaurbooks.com

Library of Congress Cataloging-in-Publication Data

Druett, Joan.
    Shark Island / Joan Druett.
       p. cm.
    ISBN-13: 978-0-312-36147-1
    ISBN-10: 0-312-36147-5
    1. United States Exploring Expedition (1838–1842)—Fiction. 2. Ship captains—Crimes against—Fiction. 3. Americans—Foreign countries—Fiction. 4. Discoveries in geography—Fiction. 5. Scientific expeditions—Fiction. 6. Shipwrecks—Fiction. 7. Explorers—Fiction. 8. Linguists—Fiction. I. Title.
PR9639.3.D68S53 2005
823'.914—dc22

                                      2005046509

First St. Martin's Minotaur Paperback Edition: October 2006

10 9 8 7 6 5 4 3 2 1

For Steve
Take care, bro.

Author's Note

On Sunday, August 18, 1838, the six ships of the first, great United States South Seas Exploring Expedition, commanded by Lieutenant Charles Wilkes, crewed by 246 officers and men, and with seven scientists and two artists on board, set sail from the Hampton Roads, Virginia, headed for the far side of the world. Almost four years later, in June 1842, the remnants of the expedition straggled into New York. One vessel had been sent back in disgrace; one had been lost with all hands; another had been wrecked at the Columbia River; and a fourth had been sold into the opium-running trade on the coast of China. Much had been accomplished—huge tracts of the ocean had been charted, plus 800 miles of scarcely known Oregon shore and 1,500 miles of entirely unknown Antarctic coast. The Stars and Stripes had fluttered off the lagoons of well over 200 tropical islands, and more than 4,000 artifacts and 2,000 scientific specimens had been collected, an enormously rich fund that became the foundation of the collection of the new Smithsonian Institution. For uncounted thousands of Pacific Islanders the Exploring Expedition had been their first introduction to the official face of the

USA. Yet, instead of returning home in triumph, Lieutenant Wilkes chose to slink on shore by hitching a ride on the pilot boat.

The strange voyage of the U.S. Exploring Expedition is the setting of the Wiki Coffin mystery series. While the novels are based on true events, and many of the participants in the stories are real, the mysteries and the people most intimately involved with them are figments of the author's overactive imagination—as is the brig *Swallow*, the seventh ship upon which most of the action takes place.

Shark Island

One

Atlantic Ocean, October 1838

The hours were dragging. After watching the boat carry Forsythe from the brig *Swallow* to the expedition flagship *Vincennes*, Wiki Coffin had waited at the taffrail for a very long time. Now, however, patience had fled, and so he paced nervously up and down the quarterdeck of the *Swallow*, while foreboding coiled inside him.

It had been dawn when Forsythe had departed, and the misty air had been relatively cool. Steam had risen lazily from newly swabbed decks as the five boats from the different ships had converged on the *Vincennes* in response to Wilkes's urgent summons for a council of war. The distant sounds of marines stamping to attention and the boatswain's piping had echoed with uncanny clarity as the five junior captains had clambered up the side of the flagship and vanished through the doorway of the lofty house on the poop.

Another flurry of activity had followed as the boats had returned to their respective ships, but since then there had been no movement on the water.

Now it was almost noon, and the hot sun was high in the sky. The ships lay quiet and still on top of their rippling reflection—the two big sloops *Vincennes* and *Peacock,* the gun brig *Porpoise,* the schooners *Flying Fish* and *Sea Gull,* and the ex-privateer brig *Swallow*. The seventh member of the discovery fleet, the storeship *Relief*, had been sent ahead long since, as she had sailed so badly that she was retarding the progress of the rest all the time she was with them; with luck, they would meet up with her again in a few weeks' time. On the *Swallow,* caulking of the deck boards was shrinking in the heat, and the acrid smell of warm tar rose up so strongly it was almost visible as Wiki paced from one rail to another. Because Forsythe's second-in-command, Lawrence J. Smith, was still on board, he was wearing boots as part of his effort to keep peace with the self-important little man. Lieutenant Smith had no authority over him, Wiki being the expedition translator and therefore a civilian, but Wiki knew perfectly well that the pompous officer would have sniffed and carped if his feet were as bare as those of any common sailor. However, he still wished he could shuck the hot footwear.

At long last, just as pipes shrilled to the tune of "Nancy Dawson" and the usual stampede for the morning ration of grog began, there was movement in the distant doorway of the house on the *Vincennes*. The tall, distinctive figure of Charles Wilkes, the expedition commander, came out on deck first, to be followed by the rest in a huddle. Signals jerked up the far-off lanyard, ordering the various ships to send boats for their captains. Behind Wiki, Lieutenant Smith raised his voice, but blocks were squealing already as the men anticipated his orders and the *Swallow* boat was lowered. Wiki leaned over and watched as it went down. The splash as it hit water was too much to resist—he gave way to impatience and vaulted over the rail, landing on his feet in the bottom of the boat.

When he looked up after settling in the stern thwarts, Lieutenant Smith's face was peering back down at him, flushed red with affront. "Wiremu," he barked, using his peculiarly irritating version of Wiki's name. "Mr. Coffin, sir! What do you think you are about? I do not believe I heard a request for your presence on the flagship."

Wiki simply lifted his hand in a silent salute. As the six men of the *Swallow* boat's crew took up their oars they wore broad approving grins, but he disregarded that, too, staring tensely forward as the boat surged rhythmically across the stretch of water that divided them from the *Vincennes*. He was desperate to know if his friend George Rochester, who had been unfairly demoted to the rank of midshipman on the *Vincennes* some weeks earlier, had been restored to the command of the *Swallow*. If not, Wiki—who had never wanted to be part of the exploring expedition in the first place, and had only consented to come because it was a chance to be on the same ship as his old comrade—was determined to jump ship at the next port the fleet touched.

The stern of the boat clicked against the hull of the *Vincennes*, and the man at bow oar reached out and snatched a dangling rope. The boat swung round with the momentum, coming side-on, and then stilled. The instant it was steady Wiki stood up, grabbed the leading edges of planks, and began to climb. Halfway up the side, it crossed his mind that while he didn't care a jot about Lawrence J. Smith's opinion, Captain Wilkes was a much more daunting proposition. Not only was he suddenly glad he was wearing boots, but he rather wished he had lashed up his long black hair, particularly when he arrived on deck and the squad of marines on duty stamped loudly to attention.

These soldiers were bravely sporting crimson coats—yet another sign of the general disaffection within the fleet, which was something that had been obvious long before the ships had sailed from Norfolk, Virginia, in August. Over the past ten years, ever since Congress had first voted to dispatch a body of explorers to the Pacific, the enterprise had stumbled along so badly that it had become known as "the deplorable expedition," and the men assigned to that expedition had felt the general scorn very deeply. Years had dragged by while the administration and the navy battled and the sailors and marines had waited around in growing frustration. Many of them had been unwelcome guests in the Norfolk Navy Yard, on board "that great ship of the line, the venerable *Constitution*"—as the newspaper reporters grandly phrased it—and had become the butt of coarse humor.

Naturally, they had taken every chance to express their disgust and disenchantment, and one of the most flamboyant mutinies had been staged by the marines. When ordered to get newfangled uniforms—uniforms that Congress expected them to pay for themselves!—they had simply pointed out that it hadn't even yet been decided what the uniform of the U.S. Marine Corps should actually be, official opinion swinging through shades of gray to hues of blue (though some of the nabobs in Washington favored a peculiarly seasick shade of olive green), and had staunchly refused to exchange their old-fashioned red jackets for anything more recent. Informed that only musicians were legally entitled to wear scarlet coats, they had all instantly taken up the drum and the fife, with the result that the *Vincennes* was the most discordant ship on the seven seas. Right now, the boatswain refused to pipe Mr. Coffin on board, Wiki Coffin being a mere civilian and a Kanaka native of some Pacific island, at that, so one of the most daring of the red-coated rebels jauntily whistled a couple of notes on his fife.

Swinging round at the sound, Captain Wilkes exclaimed, "Wiki Coffin! What brings you here?"

Wiki didn't answer. He had just clapped eyes on George Rochester, who was standing at the back of the group of captains, his face stretched wide with an enormous grin. Forsythe was also there, but looking moody and sardonic, and so Wiki deduced with a surge of joy that the command of the *Swallow* had been restored to George. Accordingly, he wasn't paying proper attention.

"How did you guess I wanted to see you?" Captain Wilkes demanded. "However, I'm glad you came," he went on without waiting for a reply. "A small conference, if you please!"

Wiki ducked his head, doing his best to hide his astonishment. The day before, when he'd done his utmost to explain a series of horrid murders that had sullied the first few weeks of voyage, Wilkes had been in a state of hysterical panic. Indeed, the sensational revelations had brought the expedition commander so close to a nervous collapse that Wiki wondered why he wanted to risk a repetition. Silently, however, he followed him into the big after house that had been built on the poop of the flagship.

A white-painted, lofty corridor divided the first part of the house into two halves. On the larboard side there was a series of varnished doors, which Wiki knew led to cabins for Wilkes himself, plus the four scientifics who lived on board the *Vincennes*, while on the starboard side a spindled partition partly hid a large dining saloon, which smelled of coffee and ham. Casters of crystal glasses hung high in the skylight above the big oblong mess table that took up much of the space, casting iridescent glitters with the slight sway of the ship. The revolving chairs screwed to the floor were turned every which way, just as the diners had left them, while a steward was gathering up dirty dishes and mugs, so Wiki gathered that this had been where Captain Wilkes had held his council of war. However, the commander kept on going, heading for the big room at the end of the passage, which was full of bookshelves and drafting tables, and lit with another skylight. It was here in this wonderfully well lit, high-ceilinged place that the scientifics worked, and the shelves were packed with jars and boxes of specimens as well as books. Right now, however, the room was vacant.

Captain Wilkes strode over to a desk, and sat down at it, facing Wiki, who remained standing, not having been offered a seat. For long minutes Wilkes didn't speak, picking up a pencil and watching it as he rolled it between his fingers instead. The sonorous tick of a chronometer punctuated the heavy silence, and when Wiki shifted uneasily his right boot let out a loud, embarrassing squeak.

When Captain Wilkes looked up at last his narrow face was pale and fraught, his large, dark, intelligent eyes unfocused. As always, his full mouth was tipped into a constant small, artificial smile, but today it looked more like a painful grimace. Looking somewhere above Wiki's head instead of meeting his inquiring gaze, he said abruptly, "I have a mission for you."

"Aye, sir?"

"I'm sending you to an island off the northeast coast of Brazil. I want it checked out, and you're the best man for the job. Go there, investigate, and report back to me."

Wiki blinked. As the expedition's "linguister"—translator—he spoke Portuguese, but he hadn't expected to use the language until they dropped anchor in Rio de Janeiro, where they were headed after the job of charting reported shoals in this part of the Atlantic was finished.

He said cautiously, "Investigate what, sir?"

"Pirates—*pirates*! Captain Hudson strongly suspects that this island harbors a nest of buccaneers—which poses a danger because the island overlooks our route to Rio. I want his report checked out—and you're the best man to do it, being one of *them,* as it were."

Wiki said blankly, "I beg your pardon, sir?"

"I can think of no one more qualified to decide if they are likely to attack the expedition—by stealth, when we least expect them. Not only do you speak Portuguese, but 'Set a thief to catch a thief'—or so the saying goes—and don't your people make a custom of cutting out ships? I've heard of infamous cases where whole crews were barbarically slaughtered by pirates in New Zealand, the ships looted and then burned while the victors feasted on the bodies of the slain—and I am sure that even Brazilians have heard of this, too."

Wiki shook his head in utter bemusement. He had often been puzzled by the strange processes of *pakeha* logic, but this was particularly baffling. He felt intrigued as well, though. The day before, the sloop *Peacock* had rejoined the fleet flying urgent signals, and since then her commander, William Hudson, had spent hours closeted in conference with Captain Wilkes. Rumors had flown about in abundance, but Wiki had heard nothing as dramatic as this. *Pirates?* He wondered why the devil Captain Hudson hadn't handled the problem himself—for, after all, the *Peacock* was a sloop of *war,* and while she didn't carry anything near her usual armament, she did have eight assorted cannon.

He ventured, "Is Captain Hudson absolutely certain they are pirates, sir?"

"It's difficult to decide what else they could be," Wilkes snapped. "According to the charts the island is uninhabited, but cannon were aimed at the *Peacock* from a fortification on a headland, and Captain Hudson's lookouts swore they spied vessels on the beach below."

Wiki thought about it. Ever since her humiliating defeat by the

Argentineans in 1827, Brazil had been in a ferment of revolt and rebellion. The country had been ruled by a succession of unpopular regents, giving unruly elements of the population all kinds of reasons for raising hell. It was perfectly credible that a revolutionary group should have taken over an uninhabited island near the coast, so he said, "Insurgents, perhaps?"

"*Warlike* insurgents, then," Captain Wilkes retorted.

"Captain Hudson didn't send in a party to investigate, sir?"

"The island lies in uncharted shoals—and the *Peacock*'s timbers are tender. It was just last year that she was almost battered to pieces at the mouth of the Persian Gulf—and did the navy yard repair her properly? *No, they bloody well did not!*"

Captain Wilkes's voice had risen, and his face flushed red with rage, while Wiki watched him in alarm. It was common knowledge that the constant delays, hostility in the navy yard, and the petty parsimony of the administration had vexed the expedition's commander sorely, so everyone was used to his testiness on the issue. However, whispers about his nervous state were flying about the fleet; one of the other scientifics had confided that when he had accidentally dropped a jar in his stateroom while Captain Wilkes was trying to rest in his cabin next door, the commander's incoherent rage had been frightening.

"It's just one more problem to add to my troubles!" Wilkes exclaimed. "It's just two months since we left the shores of home, and yet I feel as if there is a year's worth of burden on my shoulders already!" Then his stare focused on Wiki's face again, and he demanded, "Did you read what the editor of the Norfolk newspaper had the *sauce* to publish on the eve of the expedition's departure?"

Wiki had read the newspaper every day that he was in Norfolk, and thought that he remembered the editorial quite well, but warily shook his head.

"The editor of the *Norfolk Beacon* published his strong opinion that the organization of the expedition had been a disaster, and that only with strict discipline would good come out of evil, and honor out of shame. And the editor was *right*! The management of the exploring expedition has been a disgrace to the navy and those who direct its councils! The whole process has been deeply marked by both evil and dishonor—on the part of those in the corridors of power! *I've* done nothing wrong and *will* accomplish a great deal to the glory of my country, but *all* my efforts will go unrewarded—as unrecognized as ever!"

Sweat was beading on his upper lip, and he was going red and white by turns, while he rubbed his forehead as if in terrible pain. Wiki looked about desperately, hoping that someone—the steward, perhaps—would come to investigate, but there were no steps in the passage, and no one tapped on the door.

He said as calmly and reassuringly as he could, "I honestly believe that without your efforts the expedition would never have got to sea. You have accomplished a great deal, sir."

He was speaking nothing less than the truth. Captain Wilkes had never faltered in the challenge of choosing scientifics and officers and organizing the departure of the expedition; he had demonstrated a faith and optimism that the past two months of voyage had justified. A great deal of scientific data had been collected. Huge tracts of the Atlantic had been surveyed, and charts corrected. Currents had been tracked. There had been storms and squalls; twice the fleet had been scattered, and with difficulty had been assembled again, but throughout it all—and despite those ghastly murders—the job had been done. Wiki had often heard Rochester declare that Captain Wilkes was conceited, ambitious, and arrogant, but his own opinion was that there was dedication and intelligence there, too.

"Indeed, I have," the commander agreed, his face flushed with gratification. "And I will accomplish a great deal more, including an assault on the last great *unknown* continent—despite the difficulties *they* put in my way!"

Wiki concealed a grimace, because he shouldn't have been hearing this. Officially, no one save Captain Wilkes himself knew where the expedition would steer, though every sailor who dipped his mug into the scuttlebutt of fresh water by the foremast—the place where seamen traditionally gossiped—was perfectly aware that one of the goals of the exploring expedition was the formal discovery of the Antarctic continent.

He said in a neutral voice, "That would be wonderful, sir."

"You're right! It *should* be an American discovery, by right of history! And yet the *French* could easily get there first."

"The French?" Wiki echoed blankly. It was the first he had heard of it.

"Aye, the goddamned *French*! Dumont D'Urville sailed as long ago as September last year—with a well-equipped expedition of two corvettes, assembled in less than six months while our own project was dying of inertia! And, by God, if they do get there before me, who will be blamed? *Me!* I'll be the laugh of Washington! But if by some miracle this expedition *does* beat the Frenchmen to the official discovery of the continent, the glory will go to the navy and the nabobs, not to the person who truly deserves it! Did you know that the men are constantly restless?" Wilkes demanded with an abrupt change of subject. "That there was a mutiny on the *Peacock* before we even dropped down the river? That the word of *that* got back to the administration—and we had to quash it by sending a letter ashore saying that it had been nothing more than a little improper language?"

Wiki shook his head, completely at a loss to know how to respond, and the expedition commander wildly exclaimed, "They expect us to keep tight discipline, and yet they refused to give Captain Hudson—the second-in-command of the expedition!—a rank befitting his station. He is still officially a *lieutenant*! And they have been equally neglectful of *me*, goddamn it! Yet I command an expedition of seven ships that will circumnavigate the globe—will discover unknown territory, will fly the Stars and Stripes in a multitude of foreign ports! It's unbearably insulting! How *can* they expect me to maintain order when they offer me so little respect themselves?"

Wiki said with complete sincerity, "It's a damned shame, sir."

"Indeed it is—indeed! Rank is of prime importance and the whole fleet knows it! They laugh at me—*laugh!*—and defy me at every turn. But, by God, I'll exert discipline—I know how to be a martinet, I assure you! I know how to punish the witless virgins!"

Wiki could hear Wilkes's heavy breathing, but to his huge relief the rant had come to an end. Silence fell, while Captain Wilkes's restless gaze flickered about the big room, settling on jars of dead fish and seaweed and then moving on. Finally, he said, "I have taken the command of the brig *Swallow* away from Lieutenant Forsythe, and restored it to Passed Midshipman Rochester."

Though that was what Wiki had guessed already, he was still very glad to hear it. However, he checked, "May I ask which ship is carrying me to the island, sir?"

"The *Swallow*." Captain Wilkes added, "Lieutenant Forsythe will be going with you."

This came as such a shock that Wiki involuntarily exclaimed, "Surely not as Captain Rochester's second-in-command!"

It was a terrible prospect. Not only was there bad blood between Forsythe and Rochester, but it would lead to a most peculiar social situation: George Rochester would outrank Forsythe only when both were on board the brig. Away from the *Swallow*, George would be a mere passed midshipman, and Lieutenant Forsythe would be the senior officer.

"Certainly not," said Captain Wilkes tartly. "Lieutenant Forsythe will have a command of his own."

Wiki blinked in surprise. "A second craft is going with us, sir?"

"Aye. I'm giving him the *Peacock*'s big cutter."

Wiki thought of the boats he had seen stacked on chocks on the waist deck of the *Peacock*, nesting one inside the other. There had been three, he remembered—the launch at the bottom, and then the two cutters, one bigger than the other.

He asked, "How big is she?"

"The big cutter?" Captain Wilkes's tone became practical and seamanlike—at long last he seemed in control of himself. "Just a touch under thirty feet, and very fast even when beating upwind—two masts, dipping lug foresail, standing lug mainsail. I have ordered her to be decked over forward as far as the foremast, with two berths underneath, and fitted with a tarpaulin to haul over the main boom when she is at anchor. The carpenters are working on her now. She'll carry two swivel guns, and have a crew of six, with two officers." Then he added, "Captain Rochester will be in control of the mission while the brig is at sea, but once you are at the island Lieutenant Forsythe will be in charge, and you will follow *his* instructions. His orders are to get you on shore and support you with force, if necessary."

It was a dreadful plan, Wiki thought with a wince; it would take all Rochester's diplomatic skills to avoid a power struggle even before they got to the island. With foreboding, he asked, "Who will be Lieutenant Forsythe's second-in-command, sir?"

"Passed Midshipman Kingman."

This was no easier to digest. Zachary Kingman was Lieutenant Forsythe's special drinking crony; they were almost always seen together on sprees in port. Thin to the point of emaciation, and with a constant loosely stupid death's-head grin, Kingman was older than most passed midshipmen because he had wasted so much time at the gaming tables, and he was a troublemaker still. However, both he and Forsythe were handy with their weapons, Wiki silently admitted; they were men who never hesitated to charge into danger, and might be exactly what the situation demanded.

But who, then, was going to be George's second-in-command on the brig? Over the past three weeks Lawrence J. Smith had been the first officer of the *Swallow*—and loathed cordially by all, Forsythe included. Carefully, because the pompous, much detested Lieutenant Smith was a particular crony of Captain Wilkes's, Wiki said, "Will Lieutenant Smith be Captain Rochester's second-in-command, sir?"

Captain Wilkes said stiffly, "I have other plans for the good lieutenant, and have assigned Midshipman Keith to the position of Captain Rochester's first officer."

Wiki was stunned. Midshipman Keith might be wonderfully enthusiastic about ships, the sea, and the exploring expedition, but he was only seventeen years old, for God's sake! Then a thought occurred to him—Constant Keith, like Forsythe and Rochester and Wiki himself, had been deeply involved in the recent murders; he, with all of them, had witnessed Captain Wilkes's hysterical outburst when the identity of the killer had been revealed. Had Wilkes seized on Hudson's pirate story as a chance to send them out of his sight while he got over the memory of his public embarrassment?

It was impossible to ask, so Wiki said neutrally, "Is the island on the charts, sir?"

"Of course." Wilkes rose and walked to a table where a chart was already spread out. The island was a flyspeck a hundred miles from the Brazilian coast, in waters that were wickedly shoal. These were the seas where Captain David Porter of the *Essex* had hunted British shipping back in 1813, Wiki remembered. It had been good hunting ground—because it was indeed overlooking the route for Rio. Suddenly, checking out the island for pirates didn't seem quite so bizarre.

Small as it was, the island had a name. Captain Wilkes said helpfully, "It says Shark Island." On the chart, though, the name was printed in Portuguese—Ilha Tubarão.

Two

When Wiki arrived back at the *Swallow* George Rochester was already on board, and Lieutenant Smith was sulkily following his duds down into the boat that would deliver him to his new berth on the *Vincennes*. The atmosphere about the brig was festive; men wearing broad grins were lined up at the rail to watch him go.

Nodding as the boatswain cheerfully saluted him back aboard, Wiki mused that it was a testament to just how bad Captain Wilkes's judgment had been when he'd replaced Rochester with Forsythe, and then made Lawrence J. Smith the brig's first officer. Forsythe had the worst failing possible in a captain, that of being inconsistent: careless of discipline one moment, he was tyrannical the next. Lieutenant Smith had proved too self-important to moderate his superior's wildly swinging moods, and too conceited to compensate by developing rapport with the men. He was also unbearably irritating. Altogether, it was little wonder that the sailors of the *Swallow* were exceeding glad to see him go.

George Rochester couldn't hide his pleasure at the way things had turned out, either. As he led the way down the companion and through the saloon to the captain's cabin, he was grinning from ear to ear. It wasn't much of a room, being just big enough to hold the chart table, a chair, and the settee, plus a sleeping berth with lockers underneath, but he surveyed the little realm with proprietary pride. The gold epaulette that had been restored to his right shoulder positively glowed in the reflection of his radiant delight.

Then, however, he threw himself into the chart table chair, dangled his legs over one of the arms, put on a long face, and demanded of Wiki, "Where the devil are we going to put them all?"

Wiki went to the settee and settled into his favorite thinking position, slumped forward with his elbows planted on his spread thighs and his hands relaxed between them. His mind was mostly turning over the interview with Captain Wilkes, so he said vaguely, "Who?"

"Forsythe and Kingman, that's who," George retorted. "Concentrate, old man—because we have a problem. While they will be in the cutter much of the passage, they will have to berth on the brig at nights. We can put the cutter's six men into the fo'c'sle, but we can hardly do that to their officers!"

Apart from the captain's cabin, there were only two staterooms on the *Swallow,* one for the first mate, and the other for the brig's civilian scientific, who was Wiki himself. The rest of the space in the after accommodations was taken up with the saloon, which was mostly filled with a big table built about the foot of the main mast, and the pantry, where the steward worked.

Wiki guessed resignedly, "You want me to give up my room?"

"Well, if the carpenter built a second bunk in your room above the one that's there, both Forsythe and Kingman could take it over."

"That's a point," Wiki allowed.

"You wouldn't mind moving?"

"It wouldn't be the first time," Wiki pointed out.

He had lived in the forecastle of the *Swallow* for the first weeks of voyage, so that another scientific could take over his stateroom. There had been a bit of a problem at first: Knowing that Wiki was the captain's particular comrade, the sailors had strongly suspected that he was the captain's spy. After a few days of keeping a low profile he had been accepted, however, and on the whole had liked it there—because he didn't like sleeping alone. At home in the Bay of Islands his mother's people slept in a single sleeping *whare,* so that throughout his childhood the nights had been punctuated with snores, people turning restlessly on their sleeping mats, and the low voices of the wakeful. Indeed, one of the most foreign aspects of life in New England had been having a bedroom to himself.

So he said quite placidly, "Into the fo'c'sle I go"—but George immediately exclaimed, "I wasn't thinking of that!"

"So what, pray, did you have in mind?"

To Wiki's surprise, Rochester's expression became remarkably furtive. Stroking his fluffy fair side whiskers in meditative style, his friend admitted, "I thought perhaps you would share the first mate's cabin with Midshipman Keith."

Wiki burst into a roar of laughter. "So I can coach him in the duties of a first officer?"

"I was actually hoping you would carry out the duties yourself—without young Keith guessing it, of course."

"You have to be joking," Wiki said dryly. "I'm with the expedition as a civilian, remember."

"There's no better seaman on the ocean than you."

"Fiddlesticks." Wiki might be a consummate seaman on whaleships and in whaleboats, but the ways of the navy were still largely a mystery. When George had originally suggested that he should sign up with the U.S. Navy to come on the exploring expedition, Wiki had flatly refused, which was why the job of civilian linguister had been suggested.

"And you've been an officer on whalers," Rochester persuaded.

"Whaling captains don't care if a man is brown, black, white, or brindle, just so long as he has sharp eyes and wields an unerring lance," Wiki pointed out rather acidly. He'd seen Fayal Portuguese, black men from the Cape Verde Islands, and Gayhead Indians from Massachusetts walking the quarterdecks of whalers, but everyone knew that the sky would fall before a man of color—a half-caste Polynesian being a very good example—would be awarded rank in the navy.

"It would be for the good of the brig."

"Nonsense. Midshipman Keith has the makings of a good officer."

"Not the way I remember it," George said moodily. When George had been in charge of one of the cannon on the *Vincennes*, during his demotion there, Keith had proved a useful fount of knowledge about how the iron beast worked; but otherwise his closest acquaintance with the young man had been at a feast in Captain Wilkes's wardroom where he had shared the bottom of the table with Keith and another noisy young midshipman.

"He cracks terrible jokes," he complained. "And has a rotten weak head for Madeira."

Wiki's own experience had been somewhat the same. He had first met Constant Keith and his fellow mids as their specially invited guest in the midshipmen's mess, which was also where Keith and his crony, a plump lad by the name of Dicken, berthed. He remembered the room vividly, and thought that the young man was going to get quite a shock when he first clapped eyes on his new accommodations—and that he surely had a lot to learn.

He shrugged, and nodded. "If he asks me questions about seamanship, I'll answer them. But," he warned, "I can't promise any more than that."

On the *Vincennes,* Midshipman Keith was in a state of abject grief. His friend, Jack Dicken, had tears running down his red cheeks, too, and kept on sobbing, "But 'tis a signal honor," to which Keith replied, "I know, I know." Every time he looked about the luxurious berth he was leaving behind, though, more tears would fall.

The two of them had set up this room together, spending a great deal of money—not that that had been a huge sacrifice, as both hailed from rich families. Now Constant Keith, like all his friends, considered the room both beautiful and in the very best of taste; as he had written home to his family, it was the admiration of all. The bulkheads were hung with crimson-striped drapes, and decorated with a large mirror on one wall and an even larger display of weapons on another. A Brussels carpet covered the floor, and the porcelain bowl of the washstand was sprinkled with designs of green clover. Silver candelabra perched on tables, and Chinese urns full of painted feather flowers stood about in corners. The two divans where Keith and Dicken slept were upholstered in blue damask.

Still worse, Keith had invested six hundred dollars in a private store of wine and food—only staples like flour being provided by the ship—and all of this would have to be left behind, too. He was just seventeen and naturally hungry, and his spirit quailed at the thought of what the rations were apt to be like on the *Swallow.*

"But 'tis such an honor," Dicken repeated. "You should be fit to bust with joy."

"And I am, I am!" Keith cried. When Captain Wilkes had sent for him he had shuffled along reluctantly, with memories of past sins lining up in his guilty mind, and he had fully expected to be reprimanded, or even punished. Too, he'd been stricken with the nasty notion that Captain Wilkes had somehow deduced that the midshipmen didn't hero-worship him any more, not the way they had at the beginning. Where they had once revered their commodore unquestioningly, considering him a genius of the stature of Captain Cook, they now felt uneasy about many of his decisions, especially his ominous habit of changing the officers of the various ships on a whim. Not only did it make a chap wonder who he'd be taking orders from next, but it overturned the comfortable arrangements of the squadron.

Accordingly, it had taken Keith an embarrassingly long time to realize that he was being promoted to the station of first officer on the brig *Swallow*—and on such a wonderful exciting mission, too! He must have seemed sadly addleheaded, he feared. But then— probably just in time to prevent Captain Wilkes from arbitrarily changing his mind—his heart had leaped with understanding, and he had exclaimed out loud with joy. Captain Wilkes had even smiled briefly as he had dismissed him, and for a moment Keith had regarded him with something like his old admiration and awe.

"Captain Rochester will be your commanding officer," Dicken said enviously. George Rochester was the unquestioned hero of the midshipmen's mess—not only was he the paragon who had topped the class in the last set of examinations, but, because he had been given the command of one of the expedition's ships, he was living proof that mere midshipmen could aspire to wonderful things. All the junior midshipmen had mourned when George Rochester had been abruptly demoted, and all of them were exceeding glad to hear that he'd been restored to the quarterdeck of the *Swallow*.

Then Dicken lowered his voice. "One of your shipmates will be Wiki Coffin."

The two young men gazed at each other. Mr. Coffin had been a guest at one of the midshipmen's weekly feasts, and though he had turned out to be courtly, civilized, and interesting, they still considered themselves extremely daring to have invited him.

"They say he's a chief at home," Keith said uncertainly, and then went on more strongly, "And he is only *half* a savage. His father is a respectable Salem shipmaster." Though it was not really *respectable* to father a son out of wedlock in a far-off, barbaric land, and then take the lad home to New England to meet his Yankee folks—folks who included Captain William Coffin's legal, childless wife, who, according to gossip, hadn't known about the child until he appeared at her kitchen door. "They say Captain Coffin has made a fortune out of trading with the Orient," he added as a kind of excuse.

"I wonder why Wiki Coffin don't sail with his father, then?"

"He sailed on whaleships, so I hear—out of choice, because it's the best apprenticeship a cove can have. Now, he's a first-rate seaman, they tell me," Keith said, and mused that he might even find Mr. Coffin a fount of seafaring lore. "I could learn a lot from him!" he exclaimed bracingly. "Fascinating facts of human nature can be learned even from a savage—and especially from a *half*-savage. I shall apply myself to it—I shall cultivate his company!"

"They also say his folks eat people," Dicken ghoulishly warned.

Three

*O*n detailed inspection, the big cutter of the *Peacock* turned out to be just six inches under thirty feet in length, eight feet wide, and with a three-foot draft; she was of lap strake construction, with the ends of the nails that held her light planks together clinched over. Shallow runners—bilge-keels— were fixed on the outside to keep the boat upright if hauled out onto the beach, and also serve as grab-rails for anyone swimming along- side. Because they would also prevent the boat from rolling heavily or making too much leeway, Forsythe knew he would be able to sail fast close-hauled, something suited to his dashing style. Damn it, he thought, he was in love with the dashing little craft before he'd even tried her out on the water.

However, Forsythe was far too shrewd to betray this. In- stead, with Midshipman Kingman, he went over the boat and her accoutrements with nitpicking care. Sails, masts, and rigging were inspected and either approved or condemned: the first officer of the *Peacock* was so pleased that neither Forsythe nor Kingman was going to be a fixture on the sloop of war (a nasty thought that had occurred to him as he had watched the big Virginian and his crony arrive) that he sent for new canvas and the sail maker without the slightest demur. Then Forsythe raided the *Peacock*'s armory, requisitioning a bristling array of dirks, cutlasses, Bowie knives, and Hall breech-loading rifles, plus an assortment of the famous Elgin combination cutlass-pistols that had been designed expressly for the expedition.

By the time the cutter was ready to be lowered into the water, the six cutter's men who had been assigned to him had arrived, sea bags over their shoulders and noncommittal expressions on their faces. Casting an equally critical stare over them, Forsythe was just as gratified. All were able seamen, and looked strong, sturdy, and nimble. Too, they were men in their prime—like all the seamen on the exploratory expedition, they were on the young side of forty.

Having taken their names and assigned them to their places, Forsythe gave the cutter a thorough workout to assess her sailing qualities. For an hour or more he dashed back and forth through the fleet, and the sun was lowering to the horizon when he finally turned for the *Swallow*.

On board the brig, Wiki watched the smart cutter tack toward them. He was with the two other Polynesians of the crew—"*Kanakas,*" as the American seamen called them—and at his ease on the foredeck. Named Sua and Tana, his companions were both Samoan; both were handsome, muscular men, Sua being even more massive in build than Tana.

Because it was the dogwatch and they were off duty, they were sitting cross-legged on the foredeck, and because Forsythe wasn't on board yet they had their shirts off and were chatting in the Samoan language. Sua, the big one, had his trousers rolled up his tree-trunk–like legs, revealing a great deal of the intricate blue tracery of his *pe'a*—the dense tattoo which covered his thighs and extended up to his waist. Gained with physical pain and the payment of much treasure, it was a testament to his manly courage, and also to his sense of community with his home village.

He was also watching Forsythe's cutter. He said, "We sail at dawn?"

"Aye," said Wiki.

"Where are we going, do you know?"

It wasn't a secret, as far as Wiki knew, so he said readily, "Shark Island."

"Ah." Sua thought a moment and then said wisely, "With a name like that it must be a place of many legends."

"Perhaps." Wiki shrugged. "They say the island is uninhabited, though."

"Ah." He thought again. "Do you have shark legends in New Zealand?"

Wiki considered. "Only of *taniwha*."

Taniwha were fabulous monsters usually found in deep water, unseen and yet so powerful that captains of great *waka taua*—canoes of war—would steer up inconvenient creeks to avoid them, and warriors walking the trails through the forest would take a longer path to make sure that they did not have to cross a ford where a *taniwha* was reputed to lurk. There were fables of great chiefs who kept *taniwha* as pets, but other great chiefs killed them, if they could, and when their bellies were cut open whole *waka* were found inside, along with bodies of many people and their ornaments.

"What do they look like?"

"Dragons," Wiki said in English, for they were scaly monsters, some reputed to be winged. Then he added in Samoan, "Some real sea creatures are also called *taniwha*—but they have to be big."

"Te taniwha nui o te moana?"

"Aye," said Wiki. He glanced sideways at Sua, intrigued that he was familiar with the New Zealand language—*te reo Maori*. Of all the Polynesian languages, Samoan and *te reo* were two of the farthest apart, and it was news to him that he could have been comfortably chatting in his own tongue with Sua. He knew surprisingly little about the big Samoan, he realized then. Back when he had started to live in the forecastle of the brig Sua had been the first to approach him, but there had only been the briefest of formal introductions before they had settled to a wrestling match, which was the usual way for Polynesian men to get acquainted on shipboard. Sua had won easily, Wiki remembered; it had been like trying to wrestle with a battering ram. He also knew that Sua's "sailor name"—the one his first American captain had given him—was "Jackie Polo," which implied that he had been first shipped in his native island of Upolu. Too, Sua had helped save his life a couple of times, but that was about it.

He said, "We call the great white pointer *mango taniwha*. Other kinds of sharks have other names—*kuwai,* for instance." Then he added curiously, "How did you learn *te reo Maori*?"

Sua grinned. "The captain of my first American ship was a bastard, so I jumped ship in Rotuma, headed into the bush, and lived there for a couple of months with a bunch of other deserters. The lot of them were bloody New Zealanders, who taught me a lot of bad habits."

This was considered hilarious. Tana and Sua giggled in the infectious manner of Pacific Islanders, and Wiki laughed immoderately, too. Then they abruptly sobered as a consciously jocular voice said from right above, "Do I hear you talk of dragons?"

They froze, wondering how long Midshipman Keith had been listening. The lad stood over them, looking brave but bashful, a tall, skinny young man with a strong resemblance to a heron that was accentuated by his habit of holding his head on one side in inquiring fashion, and the fact that he had one arm in a sling. Sua and Tana scrambled to their feet, while Wiki followed more slowly.

Midshipman Keith looked embarrassed, waved his free arm, and said, "Please—as you were," but they remained standing, the two Samoans exchanging wary glances. If either of them turned his bare back, Keith would have seen the thin, curling scars of a vicious flogging Forsythe had ordered after he had overheard Sua and Tana speaking in Samoan. They had been shouting at a time when the brig was in great danger, but Forsythe had reckoned they could have been talking mutiny, and because of that it was a punishable offense.

"Sit down, sit down," Midshipman Keith urged when they kept silent, and led the way by sitting down himself, folding up his lanky form like a cricket. They joined him, though very reluctantly, Sua stealthily pulling down his trouser legs as he did so. Wiki wanted to advise Keith that this was not a good idea, but didn't know how to do it. When he glanced out over the water the cutter was very close; in a couple of minutes Forsythe and Kingman would be back on board.

Midshipman Keith said to Wiki, "Do you have myths of dragons in your land?"

Wiki didn't want to invoke spirits as powerful as *taniwha* by idly chatting about them to a *pakeha*, so prevaricated by saying, "We were talking about sharks."

"Sharks!" The boy had his head even farther on one side, his expression so alert and knowing that Wiki thought he might be bright enough to figure that they had been gossiping about Shark

Island. Sharing a stateroom with this young man could be a challenging experience, he mused, and wondered briefly what Keith himself thought of it. It was obvious that he enjoyed listening to yarns. Right now, he was waiting so impatiently he didn't notice Tana and Sua surreptitiously pulling on their shirts.

"You have many sharks in New Zealand?" he demanded when Wiki's silence dragged on. "Are they different from ours?"

Wiki said, "There's a certain time of the year in the Bay of Islands when the blossoms of the *pohutukawa* trees fall so thickly that they turn the water red, and the sharks come in great swarms—perhaps because they are fooled by the color into thinking that there's blood in the water. It's a time of abundance for my people—by the time the season is over there's enough preserved meat to keep the *pataka* stocked all the way up to winter and beyond."

"*Pataka?* What does that mean?"

Wiki paused, not just because he heard the cutter touch the side of the *Swallow* and Forsythe hollering for a boat fall, but because there was no easy translation. *Pataka* were low houses built on stilts to protect them from thieves and vermin, often beautifully carved and decorated. According to the size of the village, they could be either small or huge. Inside were stocks of tubers, and gourds bulging with the meat of birds and rats preserved in their own fat; it was a store representing so much community effort that it was considered a treasure.

In the end he said, "Storehouses," because he couldn't think of a better word—and Forsythe clambered up to deck, followed by Kingman's attenuated, stick-insect–like form. The burly southerner tipped back his broad hat, and then exclaimed so loudly that the whole brig heard him, "For God's sake, Midshipman, what the bloody *hell* do you think you are doing?"

Wiki was aware of Sua and Tana beating a swift retreat to the forecastle. Forsythe wasn't even looking at them, though; instead, he was glaring at young Keith as he strode toward him; his red face was sour with contempt, an expression slavishly imitated by his mindless crony, Zachary Kingman, who followed close behind.

"You reckon you're some kind of *liberal*?" Forsythe demanded, making it sound like a dirty word. "Mebbe you think that all people are equal in the eyes of the Lord? Wa-al, young man, let me tell you that folks just ain't equal in the U.S. Navy, or any other navy I can bring to mind. It jest ain't logical, because there have to be superiors and inferiors on board ship. You don't fraternize with lower ranks, and that includes goddamned Kanakas—understand? Right now, you're letting the goddamned navy down, and I don't want to see it happen again."

Then, with a jerk of his head, he turned and went aft, again followed by Kingman. When Wiki looked at Midshipman Keith the young man was white-faced—not with fear, Wiki thought, but with rage. He thought Keith was going to stalk away, but instead the boy said in a trembling voice, "I see that I am not alone in the first officer's stateroom."

"Ah," said Wiki, taken aback. He had moved in already, determined to claim the upper berth because if he had the bottom one he'd have a foot in his face every time Keith climbed in or out of bed. As far as he could remember the stateroom was tidy when he'd left it; in fact, there should have been very little evidence of his presence.

"Then I wonder much with whom I share it," said Midshipman Keith bitterly, and before Wiki could say anything he turned on his heel.

The lad had the first watch, so it was midnight before he headed for bed. Wiki was awake, stretched out on the upper berth with a lamp in a bracket by his shoulder, reading a book by a man named

Edmund Fanning. The writer was a wily old sea dog from Stonington, Connecticut, who told such wonderful tales that Wiki would have relished meeting him—and maybe he had but without knowing it, he thought, because his father, Captain William Coffin, had a lot of dealings with Stonington merchants and adventurers, and when Wiki was a lad he had taken him along there on trips for both business and pleasure. Fanning had sealed in the Falklands, and sailed south to South Georgia; he had fought pirates in the South China Sea, and frightened islanders with "Quaker" cannons made of wood; he had dealt with mandarins and been imprisoned by the Spaniards; and he had made himself a fortune out of all these adventures.

When he heard a tap at the door Wiki was so absorbed it took him a moment to come back to his surroundings. Then the door cautiously opened, and Keith's face appeared in the gap.

The junior officer looked exhausted, Wiki thought—and no wonder, because Rochester had given him a second dressing-down, though in the privacy of the captain's cabin. For Forsythe was right: Without strict divisions of rank a ship of war would never function, and so Captain Rochester—though he'd already had an icy exchange of words with the lieutenant on the undesirability of shaming fellow officers in public—had been forced to bring home the lesson.

Keith also looked remarkably apprehensive—a surprise for Wiki, who considered that the young man should have been feeling considerably relieved to find that he was not sharing the cabin with either Forsythe or Kingman. So he said with a reassuring grin, "Come in; I won't bite you." And wondered why the lad's eyes incredulously widened.

Four

Three days later, Wiki woke as eight bells rang at the start of the morning watch. Being a civilian, he had the luxurious option of turning over and going back to sleep, but this morning the dawn peace was rudely interrupted by the lookout's long-drawn-out holler of, *"Land Ho!"* Wiki looked over the edge of his bunk, saw that Midshipman Keith had left already, and swung briskly down to the floor.

When he arrived on deck the sun was just lifting above the misty horizon, and the brig and the cutter she towed behind her were floating alone in a luminous, peacock-colored sea. In contrast to the serenity of the setting, the brig was a cacophony of noise. Up until now they had seen blessedly little of Forsythe—during their passage the weather had been fair, and the lieutenant, with Kingman and the cutter's crew, had spent most of the time on board the cutter, racing her alongside the *Swallow,* and occasionally even overtaking the smart-sailing brig—but now he was making his presence abundantly felt by hollering about the decks.

George Rochester was keeping aloof from all the commotion, standing at his ease on the foredeck. Wiki, arriving beside his friend, said, "*E hoa*—my friend—what's up?"

"We've raised our landfall, and so he's taken charge, old chap. I never knew before that Forsythe was the studious type, but he quoted Wilkes's instructions word for word, by rote and without a tremor. We've sighted our goal, and so he's commanding the mission."

"He surely didn't waste time," Wiki dryly remarked: Shark Island was only just visible from the deck, a toothlike shape on the horizon. Forsythe had obviously leapt out of his berth in a hurry, because his trousers were rumpled and his braces dangling. His voice was abruptly muffled as he hauled a frock shirt over his head, and then he started yelling again.

"He's calling for battle stations," Rochester observed in disbelief. Sua, the brig's official drummer, had just run out on deck with his drum—a length of log. This was one of the *Swallow*'s eccentricities, something that Forsythe, surprisingly, had not changed when he was in charge. The Samoan hammered out a primitive, blood-stirring beat to quarters, accompanied by Forsythe's bawled orders to clear the decks for action, and Wiki and Rochester swiftly got out of the way.

Zachary Kingman echoed Forsythe's commands in an ear-splitting howl. Footsteps thumped in energetic response, and within an extraordinarily short space of time unnecessary gear had been stored belowdecks and everything movable lashed into place. The deck planks were wetted and sprinkled with sand. Rigging thrummed as men carried cases of rifles into the mast tops. Tubs of water were set about the decks for putting out flames. The boatswain busily handed out arms and measured out powder and ammunition, and soon every man had a pistol and a dirk thrust into his belt. Cutlasses were stacked into a rack on the quarterdeck, and then Lieutenant Forsythe shouted out for the brig's two nine-pounder cannon to be readied.

This was supervised by the gun captain, a mountain man by the name of Dave who brought passion to the job. The tight lashings that held the cannon housed up tight to the bulwarks were cast away, and by hauling on rope tackles attached to the sides and the rear of each iron monster, his team heaved the guns back for loading, and then up to the gunports in the rail for aiming. Five dumb shows, and Lieutenant Forsythe was satisfied—the brig *Swallow*, without a doubt, was ready to defend herself to the very last man. When George inquired gently whether the crew were to be allowed their breakfast, Forsythe nodded complacently, with the air of a man with a job well done.

By this time Shark Island was in plain sight five miles ahead, its central feature a triangular pinnacle that reared up into the vividly blue sky and was streaked with growth which was intensely emerald even at a distance. Contemplating this while he chewed the last of his bread, Forsythe announced that he would now take the cutter to the island to spy out the lay of the land. Wiki, somewhat to his surprise, was not to be one of the party—instead, he was instructed to take the helm of the *Swallow* and bring the brig to a standstill a mile from the land, where he would await the return of the cutter. A council of war would follow, Forsythe informed him, during which the details of the mission would be beaten out. Then, with no more ado, he, Kingman, and the cutter's crew took their stations in the boat, and they were off.

The *Swallow* followed under reduced sail, the slow passing of the miles punctuated by the regular swish of sea. Bright morning light bounced off the rippling surface, forcing Wiki to squint. When a flick of spray spattered over the taffrail onto his arms it dried so fast he felt stinging pricks of salt. The deck boards beneath his bare feet were sticky with warm pitch, and the locks of hair that straggled down from under his hat stuck to his neck.

Because the mainsail and foresail were clewed up, he could see all the way along the sun-scorched deck to the bows. Captain Rochester, on the foredeck, was standing in a characteristic pose, his hands lightly clasped behind the seat of his trousers, which was tucked in, so that his well-muscled calves stuck out. The peak of Shark Island was lifting in the sky as they neared, towering high above the rock-girt shore. Ahead, the cutter was dodging back and forth on uneven tacks, evidently to avoid coral heads. Its silhouette was as triangular as the peak, only double. Then it disappeared into the shadow.

Wiki frowned, and cocked his head—was that a distant shout? Others had heard it too, because heads were turning to look at George Rochester. He didn't move. The world was full of the chuckle of water passing along the hull, and the distant splash of surf on rock. Otherwise—silence. Wiki waited for the cutter to reappear. Long moments plodded by, but it was as if she had vanished forever.

As the cutter entered the dark shadow of the peak one of the men in the bow let out a warning shout. Rocks lay ahead, so close to the surface that they made the water tremble. Anticipating Forsythe's quick order, hands thrust out oars to shove the boat away. The headland slid safely past; the shadow of the pinnacle rock fell away from them—and the current in the channel carried them around the point before they could prevent it.

A big topsail schooner lay at anchor in the cove. On the beach beyond, the wreck of a sloop was piled bow-up, so high that her bowsprit disappeared in a clump of bush. The beach ended abruptly in a high cliff crowned by some kind of fort. Forsythe could see the iron snouts of cannon protruding through crenellations in the massive stone ramparts.

Jesus, he thought; *no wonder Hudson didn't want to come in any closer*. He barked orders to tack about—orders that became urgent as he spied men scurrying over the decks of the schooner, a half-mile away, and two whaleboats being hastily lowered. The cutter came about smartly, but then the headland stole their wind, and the sails hung dead. Putting out oars made little difference, as the two whaleboats were pulsing fast toward them, their crews facing forward, wielding paddles like crazy goddamned Indians, their faces twisted up with effort.

Closer they came—closer, closer. Forsythe spat more orders, and his men brought the boat around again, four of the hands sculling while the other two hastily took in sail. Then they got ready to fend off attack. Kingman crouched over the stern swivel, his expression a snarl of silent defiance, and Forsythe shouldered his rifle. The cutter's crew felt in their belts for their pistols, and then, silently, they waited for the whaleboats to approach.

The man standing at the steering oar of the first was a muscular-looking cove about thirty-five years of age, big-nosed and deeply tanned, with blond hair and whiskers. He was hatless, so that they could see that his head hair was bleached almost white by the sun. He barked out an order, and both whaleboats came to a stop.

"Who the hell are you?" he demanded, while his men stirred the water with their paddles to keep the boats still. His voice was hoarse and unmistakably American.

"Lieutenant Forsythe, U.S. Navy Exploring Expedition," Forsythe answered. "And who the bloody hell are *you*?"

"You're navy!" echoed the other with obvious relief. Then he looked both puzzled and suspicious, and said, "Where's your ship?"

Forsythe jerked his head in the direction of the headland.

"Well, I hope to God you have a carpenter on board." Then the man finally condescended to introduce himself: "Joel Hammond, first mate, sealing schooner *Annawan* of Stonington, Connecticut, lying at Shark Island in distress."

A goddamn *sealer*? Forsythe wondered why the hell a sealing schooner would drop anchor at an uninhabited, equatorial island in the Atlantic, where he was pretty certain no seals were to be found. He demanded, "Distress? What do you mean, *distress*?"

"We're leaking a thousand strokes an hour."

Jesus, Forsythe thought; if that was the truth, the *Annawan* was foundering at her anchors—and yet these men had left the pumps in order to man two boats to chase down the cutter. The schooner did look ominously low in the water, but nonetheless he wondered if he was heading into a trap; it wouldn't be the first time a buccaneer had blocked his scuppers and stopped his pumps to entice would-be Samaritans into his clutches. However, if he tried to make a run for it the whaleboats would be on him in a trice.

So he said, "How did it happen?"

"We was steering up the deep channel where she is anchored now, and sailed her onto a reef. Didn't know it was there, not until we hit it."

"You don't have a chart?"

"There's no goddamned chart." Hammond's lips thinned, and then he said, "We fothered a sail and got it over the hole, but she's still leaking like a bloody basket."

Fothering was to reinforce a piece of canvas by thrumming it—matting it with bits of unraveled rope to make it thick and strong. When it was drawn over the hole, the inward pressure of the sea would stop the leak—with luck, but it seemed that Hammond had not had any luck at all. He said, "Believe me, you've come in the goddamned nick of time."

It was certainly a fact that the U.S. Navy was supposed to come to the succor of American vessels and crews, wherever they might be. Forsythe looked up at the fort. There was no sign of movement about the walls or the cannon, not even the flicker of a flag, so he jerked his head in assent.

Five

Hammond's relief was obvious enough to be unfeigned. He leaned on his oar, and the two whaleboats spun round in the wonderfully quick way of their class of craft, and dashed off to the schooner. Casting Zack Kingman a warning look to keep his station at the swivel gun, Forsythe ordered his men to follow the two boats—but slowly, to give him time to think. They took oars and sculled gently, while he sat at the tiller and studied the two ships—one wallowing at anchor, the other wrecked high on the beach—with misgiving coiling in his belly.

What he saw was reasonably reassuring, however. The manner of the sloop's wrecking was strange—as if she'd been run up on the beach under full sail—but her name was still legible, and read "*Hero* of Stonington, CT." So both craft hailed from the same port, Forsythe mused; maybe they had come in together. The name *Annawan* was plain on the stern of the schooner, and as she rocked in the back-wash from the surf he could glimpse the top edge of the fothered canvas that had been bowsed up tight beneath the waterline on the starboard side. After the whaleboats arrived at the schooner and had been swiftly drawn up, the men who had crewed them spilled rapidly over the decks, and the silence was sundered by the rhyth-mic thud and suck of pumps. After a short pause a sick stream of water gushed down her side.

He could see Hammond striding along the quarterdeck to the stern, obviously expecting to receive the cutter there. Doing the un-expected was always good strategic sense, however, so Forsythe gave instructions to work around to the bows. No sooner had they touched planking than he swiftly swung up the chains, balanced on the bowsprit, and ran lithely along it to the foredeck. Kingman fol-lowed, and they stood together brace-legged between the knight-heads, alertly studying the scene while Forsythe unslung his rifle and Zack Kingman loosened the two pistols in his belt.

However, the appearance of the *Annawan* bore out what Ham-mond had said, too. Like almost all the merchant craft that streamed out of the ports of New England, the schooner had two deckhouses, one on the foredeck, and the other on the afterdeck. From experience, Forsythe deduced that the forward house would hold the forecastle for the seaman at the forward end, and the workshops for the sail maker and boatswain at the sternward end; while the after house would hold accommodations for the captain and first officer, plus the steward's pantry. The galley, where the ship's grub was cooked, was set in a shed on the starboard side of the foredeck, which was usual, too. Savory smells issued from its sternward-facing door, and a thin plume of smoke drifted from its smokestack. The three masts were stout, as was the rigging—which was only to be expected in a vessel that plied its trade in stormy seas and high southern latitudes.

Hammond was waiting on the afterdeck, but when he saw Forsythe and Kingman he started hurrying toward them—to be forestalled by an energetic figure who fairly leapt out of the door of the after house, waving a stick above his head. This, Forsythe immediately guessed, was the captain of the *Annawan;* a powerful-looking older man, he had gray hair that bristled all over his head, and skinny legs that were obviously lame.

"My God, salvation!" this fellow shouted, and then set himself into a rapid three-legged dance along the deck, his stick tapping lustily, and his legs swinging out to either side like a metronome. Just three yards away, however, he stopped short, evidently having second thoughts, because he said suspiciously, "Navy? That damn fool Hammond informed me you are naval officers, but you don't look like navy men to me. Where's your uniform, huh?"

Forsythe looked down at his frock shirt, a loose, shabby affair that was belted at his waist over well-worn duck trousers, and shrugged. He hadn't expected to make any kind of official visit, and he was damned if he was going to apologize for his appearance.

"And you ain't even shaved," went on the other, who was himself indecently stubbled. "What's happened to our navy, huh? Is there no martial pride any more? You could be two of those goddamned privateers that prey on this coast—*insurgents!*—for all we can tell."

Forsythe snapped, "This is Passed Midshipman Kingman, and I am Lieutenant Forsythe. We're officers with the U.S. Exploring Expedition."

"You say *sir* when you speak to me, son," the other snapped right back. "That is, if you are indeed a confounded navy man. I pay my taxes, you know—and it's no insignificant figure!—which counts me as your employer. And where's your confounded ship? Or does the navy send its men out in boats now? Where the hell did you materialize from?"

"We're with U.S. Brig *Swallow*," said Forsythe, thoroughly nettled, and again jerked his head in the direction of the headland. "She's within call, believe me."

"So you command the brig's tender?" the other said, his tone disdainful. "Well, that makes sense," he allowed, and finally unbent enough to introduce himself. "Ezekiel Reed. Owner and captain of the *Annawan*—and owner of that poor wreck on the beach, too. An exploring expedition, huh?" His little eyes had gone very sharp. "You haven't come to explore here, surely?"

Forsythe paused, and then decided that telling the truth might do more good than harm. "We're on a mission after pirates."

"You're after those goddamned insurgent privateers? You're a whole month too late, by God!" Reed stamped his foot, then jumped and cursed with the pain, which didn't appear to do his temper any good at all. "Why couldn't you have come four weeks ago, huh? Then you could have seized a prize, instead of me losing my sloop."

"The *Hero*?" Forsythe said alertly. "She was attacked by pirates?"

"She was, indeed—though the captain had the common guts to sail her right up the beach to escape 'em."

"And they looted her?"

Captain Reed let out a huge sigh instead of answering, and then turned and stumped off, waving his free arm and saying, "Come, come. Come and discuss a bottle in my cabin."

Forsythe and Kingman followed the old man along the deck, casting wary glances from side to side as they went. The crew was a weathered, surly-looking bunch; most were heavily bearded, and some had scarred hands and fingers missing, evidently the result of past battles with seals. Joel Hammond was standing by the mizzenmast, and Forsythe slowed as he came alongside him. He wanted to ask why the hell either he or Reed hadn't sent a boat after the *Peacock* to beg assistance, but instead he cast a significant glance at the fort.

He said, "What goes on up there?"

"Nothin'."

"What d'you mean, *nothin'*?"

"Exactly what I say," the mate retorted. "It used to be a prison, or so I heard, but it ain't been used for many years. The cannon have all been spiked, and the rest is in ruins. Go up there yourself, if you don't believe me."

"And what about the island?"

"It's deserted, and it ain't no use asking me more, on account of there ain't anyone left here to tell the tale." Then Hammond grimly advised, "You'd better get a move along. The old man is awaiting, and he gets uncommon angry when impatient."

The door to the after house companionway was open, and the uneven echoes of Captain Reed's progress echoed in the short passage at the bottom. Forsythe negotiated the half-dozen steps easily enough because of a shaft of sunlight that dropped down there, but then he paused, because the captain's cabin at the end of the corridor, where Ezekiel Reed had disappeared, was so dark he needed to wait while his sight adjusted. He did see that a stateroom was sited to either side of the corridor, because their doors had been left open. He glanced into the one on the larboard side; it was small and Spartan, with sea chests stowed neatly beneath the single berth. Then, when he was about to move on, Zack Kingman came up behind him, grabbed his arm, and hissed, "Bloody hell, look at that."

"What?"

"Look at that, I say." Kingman's grin was loose, his whisper lascivious. He was pointing at the second stateroom, the one on the starboard side of the corridor, a relatively spacious affair which had evidently been enlarged by taking over the steward's pantry and knocking down the partition between them.

"Wa'al, I'll be damned," said Forsythe, equally sotto voce. "The old bastard's got a woman with him!" This room had a double berth, the covers tossed and rumpled, and was otherwise cluttered with female garments. Hats and bonnets dangled from hooks, and frilly petticoats and lacy corsets trailed out of baskets and trunks. The air was dense with perfume, and the cleanest object in the room was the mirror. It looked and smelled like a bordello.

Then Reed's voice sounded out from the captain's cabin. "What are you hanging about for?" he hollered, and the two men turned reluctantly away.

Stepping over the threshold of the captain's cabin, Forsythe saw why it was almost too dim to see a goddamned thing—the sidelights in the upper parts of the fore and aft bulkheads were all blocked off with heavy furniture. *Jesus Christ,* he thought; he had never seen the like in all his seafaring life. Walls were hung with heavy drapes, and side tables perched against them. Great jars of feathers stood in corners, and fancy lamps, a box of ship's papers, and a large birdcage cluttered the top of the saloon table. The resemblance to an overfurnished New England parlor was astonishing— even to the stifling heat, because there was a low fire in the stove. The only evidence of male occupation was the collection of skinning knives, muskets, and cutlasses that hung on the forward bulkhead, with a rack of sealing bludgeons at the foot.

Captain Reed was sunk deep in an easy chair and didn't bother to get up as Forsythe and Zack walked in. They looked about hopefully, but the mysterious female wasn't present. After getting them seated, Reed lifted his voice, and a portly, prissy-looking man trotted in—Jack Winter, they were told, the ship's steward. A bottle of brandy and three tumblers were produced, and then the steward was ordered to go to the forward house, break out a bottle of grog, and entertain the cutter's crew on the foredeck.

The old man was acting surprisingly hospitable, considering he had lost one ship and was on the verge of losing another, thought Forsythe—but it was no skin off his nose, he ruminated on. Reed was the boss, and if he preferred sinking a bottle of brandy to getting the damage in the hull of the *Annawan* assessed, then that was perfectly fine by him.

"Tell me again why you're here," the old man demanded after the steward had gone.

"We was sent here by Captain Wilkes of the Exploring Expedition," Forsythe said succinctly, after sinking half the glass he'd been given. Kingman, to his right, was smacking his lips as he gazed affectionately at his own tumbler, which he'd already drained, and Reed affably leaned forward and tilted the bottle again.

"Exploring? Exploring for what?"

"Wa'al, for the continent of Antarctica, for a start," said Forsythe, who knew it was common knowledge and didn't care that it was supposed to be a secret.

"What? When most of America is still unexplored as yet?" Captain Reed shook his head in disgust. "So that's what they do with the taxes I pay, huh? Madness! And, what's more, it's bloody pointless. Antarctica has been discovered already—by Stonington sealers!—and, what's more, in that sloop of mine that lies out on the beach."

Forsythe didn't bother to hide his total disbelief. It was Wilkes's ambition to go down in history as the discoverer of Antarctica, and the idea that it had been "discovered already" was very amusing; Forsythe had never felt much love for Captain Wilkes, and having had the command of the brig *Swallow* whipped away from him hadn't improved that sentiment in the slightest. However, it was impossible to credit that the old bastard wasn't raving. The wrecked sloop on the beach wasn't much bigger than the cutter.

"It's true—and I can tell you the date right down to the day," Reed assured him. "It was November 17, 1820, when my neighbor Nat Palmer, in command of that sloop *Hero,* raised thousand-foot cliffs in a sea filled with ice. He wrote it in his logbook."

Jesus God, thought Forsythe. Just to keep this crazy conversation going, he said, "Neighbor?"

"Captain Nathaniel Palmer is a Stonington man, too."

"You're from Stonington?" Well, thought Forsythe, that figured. When the old man drained his glass instead of answering, he said, "So what the hell was he doing in the Antarctic Ocean? Looking for seals?"

"That is exactly what he was doing." Feeling around for the bottle, Captain Reed found it, lifted it, and topped up all their tumblers. "That sloop was just forty-four tons register—did you know that?"

Forsythe shrugged.

"Nat was just twenty-one when he discovered that great land mass seven hundred miles south of Cape Horn, which in the log he called 'Antarctica.' But," Ezekiel Reed added with a sigh, "he was really supposed to be looking for rookeries, and not a single seal did he find."

"So he made a losing voyage?"

"Aye—which makes me wonder what the *use* is of this so-called exploring expedition of yours. What *good* is it going to do for our great country, huh? Tell me that! Well," Reed exclaimed, forestalling anything Forsythe might want to say; "you don't need to bother!—for I know the answer already!—*none!* I know that to my

44

personal cost, because this schooner that we are setting on now—this same schooner *Annawan!*—has been on an exploring expedition already, but they didn't discover a goddamned *thing,* let alone a profitable rookery."

Forsythe was so stunned he almost dropped his glass. "But the Wilkes expedition is supposed to be the first damn American exploring expedition ever!"

"Well, it ain't," the old man snapped. "Back in 1829 a passel of Stonington merchants put up the money for a three-ship fleet to survey and discover in Antarctic seas, and I was ill-advised enough to be one of those investors. There was the *Annawan,* with Captain Nat Palmer in command, the *Penguin,* commanded by his brother, Alexander, and the *Seraph,* with Benjamin Pendleton in charge, and the fleet was called the South Sea Fur Company and Exploring Expedition. And," Reed said sourly, "we lost a whole heap of money."

"But they found Antarctica?"

"I don't know where the hell they went, but they never found nothing." Shaking his head, Captain Reed let out a grunt of angry laughter, and said, "And now the poor bloody American taxpayer is funding another of the same. And what are you doing, huh? Discovering? No! You're hunting *pirates,* for God's sake, a month too late to do any good! Why, goddamn it, *why?* "

Forsythe shrugged, and told him about the *Peacock* and Captain Hudson's report.

"So that's what it was!" Reed exclaimed. "Saw her myself, I did—*Peacock,* was she?" Then, to Forsythe's amazement, the old man's mood changed like a weathercock, and he shook with gusts of raucous laughter. "Most comical thing I'd seen in years!" he shouted between spasms of mirth. "An enormous great sloop of war taking fright at the sight of an old ruin of a fort! Oh, it was a treat to see how she kicked up her wake," he cried, as jolly as a country priest, while Zack Kingman giggled in his affable but un-comprehending way.

Forsythe, who didn't see the joke at all, watched Reed without expression, thinking this was bloody strange behavior for a man in such dire straits. When the laughter died down he said, "I would've figured you'd have signalized her—or sent boats after her, consider-ing the leak you've got there." He could hear the thump of the pumps, a dismal sound because of the soggy feel of the deck beneath his feet.

"Didn't know we had a leak then, did I?" the old man retorted. "Didn't know until I got back on board that that damn fool Ham-mond had run her on a rock. And when I arrived they was fothering a sail that he reckoned would get us to Pernambuco."

"But it didn't," Forsythe finished for him.

"Not even out of the channel where she lies."

"So what were you doin' here, anyways?"

"I called at Rio expecting to find the *Hero* there, but she wasn't. All I got was news that she'd been attacked by insurgent privateers— and run ashore in an effort to escape."

"So you came to salvage her?"

"Aye. Bad decision—bad."

Bloody bad, Forsythe mentally concurred. "And she'd been looted?"

"The holds are quite empty." Reed looked around at the night-marish clutter of the cabin, and sighed heavily. Then he looked at his drained glass and tipped the bottle over it, but with no result.

"So where are these privateers now?" Forsythe pursued.

Reed didn't answer, instead shaking the brandy bottle as if he couldn't believe it was empty. He lifted his voice, hollering for the steward, so Forsythe raised his voice, too, saying, "If you have any idea where the thieving bastards might have fled, we can go after them."

Reed said, "Don't be a bloody fool." Then he shouted out for the steward again. "Jack, goddamn it—Jack Winter! We need another bottle here, rouse it up!" Then, as the echoes died away, he looked at Forsythe, and said, "When do you expect your brig to arrive? I need to talk to the *real* boss of your outfit—the captain! I don't want you chasing off after insurgent privateers and creating all kinds of international situations, I want to claim my rights of succor as a citizen of the United States—a taxpayer, damn it! What's his name?"

"George Rochester," Forsythe bit out sourly. "But I gave him orders to lay off and on until the cutter returns."

"What? Who the hell are you to order your captain about?" Without waiting for a reply, Reed heaved himself out of his chair, grabbed his stick, stumped along the passage to the foot of the stairs, and shouted, "Goddamn it, you stringshanked bastard of a steward, don't you hear me? Brandy, more brandy!" Then he turned, looked at Forsythe, and said, "The brig don't come until summoned, huh? Well, I know how to fix that." And he lifted his voice again, hollering, "Hammond, there! Where's the mate, damn him? Hammond!"

"Don't bother," said Forsythe, coming out of his chair in an angry rush, and heaving past Reed up the stairs. "Zack," he ordered over his shoulder as he arrived out on deck. "Tell the men to get ready to get under way for the brig."

"What?" said Captain Reed, hurrying up the companionway after him. "You're going? But you ain't even looked at the damage yet. Write a note for your captain—this Rochester—and appraise him of the sad situation. Hammond will carry it for you."

Like hell, thought Forsythe; he couldn't wait to get off this sinking tub and away from this crazy old man. He opened his mouth—and saw the young woman who was walking along the deck toward them. She was carrying a bottle of brandy in one hand, and a tray of edibles in the other; and she was the most beautiful girl he'd ever clapped eyes on in the whole of his life. Her uncovered hair, thickly braided, was as smooth as black silk; she was small and voluptuous, with a tiny, nipped-in waist, and large round breasts that were only half-concealed by the low bodice of her gown. Her eyes, huge and lambent in a pale, heart-shaped face, were fixed on Forsythe as she walked with swaying hips toward him.

So he shut his mouth and didn't complain, even when Hammond set off for the brig *Swallow* with both whaleboats—a total of twelve men, which seemed rather too many for the simple delivery of a message.

Six

*E*ven after they returned to the cabin, Captain Reed didn't bother to introduce the woman, instead addressing her as Annabelle. Forsythe took the same chair he had before, avidly watching her as she filled the brandy glasses and then handed around a plate of small savory pies. Every now and then her dark gaze slid sideways to meet his hot stare, while a slow smile tugged at the corners of her lips. The implied invitation was incredibly arousing. Forsythe shifted about restlessly, crossing one meaty thigh over the other and then changing back, thinking that it was a long time since he had been with a woman—it was two months since the expedition had left Norfolk, Virginia, and he had not been on shore even once.

The miniature pies were delicious. "Our cook is a Frenchie—or some other kind of foreigner," Captain Reed said, back to being affable. "Picked him up in Rio after our old cook ran away, so we ain't had him on board much more than a week. He don't speak a goddamned word of English—or any other language so far as we can tell, and don't understand much, either. Mebbe the knock he took on his head addled his wits," he added.

"You had to knock him on the head to persuade 'im to ship with you?" queried Zack Kingman, who was not noted for his tact.

"Nope," said Reed. "Whosoever did his best to brain him did it before we arrived on the scene. Been in some kind of brawl, perhaps? But he can cook—my God, he can cook."

Forsythe wasn't listening. Instead, he was watching the girl—Annabelle—go through a strange little ritual. Taking a bit of pie and a hollow straw, she went over to the table and uncovered the birdcage, revealing a large, white parrot. Crouching, she cooed, and then put the straw between her pursed lips and sucked the pastry fast to the end of it. After pushing that end between the bars, she held the straw with her full, pouted mouth while the parrot pecked the tidbit free.

"It's her pet," said Captain Reed. "Would take the damn bird to bed, if she could."

Bed. The light from the low fire on the other side of the table illuminated Annabelle as she crouched, silhouetting the shape of her breasts. The fabric of her single gown and petticoat was so translucent in the reflection of the flames that Forsythe could distinguish the inward curve at the base of her spine, and the fullness of her buttocks. *Oh, Jesus.* He thought of the tumbled double berth in the starboard stateroom. *God*, he thought, *give me an hour with her in that bed*—and pictured what would happen.

When she straightened, she smiled first at Zack and then at Forsythe, so teasing that Forsythe wondered if the crazy old man would be willing to share her with them. Kingman was staring at her with a slack, lustful grin, making no attempt to hide the bulge in his breeches. Dirty bastard, thought Forsythe, even though they had shared the occasional woman in the past. He wished very much they were both wearing uniform—not only would he look so much finer, but the girl would see that he, Lieutenant Forsythe, had the higher rank.

Coming over, she perched on a "lady chair" that was so low-legged Forsythe could see down the front of her dress. Because her head was in front of the birdcage, he couldn't see the parrot any more, but he could hear it pecking—tap, tap, tap—at the crumbs that had fallen to the bottom. Above the hard, clicking noise, he heard her say, "Tell me about your expedition, pray—what you do, and where you sail. Will it be dangerous, perhaps?"

It was the first time Forsythe had heard her speak. He was so surprised by the rise and fall of her accent and her foreign choice of phrasing that for a moment he didn't take in the words. What the hell was she? French, he thought—Creole, perhaps, because there was a southern rhythm in her speech.

"Where are we going? Why, to distant seas and far-off lands." His tone was sardonic when he finally replied, because he was echoing a phrase that Captain Wilkes was overfond of repeating. "To the Antarctic and the Pacific," he elaborated.

She clasped her hands in the lush hollow of her lap and said, "To the Pacific islands?"

"Aye."

"Oh, how do I envy you!"

"Why?"

When her lips parted he expected her to say something about the romance of tropical paradises, but instead she confided, "Once I knew a young man from the south Pacific who told me wonderful tales of the land of his birth."

Forsythe frowned. "A Kanaka?"

"*Kanaka?* What is that?"

"A native—an islander from the Pacific. You'd recognize him by his brown skin," Forsythe said ironically.

She looked at Captain Reed, her expression oddly taunting, and then back at Forsythe. "His skin was brown, yes—a warm gold, and very smooth, like satin. He was very handsome. His face creased up into an absolute picture of humor when he laughed—just so." Annabelle lifted her fingers and pulled her cheeks upward and outward into an urchin grin, while her dark eyes sparkled wickedly.

Jesus Christ, thought Forsythe without returning the smile, what the hell was she telling him? Anger stirred, and he demanded, "And did this native inform you that the Pacific islands pose a danger for Americans? That every year whaleships from Nantucket and New Bedford are cut out by treacherous Kanakas, and whole crews of Salem traders are trapped and slaughtered?" Turning to Reed, he exclaimed, "You told me you reckon the American taxpayer is funding a senseless mission—that the exploring expedition is just an expensive joke! Wa'al, jest let me inform you, sir, that we will fly the U.S. flag in a thousand lagoons, and teach those bloody upstart Kanakas to respect it! We'll seize the bloody perpetrators, and hang 'em if necessary; we'll burn down their villages, and learn them a lesson. Our job is to make the Pacific safe for shipmasters like you, sir!"

"And I'm right glad to hear it!" Captain Reed replied with spirit. "Why didn't you tell me that before, you bloody fool?" he demanded, his tone jocular rather than insulting, and leaned forward to top up their tumblers. "For too many goddamned years the East India Marine Society has been lobbying for ships of war to patrol the Pacific, with no response at all from those jackasses in our government! My God, friend Coffin will be glad to hear of this!" Reed cried, and swigged brandy with gusto.

Forsythe and Kingman drank deeply, too, but at the same time they looked at each other with identically lifted brows. Then Zack lowered his glass to query, "Coffin?"

"Aye—Captain William Coffin, who has made many a journey to Washington to talk those jackasses into understanding the hazards that the pioneers of American commerce face. He's a Salem man himself, who knows from personal experience what it's like to lose a portion of his crew to bloodthirsty cannibals. By God, he'll be pleased—I wonder if he knows it?"

Again, Forsythe and Kingman exchanged looks. Then the girl interrupted. "But how will you know that you punish the right natives?"

Forsythe blinked and said, "What?"

"Perhaps you will punish the innocent, not being able to distinguish them from the guilty. Perhaps to you they all look alike?" Her tone was derisive. "And even if you can tell one from another, it is certain that you cannot understand their speech, and therefore they cannot plead for themselves. So how can you know that you are dealing out justice, instead of committing crimes of your own, and disgracing the American flag?"

Forsythe bit out angrily, "We have a linguister—a translator—on board."

"Wiki Coffin," said Zack helpfully.

"Wiki!" she exclaimed. Her mouth fell open and her eyes widened. "But he is the same young man of whom I spoke!"

Somehow, thought Forsythe, that did not come as a surprise. Nonetheless, it made him furious. Wiki Coffin had strolled the streets of many a port, and didn't exercise nearly enough goddamned caution about where his amorous glance might fall. In Norfolk, Virginia, Forsythe had picked a fight with the upstart half-breed after seeing him keeping company with a fair-haired southern girl, a quarrel that he reckoned was wholly justifiable.

Annabelle said softly, her smile mysterious, "I taught Wiki how to waltz. I was just eighteen; he was sixteen . . . and already a man."

Her long, black lashes lowered secretively as she murmured the last phrase, and when she raised them she was not looking at Forsythe, but at Captain Reed, her expression alive with mischief. It was as plain as if she had said it out loud that she and Wiki Coffin had done a damn sight more together than waltz, and that it had been highly enjoyable, too. The look Ezekiel Reed cast back at her was nothing less than vicious—and understandably so, in Forsythe's opinion. In Reed's place, he would have slapped her, and then, by God, he would have thrown her onto the double berth, flipped her petticoats over her face, and learned her a lesson she would take a bloody long time to forget.

Then all at once, in the midst of his anger, Forsythe placed Annabelle's accent. Damn, he thought, she'd been born in some Louisiana bayou—she was Cajun! He tossed brandy into his mouth, swallowed, and then said with contempt, "You know the waterfront of New Orleans better than even I do, I'd be prepared to place a bet on it."

To his surprise, it was Ezekiel Reed who snapped back. Belatedly, he saw that the old shipmaster had gone white with rage, his tight lips rimmed with blue. "Your manners are a bloody disgrace!" Reed exclaimed. "I'll have you know that my wife was convent-educated! And she met Wiki Coffin at our wedding!"

This little tart was Reed's *wife*? Bloody hell, thought Forsythe. If Reed was telling the truth, he was a substantial Stonington merchant—and yet he had married nothing better than a swamp rat, and a Kanaka-lover at that! Then he realized that marriage must have been the price for letting him into her bed. Ezekiel Reed was twice her age at the very least, so without a doubt she'd done it for his fortune. By God, though, his hot thoughts ran on, she surely was a tasty morsel, and he would have been sorely tempted himself, in the old man's situation.

Then Zack Kingman spoke up, immediately demonstrating that not only was he lagging behind in the conversation, but was impervious to atmosphere, too. "Convent? That's a new name for it," he said, and giggled.

Forsythe thought the joke amusing. Not so Captain Reed. "You goddamned insulting dog!" he roared. He staggered drunkenly as he flung himself out of his chair, but the swish of his stick was eloquent enough.

"*Jesus,*" said Zack Kingman as he dodged the blow. "Let's get the hell outta here!"

Seven

A sailor stood in the chains beneath the bow of the *Swallow*, holding himself in place with a crooked elbow, the coil of the sounding line in his left hand and the other fist gripping the end of the twenty-fathom rope. For Wiki, he was a black shape beneath the forward curve of the starboard bow, silhouetted against brilliant ripples and the purple and turquoise shadows of underwater coral. As he watched, the seaman swung the line back and forth in widening arcs, the ten-pound lead weight a black blob at the end. The rope whirled three times, audibly whistling, and then was expertly dropped dead ahead of the brig. The *Swallow* glided forward while every man on deck held his breath. When the bow was level with the line the leadsman hauled it in, muttering as the bits of leather and bunting that marked off the fathoms threaded through his right hand.

"By the deep . . . *nine!*" Cautiously they sailed on. There had been no sign of the cutter for so long that Captain Rochester had determined to forget Forsythe's instructions, and mount a search. However, he was even more determined not to endanger the brig.

Time passed . . . passed. "By the deep—*four!*"

George Rochester drew in a deep breath. "Clew up tops'ls!"

"Aye, sir!" hollered Midshipman Keith. His voice squeaked as he relayed the order. Bare feet thudded on deck planks, and men grunted as they hauled at ropes. A quick cry from the man in the chains, and Rochester shouted, "Starboard the wheel!"

Wiki heaved down on the helm, one foot on a spoke for greater leverage. He heard rapid orders, and then the headland slid past and the vista opened out. A large cove lay before them, edged with rocks and white sand, backed by a towering cliff face. A three-masted topsail schooner floated at anchor a hundred yards from the shore, Forsythe's cutter tied up to the martingale chains. Beyond her, the wreck of a sloop lay well up on the beach, and high above the wreck stone ramparts loomed at the top of a sheer cliff—Wiki could see the iron snouts of cannon, just as Captain Hudson of the *Peacock* had reported. On the half-mile of water that separated the brig from the anchored schooner, two whaleboats were pulling toward them with what looked like frantic haste.

Wiki heard Rochester's urgent shout: *"Wear ship!"* The brig had to come around on her heel so that the two guns on the quarterdeck could be brought to bear on the schooner and the oncoming boats. The deck boards thudded with the sounds of well-drilled response. Marksmen ran up the rigging hand over fist, while other seamen chanted at the halyards. The two big stern-chasers were run out, already primed, powdered, and loaded. Dave the gunner bawled, and brawny men grunted as crowbars were wielded and the cannon aimed.

The brig rocked and stilled, ready for action. The two whaleboats kept on a-coming. Then, when they were just a few yards off, the two steersmen leaned on their oars, and the boats turned and came to a stop, side-on to the brig. The men inside them were tough-looking fellows of a variety of ages. They didn't appear to be armed, but the thicket of rifle barrels poked over the bulwarks of the *Swallow* didn't waver.

The man at the steering oar of the nearest boat held one hand up to shade his eyes. Wiki saw him give the brig an assessing look all the way along the lean black hull from the sharp bow to the flamboyant sheer of the stern, and then up to the two tall, dashingly raked masts and the long spars designed to carry an enormous breadth of canvas. Then, carefully, he summed up the two cannon and the rifles aimed unwaveringly at his boats' crews.

"Brig *Swallow* ahoy!" he finally shouted.

"Ahoy, sir," replied Captain Rochester, arriving at the gangway rail.

"Sealing schooner *Annawan* of Stonington, Connecticut, Captain Ezekiel Reed."

"You're *American*?"

"Aye," said the other. "I carry a message from Lieutenant Forsythe. Permission to come aboard?"

Captain Rochester paused, looking up to check the fort. The sun struck light from the distant snouts of cannon.

Following his gaze, the blond man said with a touch of derision, "You can set your mind to rest—it's deserted. Ain't anyone left alive to tell the tale of why it was abandoned, but we do believe it was once a prison. Permission to board?" he asked again, and Rochester at last nodded—but without ordering his men to stand down from their stations.

All twelve men arrived on the deck in a bunch, leaving their boats emptily swinging about at the ends of their painters, so that the brig seemed suddenly very crowded. Their spokesman stepped forward, and said, "Hammond's the name, Captain Rochester— Joel Hammond, first officer. Beautiful craft, you have here," he added, as if he couldn't help himself. There was rank envy in his tone. "The U.S. Navy has done you proud."

"Aye," George Rochester complacently agreed. "Lieutenant Forsythe has told you we're with the U.S. Exploring Expedition?"

"He's with Captain Reed right now."

Hammond's reply was strangely evasive, Wiki thought as he studied the intruders warily. That they were sealers was logical, because the best of them came from Stonington, Connecticut—but what the devil were they doing at this equatorial island? The Stonington sealers were the anonymous kings of the farthest, coldest, most tempestuous reaches of the world; they sailed their small, sturdy craft into wild, uncharted seas, and landed on icy, surf-battered rocks in pursuit of their prey. Even the whalemen regarded them with awe. So why were they so far from their regular sealing grounds? It was late October, the start of the southern sealing season, and by rights they should be south of the Falklands. Too, he didn't like the fact that two whaleboats had come when only one was necessary.

George Rochester, who was even more acutely aware of the danger of having so many suspicious-looking strangers on board at once, said blandly, "A message?"

"Aye, sir." And Hammond handed over a sheet of paper.

Rochester read it, looked up, frowned, and said, "You have a leak?"

"We're pumping a thousand strokes an hour, just to keep her afloat."

"My God!" said Rochester, appalled. "It sounds as if we've

arrived in the nick of time." He paused, frowning down at the deck planks between his boots, and then looked up with an air of decision. "We've yet to get the brig anchored, but I'll be over with our carpenter as soon as humanly possible. Your captain must be pacing the deck, poor chap! Normally, I'd dispense hospitality, but I mustn't delay you—you must get these men back to the pumps!"

He turned his head, caught Wiki's eye with a meaningful look, and then turned back to the visitor. "Mr. Hammond, this is Mr. William Coffin, our shipboard scientific."

Wiki stepped forward. Hammond's expression was a study in baffled astonishment, his small eyes suspicious as he scanned Wiki all the way from snaky black hair flowing about brown-skinned shoulders to bare, broad feet sturdily pressed against the warm planks of the deck. He said nothing, and did not offer to shake hands. Instead, his manner became stiff and offended, as if he thought he might be the unwitting butt of some strange practical joke.

"Wiki, my good fellow," said George, his smile guileless. "Would you do me the honor of accompanying Mr. Hammond and his men to the schooner? Give Captain Reed my compliments, and convey my sincerest sympathies that he should find himself in such a plight. Reassure him that I will be along the *instant* the brig is snug. And—if you get the chance—do have a preliminary look at the damage. If it's not going to be possible to fix her, then the sooner I know it, the better."

Wiki, knowing without being told that George did not trust Hammond an inch, and that he was being sent ahead as a spy, couldn't help a small conspiratorial grin as he retrieved his boots from where he had stowed them in a corner by the helm. Then, with a farewell nod, he jumped down into Hammond's boat. No one said a word, though the oarsmen's faces were expressive enough.

As the whaleboat was rowed steadily across the insistent shoreward current, he avoided the inquisitive stares by studying the schooner. He saw the two taut ropes stretched down the starboard side, and then, underwater, the dark square of a fothered sail. So there really was a leak, he thought; the figure of a thousand strokes stretched belief to the limit, but there was a chance Hammond was telling the truth.

He said to Hammond, "You ran onto a rock?"

"In the middle of what appeared to be a clear channel, close to where she lies now."

"Unlucky—but then again, you took quite a risk coming in."

"We came in for water. There's a good stream farther up the coast."

Wiki was still very curious about why a sealing schooner should come to Shark Island, but before he could frame a question his attention was seized by an overwhelming impression of panic on board. He heard a loud, curiously shrill cry, and the thump of hurrying feet.

He glanced quickly at the oarsmen's faces, but they didn't look as if they had heard anything out of the usual. The boat had entered the channel where the schooner lay, and because it jinked about in the current they had redoubled their work at the oars. Then the side of the *Annawan* loomed over them, the bulwarks hiding whatever might be happening on deck. The copper sheathing below the waterline gleamed a ghostly green in the dark water, and the reflections of ripples danced on the black paint of the hull.

Two men reached out, grabbed dangling boat falls, and hooked on, while others steadied the boat by gripping the side of the hull. Hammond, standing in the stern, hollered, "Ahoy the deck!"

There was a long pause, and then a man arrived at the open gangway above them. "Sir?" he said. His tone was oddly wooden. Because the sun was behind him, it was hard to see his face.

"Tell Captain Reed a visitor has arrived from the U.S. brig *Swallow*."

"Sir." But the man did not move—it was as if he had no idea what the first mate had said. Wiki stood up to see him better, and then saw that the sailor's face was ashen.

Something has happened. Trouble. Wiki thought immediately. *Forsythe.* He jumped, grabbed the leading edge of a strake, scrambled urgently up the side—and then stood rigidly still, frozen by the utter unexpectedness of the scene.

A young woman was walking unsteadily toward him, her movements stiff. She was small but voluptuously built, her half-exposed breasts thrusting out the bodice of her dress. Her night-black hair was neatly braided into the nape of her tender neck, and her gown was a shimmering dove gray, a color that he knew exactly matched the translucent irises of her eyes. She was still young, just two years older than Wiki himself, and still remarkably beautiful; those huge black-fringed eyes were still the dominant feature of her small, white, heart-shaped face.

Annabelle! She blinked as she met his incredulous stare, but her expression was blank. Blood dripped from her arms and hands.

"You catch me at an inconvenient moment, I'm afraid," she said in a queer, numb, formal voice. "My husband's just been stabbed to death."

Eight

As if in a blur, Wiki heard rapid strides, and when he looked past Annabelle he saw Forsythe hurrying along the deck toward him, evidently from somewhere forward. Behind the lieutenant's bulky, powerful form scurried the much skinnier, more ropey shape of Passed Midshipman Kingman. Kingman's mouth was hanging open. Forsythe's frown darkened when he saw Wiki. "What's she screaming on about? And what the hell are *you* doing here?"

Wiki said dazedly, "Did you hear her say that Captain Reed's been stabbed to death?"

"What!"

Forsythe spun on his heel and headed rapidly for the after house door, with Wiki close behind him. They jumped down the companionway in a clatter of boots, and Forsythe led the way along a short corridor. At the threshold of the captain's cabin Wiki stopped short, stunned by the sight of the dark, grotesquely over-furnished room, but Forsythe ran straight over to the body that lay sprawled on the floor. Ezekiel Reed. The light was dull on the handle of the knife that was stuck deep into his back.

Captain Reed lay facedown, his feet toward the after bulkhead where an array of sealing weapons hung, and his head toward the companionway stairs; he was lying alongside a rucked-up rug which was soaked with his blood. It was obvious without looking that he was dead—and yet there was a strong sense of a living presence in the room. This was the dangerous time, when the *kehua*—the shocked ghost—had just been freed from its earthly shell. Forsythe hunkered down by the corpse, but Wiki seemed frozen to the spot.

There was a mixed reek of brandy, female scent, tobacco, bird-seed . . . and spilled blood like hot, wet rust. The nape of Wiki's neck crawled with a preternatural sense of being watched; he thought he heard a stealthy scrape and rustle. He looked around—at heavy drapes on every bulkhead, the massive furniture, and the clutter on the table: lamps, a covered cage, a box of ship's papers. There were too many crooks and crannies in this room, he thought with a grimace. The ship's rats were responding to the smell of blood.

Then at last he moved, very stiffly. He had to steel himself to go over to the body and lay a hand on Captain Reed's neck. The rough skin was warm, but, as expected, there was not the slightest flutter of life inside.

He said to Forsythe, "Bear a hand here." Together, they heaved the corpse up to its side. The congested face, though contorted with what looked like rage and fury, was perfectly recognizable. Ezekiel Reed. The last time Wiki had seen him was at his wedding; now he was dead.

"Jesus," said Forsythe. The knife had been shoved into Reed's back with such solid force that the point had penetrated all the way through his chest, so that his shirt was completely sodden with blood, back and front. As they lowered the body again, Wiki could smell brandy on the southerner's breath. Had he killed Captain Reed in a drunken fight? It wouldn't be the first time the hot-tempered Virginian had got into a brawl with a drinking partner, he thought as he straightened. The knife had penetrated Reed's bulky torso as if it were butter, and Forsythe was a powerful man.

Instead of speaking, however, Wiki concentrated on hauling a handkerchief out of his pants pocket. When he wiped his hands the cloth became smirched with blood. Looking down at it, he said, "My father and Ezekiel Reed were close friends."

"You were closer friends with Annabelle." Forsythe's tone was thick with contempt.

Wiki said warily, "Why, what did she tell you?"

"She taught you to *waltz*, she said." Forsythe made *waltz* sound like a dirty word.

Wiki winced, but instead of answering he looked about the room again, studying the way the slack, bloodied corpse of Annabelle's husband lay on the floor. Finally, he said in matter-of-fact tones, "There's no berth in here. So where did they sleep?"

"In those two staterooms down there." Forsythe nodded back at the passage.

"So where did Hammond berth?" It was usual for the first and second mates to live in the after house.

"You'll have to ask him," Forsythe grunted—and as if he had heard his name Joel Hammond came running down the stairs, his weather-reddened face confused.

He said, "What the hell has happened? Mrs. Reed is having hysterics and there is blood—*blood!*—but I can't get a word out of her, and . . ." Then, sighting the corpse, he gasped, "Oh, sweet Jesus." He seemed to recover fast, though—swinging round on Forsythe, he shouted, "So you killed him!"

"*What?*"

"You got into a fight!"

"I didn't lay a hand on the old bastard," Forsythe retorted. "And neither did Zack Kingman. If you think I was the one who knifed him, you can put that little notion right out to pasture, because we wasn't even here—just ask Zack, if you don't believe me! The first we knew that anythin' had happened was when *she* come out onto deck screamin' hell and bloody murder."

"But I heard you quarreling before we left for the *Swallow*."

"He was making aspersions about the exploring expedition! If you want to know what he was really riled up about, it was you! It was *you* who ran his precious schooner on a rock and then made a cock-up of fixing the leak! Oh, for God's sake," Forsythe said in disgust. "What kind of seaman are you? You're in *charge* here now. Instead of making wild goddamned accusations, exert a little authority. Try and behave like a captain."

Hammond's mouth sagged open. It was as if it were the first time the implications of Reed's death had dawned on him.

Forsythe looked at him with utter scorn as the blank silence drew on, and then said with an elaborately patient sigh, "For a start, it would be a bloody good idea to order this room cleaned up, so Mrs. Reed can come back inside."

Hammond stuttered, "But what do I do with the c-corpse?"

"*Jesus,*" said Forsythe, sotto voce, and then, raising his voice, said, "Send for the steward, and get him to sew it into a winding sheet, and then stow it somewhere while you get a coffin built. You have a carpenter, don't you?—or mebbe not, considering you weren't capable of fixing your own leak. But you must have a bo'sun—get him to build a coffin. Tell him to save the knife for when we inform the Brazilian authorities, because they are bound to ask for it. But the most important thing is to get this cabin cleaned up so you can get Mrs. Reed out of sight of the men. The quicker she's down here, the better for morale. And she's Roman Catholic, so you'd better get ready to hold a wake tonight. I presume you have a Bible on board?"

"Of *course* we damn well have a Bible on board!" Hammond shouted. For some reason this seemed to cause him more affront than anything else Forsythe had said.

Wiki, delighted to leave Forsythe in charge, removed himself without a word. It was a relief to get out into the bright light at the top of the companionway. Both boats' crews had arrived back on board in the interval, while the six cutter's crew were huddled with Kingman on the foredeck, so that the decks seemed packed. The racket was deafening. Men asked each other what the hell was going to happen next—that the ship was sinking under them was bad enough, but now the *captain* was dead. He'd been murdered while most of them were away from the ship—which cut the list of suspects down to a handful, and most of them could guess the name of the foul killer, or so they reckoned. The ship's pigs and hens clucked and squealed agitatedly, infected by the panicked atmosphere.

When Wiki looked around to see where Annabelle had got to she was collapsed onto a bench set against the after house, weeping wildly. There were streaks of blood on her face where she'd cradled it in her hands. He stood watching her, at a complete loss to know what to do, wondering what in God's name she was doing here on this sinking tub. Every time he had thought about her over the past eight years, he had pictured her presiding over Reed's substantial house in Stonington. It would have been a prosperous and comfortable way of life, and he had assumed that she would realize her remarkable luck, forget her wild past, and gracefully take on the role of a decent matron.

Instead, it seemed that she had taken up the dangerous and uncomfortable existence of a captain's wife at sea. It was a crazy decision—and yet Annabelle had always been madly daring, he wryly recollected; it was something he had learned in detail during the week before her wedding. Because Ezekiel Reed was rich and delighted with himself for landing such a delectable bride, he had lavishly entertained his guests for seven days of festivities before the actual ceremony—seven days that included seven nights, as Wiki vividly remembered.

The mad affair had been sparked the instant they had met; while her small hand rested in his big one, he had been engulfed by her wide-eyed, black-lashed, admiring gaze. Like his mother's people, Wiki had matured early, and when he had arrived in Stonington at the start of that week-long prewedding party, he had already learned a deep appreciation of women and their beauty. Never, however, had he experienced a girl as reckless as Annabelle Green—who was determined to make the most of her last week of liberty, and had swept him along with her wild exuberance. Already a man, he had found her utterly irresistible.

The risks she had taken were crazy—as witness that last waltz, he thought, and wondered why the devil she'd told Forsythe about it, because it had created enough of a sensation at the time. Just an hour before the actual ceremony, Annabelle had danced onto the floor of the huge reception room while half of respectable New England stared. Wiki had been leaning against a wall, content to watch her as a small orchestra played the fast three-step tune of the Boston waltz that was fashionable then, assuming that she was simply showing off her wedding dress to the host of assembled guests. Instead, she had pirouetted right up to him. "Handsome young man," she had murmured in his ear, enfolding him with her scent, "will you dance my last waltz with me?"

At the time, he had readily accepted the challenge, his face creased up into a wide conspiratorial grin—not only was he just sixteen and utterly obsessed, but he knew how she hated being thwarted. Now, eight years later, he grimly reflected that she could have got him lynched. She'd known it, too, he thought, because he remembered how wickedly her eyes had sparkled as she had leaned back in the muscular circle of his arms as they danced; just for the hell of it, she had deliberately and mischievously put them both in terrible danger. Was she still up to the same tricks? Had she dared Forsythe with her lush body and her dancing eyes—had he quarreled with Captain Reed because of her? And killed him, perhaps?

Then Wiki was distracted by the sight of movement on the half-mile stretch of water between the schooner and the *Swallow*. The brig was safely anchored now, the sails furled, and so a boat was heading their way. Captain Rochester had taken time to get himself into uniform, because Wiki could see the twinkle of gold lace in the stern sheets. Abruptly remembering that George had asked him to have a look at the damage to the *Annawan*, he left Annabelle without a word, heading for the hatch to the holds.

Nine

As Wiki descended the first rungs of the ladder that led below deck, the babble became muffled. At the midway point there was a landing that led to a between-decks space, and he paused to look around. In a whaleship this would have been the steerage—the place where the boatsteerers lived, and whaling gear was stored. Here, it was very cramped, because much of the area was used up by the after house and the forward house, where they were sunk into the deck. There was very little headroom, too, so that he had to stand in a crouched position. It was surprisingly light, though. Sun slanted through the forward hatch above, enhanced by light from another hatch forty feet farther aft, which had its own ladder. Wiki could distinctly see the many bags and barrels that were stored between the two hatchways. Provisions, he thought—the cook and the steward would have easy access to them because the forward hatch was so close to the forward house and the galley. Indeed, the steward would be able to reach the captain's cabin in rainy weather by detouring through here, as the second hatchway, aft, was close to the doorway to the after house.

Then Wiki tensed at the sound of deliberate footsteps echoing from below and coming closer. He realized that someone was coming up the ladder from the hold just as a dark-haired head poked up, followed by the body of a sturdy man in seaman's working rig.

Because he had been thinking so much about Annabelle, Wiki recognized her cousin at once. He exclaimed, "Alphabet—Alphabet Green!"

"Jesus Christ," said the other, his Cajun accent immediately apparent. "Wiki Coffin, what the hell are you doing here? I haven't clapped eyes on you since—hell, it must have been at Annabelle's wedding."

They shook hands, delighted to see each other. "You remember my famous nickname," Alphabet observed.

"I certainly can't remember your real name," Wiki confessed. "Only your initials—X.Y.Z., isn't that right?"

"Xavier York Zimri Green—and it surely ain't right to lumber a poor innocent infant with a label like that."

They both laughed, but then Wiki abruptly sobered. "I guess you know that Ezekiel has been killed?"

"Aye." Annabelle's cousin silenced, his expression very grim, and Wiki was struck by how much he had aged in the past eight years. Alphabet Green's face was darkened by the sun to the color of mahogany, and the creases about his squinting eyes and thin cheeks were so deep they looked as if they bit to the bone.

He sighed, and said, "Have they pinned the blame on anyone yet?"

"I don't think so." Though it would only be a matter of time before Hammond's accusation of Forsythe would become a chorus, Wiki thought grimly, because Forsythe was, without a doubt, the most likely culprit. If he was telling the truth, and had not been in the cabin at the time Captain Reed was attacked, it was lucky for him that he had two witnesses to that—Annabelle Reed, and Zachary Kingman.

"You're with the brig *Swallow*?"

"Aye." Wiki hadn't noticed Alphabet Green in the host of twelve *Annawan* men who had arrived on board the brig, but then, he thought, he'd had no reason to recognize him before having seen Annabelle.

"You've joined the U.S. Navy?"

"Never! I'm a civilian with the expedition—a translator, what they call 'linguister.' Of Pacific languages, mostly." Wiki joked in response to Alphabet's incredulous expression, "It's easier than it sounds—did you know that the Tahitian alphabet has only thirteen letters?"

Alphabet laughed. Then he waved an arm around the between-decks space, and said, "So what are you doing in here?"

Wiki roused, reminded of his task. Turning back to the ladder, he said, "I've been asked to assess the damage in the holds."

He headed downward. It was very dark, and when he stepped off at the bottom it was a surprise to find that the water was knee-deep, and the ballast was loose. He paused, frowning as he looked around, his sight adjusting. Save for a few casks stacked in tiers, and a big iron freshwater tank amidships by the ladder, the dank, echoing cavern was empty, which was usual enough in a sealer that was still on the way to the sealing ground. There was a strong, breath-catching stink of bilge. It was possible to see where the seamen had tried to fix the leak, as ripples of light seeped upward from beyond the fothered sail—but there was a hint of more light flickering farther beyond. It looked ominously as if the whole strake had splintered and started. Wiki took out his jackknife, unfolded it, and sloshed over to that side of the hull. The top layer of the loose ballast shifted and grated in the dark water as he moved, making a strangely metallic scraping noise.

As he tested the wood with the tip of his knife, he was aware that Alphabet had followed him, but was so absorbed he did not turn round. Then, when Alphabet finally spoke, his voice came from so unexpectedly close behind him that Wiki jumped with surprise.

Alphabet said, "How does it look?"

"Not good." Wiki waded along in the darkness, and set to testing wood again.

Alphabet sighed, coming close again, and said, "She's old."

"Aye—and has seen a lot of hard usage, too." Which was only to be expected, with sealers. "But she was built to last," Wiki mused aloud. If they could somehow careen her, all might not be lost—if only they could find replacement planking. Thinking that he might know of a source, he said, "That wreck on the beach—have you looked at it?"

"Of course," said Alphabet, and laughed rather strangely, Wiki thought. "That wrecked sloop belonged to Ezekiel, too," he said.

"She did?" Wiki was startled.

"Aye." Then Alphabet silenced. Again, he was too close for comfort; Wiki could smell the onions on his breath. The Greens were Cajun fisher folk from Louisiana—a kind of sea-gypsy people, originally from Acadia on the seaboard of Canada, who had been expelled by the British five or six generations ago, and who now fished the swamps of the Gulf of Mexico, and swarmed about the waterfront of New Orleans. They kept to themselves, and spoke their own dialect, and had different standards of behavior. No doubt they had their own ideas of proximity—Annabelle had delighted in physical intimacy more than any other girl Wiki had ever known.

Completely spontaneously, without knowing he was going to ask it, Wiki said, "Was it truly Annabelle's last chance to waltz?"

"Waltz?" Alphabet sounded jolted. "At her wedding?"

"Aye."

"New England wives are not allowed to dance at all."

"So she hasn't danced since?"

"Hell, no. It ain't considered decent. In fact," Alphabet Green said, "she shouldn't have danced at her wedding, either—and certainly not with a handsome young man who was *not* her fiancé." His tone was knowing as he went on, "That week before her wedding, there was a *hell* of a lot she should not have done. She took crazy risks—and so did you. The family considers her mad, you know."

Wiki said softly as he folded up his jackknife, "I thought she was enchanting."

"Truly?"

"Truth to tell, I was madly in love with her. Absolutely enslaved."

"Poor Wiki," said Alphabet. He laughed and took a step away.

"Poor Annabelle," said Wiki. She who had been so passionate and alive was a weeping widow, now. He turned and set his boot on the first rung of the ladder.

As he climbed, his knuckles accidentally hit the water tank. The cold, wet iron gave out a dull bang rather than the half-empty boom had expected. That's odd, Wiki thought, and said over his shoulder, "I thought you came here for water."

Alphabet's voice echoed from a dozen feet below. "Who the hell told you that?"

"Hammond."

"That's crazy. We came in to salvage the *Hero*—he knows that."

So here at last was a plausible reason for coming into Shark Island. "How did Captain Reed learn that she'd been wrecked?"

"He got the news at Rio. He expected to meet up with the *Hero* there, but instead learned that she'd been chased up the beach here—to escape a bunch of privateers."

"Insurgents?" Watching Alphabet nod, Wiki thought that when he had suggested to Captain Wilkes that the so-called pirates could be local revolutionaries, he'd been right on the mark. It had been wildly optimistic of Ezekiel Reed to hope the *Hero* had not been looted, but still worth checking. For the first time the situation made some kind of sense.

Again it was a relief to emerge into the bright, late sunshine. Looking around, Wiki saw George Rochester on the quarterdeck talking to Joel Hammond. George had a box under his arm—perhaps the same box of ship's papers that Wiki had noticed on the table in the captain's cabin. When he saw Wiki, he lifted his free hand in salute. Annabelle was nowhere in sight, so Wiki deduced that Forsythe's peremptory advice had been followed, and the corpse had been removed and the cabin cleaned up.

He turned to Alphabet and asked, "Have you always sailed for Ezekiel Reed?"

"Hell, no. I started out as a clerk—went to sea as a super-cargo—tried out life as a ship's agent in various ports." Alphabet Green sighed, and said, "But it all came to naught. I ended up the way you see me, at work on my cousin-in-law's sinking schooner."

The bitterness was understandable, thought Wiki. A super-cargo was an important man who sailed with all the privileges of a passenger, and was in charge of selling and buying cargoes in port. For Green, ending up as a seaman was indeed a failure—and all the more so if he'd got the job only because he was cousin to the captain's wife.

He said rather awkwardly, "Ezekiel's death must be a terrible loss to you."

"It's a blow for just about everyone on board the *Annawan*."

Wiki wondered what he meant, and then remembered that sealers, like whalemen, were very superstitious. "Was he considered a lucky skipper?"

"He made a lot of money for a lot of people, including himself," Alphabet said dryly.

"So what will happen now?"

Alphabet shrugged, looked down at the deck, and said, "I expect the *Annawan* will founder within the next few days, and somehow the *Swallow* will get us all to Rio."

Again, Wiki was conscious of the heavy wallowing feel beneath his feet. Alphabet could indeed be right—the schooner could be in such terrible shape that George would be forced to take the entire complement of the *Annawan* on board the *Swallow* and ferry them to the nearest civilized port. It was only what the U.S. Navy would have expected of any of their officers in similar circumstances, he knew, but nonetheless he disliked the idea extremely.

He remembered how crowded the decks of the *Swallow* had seemed as the two boats' crews had boarded, and how threatened he'd felt, and exclaimed angrily, "The *Peacock* reported your ship as a pirate because no one even *tried* to signal the ship. Hammond told us that the fort is nothing more than a ruined prison, but Captain Hudson of the *Peacock* didn't know that—because no one bothered to contact him. I can't understand why Ezekiel Reed didn't send a boat after the *Peacock*—or fly a signal of distress, even. It seems so brainless!"

There was a pause while Alphabet stared into the distance, his eyes narrow and his expression grimly withdrawn. Then he said with distinct bitterness, "Nothing he has ever done could be a fraction as brainless as bringing his wife to sea."

Ten

*W*hen Wiki left the schooner in the brig's boat with George, the sounds of the *Annawan* seemed normal, almost. There were men at work in the rigging, and a pumping gang forward of the mainmast. After a moment Wiki could hear the thudding of the pumps at work again. The air was rent with loud hammer blows as someone worked on a coffin.

Then they were off, and the echoes gradually faded. The late afternoon light glittered on the surface of the water, and the shape of the ruined fort at the top of the cliff was black as the sun lowered behind it. The cutter followed them out to the brig, but, after pausing so Forsythe could scramble on board the *Swallow,* the big boat veered off and headed for a cove at the far side of a rock fall from the beach where the sloop had been wrecked.

Rochester didn't comment on this for a moment or two, instead checking the state of the brig with Midshipman Keith, who was all importance at having been left in sole charge. Then he turned to Forsythe, who had his fists propped on his belt and was scowling as he watched his cutter disappear, and said mildly, "What's up?"

"Sent her off with Zack Kingman in charge to set up camp on the beach," the southerner replied. "Seems the best idea, if we're goin' to be here a while."

Rochester nodded. Indeed, it was an excellent idea. Provided with a couple of bags of flour and biscuit, the cutter's men could fend for themselves and live much more comfortably than when crowded on the brig—and it did seem likely that they would be here quite a while, unless the schooner foundered in the night.

"You're not going with them?" he inquired.

Forsythe said expressionlessly, "In an hour or so I'm heading back to the *Annawan* with Zack. We've been invited to the wake, seeing as we was acquainted with the deceased. After that, I'll go to the camp on the beach."

Acquainted? That was an odd way of phrasing it, Wiki thought, and still wondered why Forsythe was here, instead of with the cutter. George looked both intrigued and startled, but was too well bred to make any remark, instead heading for the companionway and shouting out for the steward of the *Swallow*. This fellow, a long, lugubrious man from Maine by the name of Stoker, was what George often labeled a *gem:* not only was everything neat and clean in the small saloon, but the coffee that swiftly arrived was ambrosial. Platters of sliced cold meats, hot baked beans, and warm new bread followed, and Rochester, Wiki, and Forsythe settled to their places about the table, leaving young Keith still in charge of the deck.

"Now," said Rochester to the lieutenant, "I've only heard Joel Hammond's version so far, so you'd better tell me what happened."

"Version of what?" Forsythe said cagily.

"The murder."

"I don't know any more than he does—except that I saw the corpse before he did. Wiki can tell you all about that, because he was there, too."

"Perhaps if you started at the beginning," George said patiently. "What happened when you arrived at the schooner? What was Captain Reed like?"

Forsythe shrugged, thought, chewed, and then said, "He was damn pleased to see us, at first. Hailed us as his saviors."

"I'm not surprised!"

"Then he complained that we should've arrived four weeks ago."

Rochester frowned. "But the *Annawan* has been here just a couple of days."

"Aye, but that sloop—*Hero*—lying up there on the beach belonged to Captain Reed, too. According to what he said, she was attacked by privateers about a month ago, which was when she was wrecked, and so he heartily wished that we had been here then."

Rochester said alertly, "So where are these privateers now?"

"God knows, because he wouldn't tell us. Once he'd got that little complaint off his chest all he wanted to do was get down into his cabin, open a bottle of brandy, and gossip."

"*Gossip?*"

"He was in a sociable frame of mind—ready to party, anxious for a spree. Rattled like a carriage on a rutted road. Jolly as a country priest." And Forsythe, his expression sardonic, swigged coffee and set the mug down.

"*Jolly?*" George echoed incredulously. "When he'd lost his sloop, fouled his schooner, and was on the verge of foundering?"

"The way he sank that brandy, it was almost like he had somethin' to celebrate. As I just told you, when he arrived on deck to hail us he was waving his stick and shouting *Salvation!*—but once we were settled he didn't even think of begging for a carpenter. Instead of hurrying us up, he was as hospitable as you please—sent the steward forward with grog for the cutter's crew. Told us how he watched the *Peacock* take fright at the sight of the old fort and kick up her wake to get out of cannon shot. Thought it the best god-damned joke he'd enjoyed in years." Forsythe added candidly, "If I'd been that boneheaded Hammond, I'd have sent a boat a-beggin' for a surgeon. The old man looked as out of touch as a hound dog in a fit."

George shook his head in bemusement, and said, "Did he make any sense *at all?*"

"Sometimes—but his mood swung all about the compass. Quarrelsome one moment, affable the next. Unpredictable as hell."

"You told Hammond he'd made aspersions about the exploring expedition," said Wiki.

"He had the bloody sauce to inform me that it was a waste of money because Stonington sealers have already established the continent of Antarctica—in that little sloop *Hero* that's lyin' out there on the beach!"

George exclaimed, "Did you believe him?"

"I'm just tellin' you what the old man told me—that the *Hero* reached Antarctica in 1820, no less, commanded by some Stonington cove by the name of Nat Palmer. And then he reckoned that the *Annawan*—again with Palmer in command—headed off with a three-ship fleet called something like 'South Sea Fur Company' for an exploring expedition in high southern latitudes, but that they came back without finding a thing."

Wiki vividly remembered Nathaniel Palmer, who had been one of the most prominent guests at Annabelle's wedding. A tall, dark, elegant man, with a long nose and piercing eyes, he had inspired awe and admiration. However, he did not remember any mention of either the *Hero* or Antarctica. The lively chatter about Nathaniel Palmer had been much more sensational than that—that he had sailed in the service of the great Simón Bolívar in the fight to free South America from the clutches of colonial Spain! In fact, Wiki thought ironically now, Nat Palmer had been nothing more or less than an insurgent privateersman.

Forsythe went on, "Reed kept on telling me he was a big heap taxpayer, and that the exploring expedition was a big heap waste of his taxes. Then he ranted on about what a misjudgment it had been for him and the other Stonington merchants who funded that South Seas expedition, because they didn't find a goddamned seal or catch even a single fur."

"So you spoke up in defense of the Wilkes expedition?" Rochester queried.

"I was angry enough to get up and walk out, to tell the truth," Forsythe admitted. "Aye, I do confess he got me pretty riled up about it—but when I was right on the verge of headin' forward and jumpin' down into the cutter he talked me into sending a note, instead."

"And you saw Hammond head off with the message?"

"Aye."

"Any idea why he took *two* boats instead of one?"

Forsythe shook his head. "Though it did strike me as odd at the time," he allowed.

"But you went back to the cabin instead of asking why?"

Forsythe hesitated, and then confessed, "His wife joined us, and I guess she kinda took my mind away from asking pertinent questions."

Wiki was frowning down at his coffee. Looking up, he said, "Where had she been up until then?"

"I haven't a notion—but she came from someplace forward, carrying a new bottle of brandy and a tray of snacks."

"And what happened then?"

"What happened then," Forsythe said sardonically, "is that after a bit of conversation Reed suddenly turned nasty—flew into a rage and threw me and Zack out."

Rochester exclaimed, "What triggered that?"

"The woman. She's a goddamned mischief maker."

"What do you mean, a mischief maker?"

Forsythe's brooding stare slid to Wiki's face, and he said, "She's a—a *taunter*. She taunted her husband with allusions to other men in her past, and then she taunted me. She asked what the expedition would be doing in the Pacific islands, and when I told her about making the ocean safe for American mariners she prophesied that we would disgrace the American flag by punishing the wrong goddamned Kanakas."

Rochester exclaimed with horror, *"What?"*

"Wa'al," said Forsythe while his gaze shifted to Wiki's face again, "she ain't nothin' but a Cajun swamp rat, herself, so it's only to be expected she should be a darkie-lover."

"Oh God," said Rochester, and put his head in his hands. "Surely you didn't tell her that?" he groaned. As a meeting between the U.S. Navy and the merchant service, this sounded like nothing less than a disaster. Looking at the lieutenant again, he demanded, "Is that why he threw you out?"

Forsythe shook his head.

"Why, then?"

"He took extreme exception to somethin' Zack Kingman said."

"And that was . . . ?" said Wiki. He was not at all sure what to expect but, knowing Passed Midshipman Kingman, was sure it was grossly offensive.

"It was nothing but a joke—and a very amusin' joke, at that. But the old man took offense—yelled a few obscenities and ordered us out of the cabin."

"And you argued about it?"

"We bloody well did not! We left like tender little lambs, and his wife was still there when we left—so if you're picturin' me gettin' into a brawl with him, forget it. She—and Zack—can confirm it if you don't believe me."

Rochester said, "So what happened after you left the cabin?"

"Zack and I headed forward, me yelling at the cutter's men to ready the boat to get under way, seeing as what we wasn't welcome any more. They had been on the foredeck all the time, and when they heard us they stood up and turned around."

"And then?"

"Just as we got abreast of the mainmast, I heard Captain Reed shout, *Get out, you goddamned bitch!* And out Mrs. Reed come, bursting from the after house so quick I figured he give her a kick to help her along. The way she taunts, she most surely deserves it. Wa-al, Zack and I wasn't anxious for her company, neither—not right at that moment—so we headed forward brisker than ever. We was heading down the starboard side, while she ran down the larboard side, heading for the galley."

"The *galley?*" Wiki was flabbergasted. The galley, a shed with a chimney which was set on the forward deck to keep the smoke away from the helmsman's eyes, was the ship's kitchen. Furnished with a big iron stove, it was the realm of the cook. Though he knew very little about captains' wives at sea, he'd never imagined one using the galley as a refuge—on all the ships he'd sailed, the crew had considered the ship's cook the lowest of the low.

"You heard me—the goddamned *galley,*" Forsythe repeated. "God alone knows what drove her there, but at that moment it was probably the best place for her, considerin' her husband's mood. But when she'd just about got there the silly bitch turned around, and ran back to the quarterdeck and back down into the cabin, the devil alone knows why. Next thing, out she come yellin' bloody murder. By that time, Zack and me are just about on the foredeck. We come running back aft, Wiki hove into sight, and I asked what the noise was about."

There was dead silence while Wiki and Rochester stared at him, but Forsythe said nothing more. "And that's it?" said George at last.

"Aye—and it's the goddamned truth!" Forsythe snapped.

"So who the devil knifed Captain Reed?"

"Not *me*, that's for bloody sure."

"But it sounds as if no one else was there!"

There was another blank silence, while Forsythe looked aggressively from Rochester to Wiki and back again. Then he repeated, "It wasn't me," and slammed down his mug and left the table. "I'm gettin' into uniform," he snapped. "It's high time I got away."

The quick equatorial dusk was falling. As Forsythe went into his stateroom off the larboard side of the saloon, Stoker came out of the pantry and drew down the lamp that hung in the skylight. He lit it, and pushed it back on its hook, and then, after lifting the coffeepot to check its weight, he headed off to refill it.

George said very quietly, "It does sound horribly like a drunken brawl, old chap. Do you think Forsythe was so drunk he's forgotten he drew a knife on Reed?"

"He wasn't *that* intoxicated," Wiki objected, remembering that Forsythe had seemed quite rational when they checked Captain Reed's corpse. "And then there is Passed Midshipman Kingman," he added. "It sounds as if he'll confirm his story."

"They're close cronies," George pointed out, still talking softly so that Forsythe, changing into uniform in his stateroom right next door, couldn't overhear.

"You think he would lie to protect his friend?"

"It has happened in the past—and I don't see how anyone else could have got into the captain's cabin without being seen. After all, according to Forsythe's account, the deck was busy, with Mrs. Reed running to the galley along one side, and Kingman with Forsythe himself hastening to the cutter on the other."

"Ah, but there is a way," said Wiki, and described the between-decks storage area, concluding by saying, "There are two hatches leading down into it, one close to the galley and another near the after house."

"So it's possible to get from the foredeck to the captain's cabin by going between decks?"

"Definitely."

"So any of the men still on board could have done it?"

"Anyone who was powerful enough to drive a knife all the way through Captain Reed's chest," said Wiki, and nodded grimly in reply to Rochester's startled, questioning look.

Then they were interrupted by the opening of Forsythe's stateroom door. The southerner's burly form was a splendid sight in a claw hammer lieutenant's blue coat with gold trimmings, white satin breeches hugging his muscular thighs. Wiki suddenly thought he knew why he had come on board alone, and sent Kingman off with the cutter—so that he, Lieutenant Forsythe, would cut a much finer figure than his subordinate at the wake.

Annabelle had certainly worked her wiles. The thought was an ominous one.

Eleven

orsythe had got ready just in time, because Midshipman Keith came clattering down the companionway to inform him that the cutter had arrived to take him to the schooner. As they both disappeared up to deck, Stoker arrived back in the saloon with the replenished coffeepot, filled both Wiki's and George's mugs, and then went back into the pantry.

George said to Wiki, "Let's take our coffee into my cabin. I'd like you to help me with something."

Wiki bit back a sigh, because it had been a long day, and he had a lot to think about. When he took his customary seat on the transom sofa in the captain's cabin, however, his interest was immediately revived. A box stood on the chart desk—the same box that had been under Rochester's arm as they had left the schooner.

He said alertly, "The *Annawan*'s papers?"

"Aye. I was forced to confiscate them in the name of the U.S. Navy."

"Confiscate them? Officially? But why?"

"Because Mrs. Reed seemed determined to destroy them."

"*What?*"

"When I arrived on board she was sitting on a bench by the after house and incapable of speech, but not long after that the corpse came up in a winding sheet, and the steward went back down with a bucket and a mop. Five minutes after that, he came back up to deck and announced that the cabin was clean, and Joel Hammond persuaded Madame to return to her sanctum. I gave her a few minutes more to calm herself, and then I went down to express my sympathy and offer her any assistance that lay within my power—to find her taking papers out of this box, looking at each one briefly, and then throwing them into the cabin fire."

"Dear God," said Wiki, shocked. "*All* the papers, or just certain ones?"

George put his head on one side. "Interesting question," he said at last. "I confiscated the box as soon as I realized what was happening—but I had the impression that she was looking for a certain document, and was burning everything else while she hunted."

"But why?"

George shrugged. "No idea, old chap. Perhaps she was just clearing out what she considered rubbish while she looked for whatever was important."

Wiki, wondering uneasily what Annabelle might consider important, watched Rochester open the box, which turned out to be an intricate affair. Inside the lid there was a special slot for the customhouse papers, crew list, and registration papers, while the body of the box itself was neatly divided by partitions. George picked up a handful from the nearest niche, gave half to Wiki, and then they settled to reading.

Wiki said at length, "These are letters relating to Ezekiel Reed's commercial dealings."

"Mine are the same," said Rochester, looking up with one eyebrow raised rather quizzically. "Letters from captains with reports of cargoes sold, and requests for instructions. According to what I see here, Captain Reed seems to have been what my grandfather calls a 'substantial' man—he owned not just the *Annawan*, but at least ten other ships."

Wiki shook his head in wonder. "I knew Ezekiel Reed was rich, but had no idea *how* rich—though probably my father did."

"Your father?"

"Aye. He and Ezekiel Reed were great friends."

"You knew Captain Reed?"

"My father took me to Stonington quite often."

"And Mrs. Reed?"

"I was there when Captain Reed married Annabelle—Annabelle Green, she was then."

"Good God. It's a small world—though I suppose that those who ply the oceans are all brothers, in a sense." Rochester considered, and then said, "How long ago was this?"

"The wedding? Eight years ago."

"She'd been married that long? She struck me as quite young."

"She was only eighteen at the time."

George said, "Ah," and sank into thought again. Then he said, "So you attended the wedding with your father—and your stepmother?"

"My father's wife refused to attend the wedding," Wiki said without expression.

"What? Why so?"

"She reckoned that Annabelle Green was a fortune hunter who

had trapped Ezekiel Reed into a highly unsuitable match, and so she refused to honor it with her presence."

There was a speculative pause, and then George remarked, "I haven't seen Mrs. Reed at her best, but it seems to me that she's a re-markably good-looking young woman."

Wiki said dryly, "She was a very lovely young bride—and Ezekiel Reed was twice her age at the very least."

"So it's easy to guess how she did trap him—if Mrs. Coffin was right. But maybe it was a love match. Did it look like a love match to you?"

Wiki paused. The tide was changing, and the brig creaked comfortably as an accompaniment to his memories. Finally he shook his head.

"You were—how old at the time? Sixteen? So it was just before you and I were sent to the college at Dartmouth—and if I remem-ber correct, you already had an extremely well-developed apprecia-tion of a well-turned ankle." George said shrewdly, "Are you sure you didn't fall in love with her yourself, my friend?"

Instead of saying anything, Wiki looked down at the letters he was sorting.

Then he heard Rochester say, "Maybe she did love her hus-band. We have to remember that she chose to come on a sealing voyage, which is quite a test of loyalty."

"Unless it was on his orders," Wiki said rather quickly.

"Perhaps—but it seems bizarre that *he* should embark, for that matter. For the life of me I can't imagine why a rich old merchant would take it into his head to undertake a chilly voyage south after seals when he could be sitting in luxury counting his money at home."

"Neither can I," Wiki admitted, and, having finished looking through the handful of papers, he handed them to George, who put them away and then gave him more.

"They say that some men never think they're rich enough, no matter how much money they've got salted away," George mused.

"True," said Wiki.

"Did you *like* Ezekiel Reed?"

The question was so abrupt Wiki looked up in surprise. He thought about the times he and his father had visited Ezekiel Reed, and then shook his head. "He was always jovial, but I didn't really see all that much of him," he said. "He and my father spent most of their time doing what they called 'discussing bottles,' either together, or with ship captains close to their own age. At times he was drunk and undignified. Truth to tell, he seemed terribly old to me."

"Hmm," said George, and Wiki knew that he was wondering if Captain Coffin had got drunk, too. However, he said nothing more, and there was silence for a few minutes, except for the rustling of paper and the creak of the brig. Then George threw them back in the box and said, "These are letters about commercial dealings, too."

"Likewise," said Wiki, and wondered what Annabelle could have been hunting for that was so important that everything else could be readily burned. Surely she must have realized that these letters, being evidence of cargoes in transit and financial deals in port, could make a difference to the fortune she would inherit?

The next section of the box was devoted to accounts with impressive totals at the bottom of the columns. Rochester observed pensively, "Captain Reed's vast wealth might provide a motive for his murder. Whoever marries his widow will be doing nicely."

"Ko nga take whawhai, he whenua, he wahine, " Wiki agreed.

"If you want to look for trouble, look for wealth and women, ha?" said George, who even if he did not speak *te reo Maori* could recognize quite a number of Wiki's favorite proverbs. He sighed deeply, returning the accounts to the box. It was getting late, and the next section yielded nothing more interesting than provisioning receipts. Then, just as they were thinking of putting off the rest of the job until the morning, Rochester spied three folded, sealed, addressed letters that had been thrust into an inconspicuous slot at the side of the box, evidently until Reed had a chance to put them on board a States-bound ship.

"Halloa," he said. "*This* could be what she was looking for." As Wiki watched, he took out a knife and without the slightest compunction heated it in the lamp, worked the seals loose, and opened the pages out. Two were to captains replying to their queries about freights. George folded them up again and replaced the seals, which were still warm and sticky.

The third, which was much longer and much more informal, was addressed to Stonington, and had been written six days before. He beckoned to Wiki. "My God," he said. "Look at this!" Then he read it more slowly, while Wiki looked over his shoulder.

"My dear brother," it began:

> *Through the blessings of Providence I have arrived off the northeast coast of Brazil at an island group in the region of Pernambuco after a passage of ten days from Rio, where our freight of iron found a good market and no duty to pay as they do not weigh iron for the duty. Otherwise Rio is a disagreeable place to say the least and a nest of rogues and charlatans. I was in hopes of getting rid of my Mate Hammond there, he is a disagreeable thing, even if he is a Stonington man I long to get clear of him, he has no more manners than a——and I dislike the way he speaks to Mrs. Reed my wife but there were no prospects in Rio for finding another officer and so he will stay though he does not appear to care whether he gets any skins or not, he would make a better horse jockey than a first*

officer of a ship or a master of a sealing gang. I had two men run away in Rio, one being the cook, the other that New Jerseyman greenhand that was not good for nothing, and I had trouble enough replacing them and the new cook has addled egg instead of brains. Worst of all though I had every reason to have expected intelligence from the "Hero" which is carrying 100,000$ for the Canton venture, all in silver specie, but alas! all I found was the hardest of news, that she had been wrecked on an island off the northeast coast in the region of Pernambuco during attack by the privateers which abound on the coast. The crew all escaped in the boat and put into Pernambuco and so to Rio, and I am left to my solitary apprehensions as to whether to give up the sealing and invest in a cargo of cotton or to forge on with the venture, trusting to Providence that we shall fill the holds with skins at the Galapagos or the Leeward Islands, and then proceed to Canton and make some kind of profit, but in meantime I have taken on board 20 tons of ballast copper dross for which I paid 30$ and then steered north to see if I can find the wreck of the "Hero" and will apprise you as soon as I find anything about the fate of her specie, this is just for your information in the meantime. With best respects from your brother Ezekiel Reed.

"My God," said Wiki. He was stunned.

George observed, "The *Hero* was a rich prize, indeed."

"Aye," said Wiki slowly. While it was typically cunning for a shrewd ship merchant to put such a valuable cargo on the most insignificant vessel possible for the hazardous voyage around Cape Horn, in this case the ploy hadn't worked. So who else had known about the rich lading of the *Hero*? He and George stared at each other.

Twelve

*S*o this is the famous sloop *Hero*," said George Rochester.

It was early the next morning, and he and Wiki Coffin were standing on the ripple-marked sand staring at the wreck. Though the paintwork on the stern was faded, the name *Hero* was plain. Close up, it was even more obvious that she had been sailed straight at the beach. Her bowsprit was jammed deep into a thicket of scrubby low growth, and the sand between her stern and the high tide mark was gouged deep.

She was in surprisingly good shape, though. The boat and sails were gone, but the single mast and standing rigging were entire. The *Hero* had carried a forestaysail and two jibs, and there was a boom for a huge gaff sail and a couple of spars for a small square topsail—a lot of canvas for her size. The upper part of the hull was reinforced with belts of thick planking, but several of the strakes had fallen in on the larboard side, so that the wreck had slumped that way. However, the planking on the starboard side was sound.

A board led up to the gangway rail, evidence of other visitors. When Wiki tested it with a boot it took his weight, so he strode up. Then, as he stood looking about the splintered, sloping deck, he heard George join him. His friend was a magnificent sight, dressed to the nines in a lieutenant's blue claw hammer coat, its broad lapels embellished with gold buttons and lace, a gold epaulette on the right shoulder. His long neck was encompassed by a stand-up collar lavishly embroidered with gold oak leaves and acorns and fouled anchors, and three more buttons decorated the cuff of each sleeve, which was laced with still more gold. He must be uncomfortably hot, Wiki thought, and wondered if George realized how bizarre he looked in this setting of wreck, sand, and scrub.

George said with disbelief, "Nathaniel Palmer sailed seven hundred miles south of Cape Horn in *this*? She's not much bigger than the cutter!"

Wiki lifted an eyebrow, thinking that that was exactly what the U.S. Navy and Captain Wilkes expected of the small brig *Swallow*, but refrained from comment, instead leading the way to the amidships hatch. They clambered down to the hold. It was obvious at once that whatever had been there had been taken away. Rays of sun seeped in where planks gaped open on the side where the sloop had slumped, and lit up empty spaces and drifting sand. The lost air of an abandoned hulk surrounded them, along with the ammoniac smell of sea wrack.

"Cleaned out as though she's been broomed," Rochester concluded with a sigh. They returned to the deck and then went aft, where a set of steps led down to the cramped after cabin. Boards creaked ominously as they moved, and sand slid audibly in the hold below. The cabin had been ransacked, too. The table had been scarred with knife marks, and all the lockers broken open. The mattresses in the two narrow berths leaked mildewed straw.

Going back up the stairs, they walked along the sunbaked deck to the galley hatch. Wiki, going first, had to feel his way down the half-dozen rungs into the dark forecastle. It was bigger than the after cabin, designed to accommodate six. Berths were set into the bulkheads that led fore and aft, looking like half-open drawers, all of them a clutter of straw from broken mattresses. The galley stove was built against the aftermost wall—a sensible place, since it would provide heating in the icy realms where this little craft sailed. There was a smell of animal droppings, and when Wiki's sight adjusted he could see tracks on the floor. There was nothing for them here, either.

Back on deck, the sun beat down on them. Wiki turned and surveyed the bay. The *Annawan* floated heavily a hundred yards away, her bow toward them as if she were thinking about climbing up the beach, too—if she didn't founder first. A half-mile farther out, the brig *Swallow* lay poised on her rippling reflection, the Stars and Stripes waving lazily from her peak. The boat that had brought Wiki and George to shore was hauled up high on the sand. There were marks where another boat had landed sometime since the last high tide, and then been pushed back into the water.

Wiki turned and shook back his long hair to look up at the fortified prison ruins on the cliff high above. A narrow trail zigzagged up through the brush toward it. In contrast to all the other times he'd checked out the forbidding silhouette, there was movement in the lofty ramparts—the four seamen who had rowed them here were digging a grave in the burying ground sited alongside the prison. Hammering sounds echoed over the water from the *Annawan*, where the boatswain's mate was nailing down the lid of the coffin.

From behind him, Rochester's pensive voice remarked, "So there was just eight in the crew—two officers in the after cabin, and six sailors in the fo'c'sle. And a hundred thousand dollar coins in the hold! A devil of a haul—particularly when there were just eight men to overcome."

Nine or ten would have been plenty to overwhelm eight, even if they didn't have surprise on their side, Wiki thought uneasily. He looked around again, and said, "Ezekiel Reed must be one of the most unlucky skippers in history."

"Why do you say that?"

"Sealing, like whaling, depends on luck—and Ezekiel Reed not only lost his sloop, but his life in the bargain. The crew must think themselves incredibly unfortunate—not only is their captain killed, but their ship is foundering fast."

"True," said Rochester with a heavy sigh. "We'll end up taking the whole damn complement to Rio—seventeen souls!—and God alone knows where I'm going to accommodate 'em all."

Involuntarily, remembering what it had been like when the schooner's men had invaded the *Swallow*, Wiki ejaculated, "No!" Then, calming as he saw George's startled expression, he said, "*E hoa*, some of the planking of this wreck is good. If we can get at the damage in the hull of the *Annawan* we could use the planks to repair her."

"The *Annawan*'s old—I don't know if it would be possible, old chap."

"But they built her strong," Wiki argued. "They had to, if they expected her to get all the way to Antarctica on that strange so-called exploring expedition."

"Even if we hauled her out on the beach, I just don't think her timbers could stand it. Her damaged side would slump, just like this wreck here. It would be an awful lot of work, just to finish her off."

George was right, Wiki thought, and was washed with a wave of depression. The two *Annawan* whaleboats were pulling for the beach, followed by another boat from the *Swallow*. Captain Reed's coffin was balanced on the middle thwarts of one of the whaleboats, and Annabelle was in the stern sheets of the other. Men jumped out as the boats grated on shingle, and hauled them up the strand. Then six sailors hefted the coffin onto their shoulders and set off up the winding track, while the rest straggled after them, Annabelle Reed in the center.

Without a word, Wiki and George loped down the gangway board to tail onto the procession. Then they slowed to match the funereal pace of the rest. Dust puffed up with every step. Insects hummed and twigs crackled against their legs, while the walls of the fortified prison frowned down upon them. A hot little wind blew leaves about, creating a constant whisper. The slope was steep, the winding path very narrow, and everything shimmered in the rising heat. Wiki could see ruts where heavy objects—blocks of building stone, perhaps—had been laboriously dragged up this track. As the going became harder men lagged behind, so that the procession lengthened with each zigzag.

It was a curiously medieval scene, the oblong shape of the coffin stark against the hot, dry background, bobbing with the movements of the six sailor-bearers, the cavalcade strung out behind. Black-cloaked Annabelle Reed was supported by Alphabet Green's arm, but they spoke very seldom. Hammond walked several paces behind them, his head down, a moody, preoccupied figure; unlike Alphabet Green, he was wearing a broadcloth suit. Annabelle's cousin was wearing seaman's dungarees, which though clean were well worn, and Wiki thought again about how badly life seemed to have treated him. Then came a straggle of sailors from both ships. Midshipman Keith was not there, being in charge of the brig. Also absent were Lieutenant Forsythe and Passed Midshipman King-man, and Wiki wondered where they were. At the camp the cutter's men had set up, he supposed—the sounds of the wake had drifted across the water for a long time the night before.

Then they were at the top of the cliff. The shadow of the arched gate fell over Wiki as he turned through it; a crumbling stone wall led off to either side. The arch was adobe, with a few terra-cotta tiles on top. The slabs of rock that paved the path had cracked, lifted, and become treacherous, but at least the walk was level. Gravestones leaned here and there, some as tall as a man, while other slabs were set into the ground, a couple of them big enough to cover several coffins. Crypts, Wiki thought—and one did look as if it had often been lifted to receive more coffins before being closed again. Feeling curious, he strayed over to look. The inscription beneath his boots was worn and scratched, but seemed to belong to the family of a general, who had undoubtedly been the commander of the prison. Other inscriptions marked the graves of soldiers—the prison guards, most of whom had died at a very young age a hundred years ago. Prisoners were commemorated with small squared rocks set into the turf, many with just the initials and the death year.

To his right, the walls of the old prison reared up against the serene blue of the sky, spotted with gaps that had served as windows, the rods of iron that had barred them rusted and broken like rotting teeth. Over to the left side of the burying ground a clump of dusty trees rose up against a half-fallen-in boundary wall. It was there, in the shade, that the seamen had dug the grave. Now they leaned on their shovels watching the procession arrive, their shapes muddled and blurred by the heat. First the coffin bearers joined them, and then the mourners straggled up, coalescing into a single group as they came.

Wiki and George brought up the rear, joining the huddle just as the coffin was dropped with a loud thump into the grave. There was a bit of a hitch, as one end of the hole had not been dug deeply enough. With a few muttered curses the seamen hauled the coffin out again, and one of the diggers jumped into the hole to ply his shovel. Dirt was thrown up busily while everyone watched.

Wiki said in an undertone to George, "*E hoa,* did you bring your prayer book?"

"What?" Rochester looked first startled, and then horrified. "No—why?"

"Because I don't think Joel Hammond has come prepared, even though he certainly owns a Bible. He loathed Captain Reed, and won't want to recite the obsequies. I strongly suspect you'll be asked to do the honors."

"Oh God," said George, but so it proved. The coffin was dropped back into the hole, successfully this time, and Hammond, his thin mouth twisted into his strange, secret smile, invited Captain Rochester, as the highest-ranking American here, to hold the service.

For a little while George tried to argue his way out of it, but then his natural good manners prevailed, and after casting a hunted look about at the sky and the ruined walls, he stepped up to the graveside. A muttered rendition of the Lord's Prayer followed, echoed by most of those present. George's air, as he pronounced, "In the midst of life, we are in death," was convincingly solemn, Wiki thought. Then, however, his friend ran to a stop.

Silence took over, punctuated with Annabelle Reed's stifled sobs, the creaking of boots as men shifted from foot to foot, and a sudden wet cough and spit as one of the grave diggers cleared his lungs. Wiki wondered if George's mind had gone blank. As Rochester began hesitantly to speak again, however, he realized that his friend was frantically trying to adapt the rite for burial at sea—which he, like every naval officer, knew by heart—to the one for interment on land.

"We therefore commit his body to—to the ground, to be turned into—into—ashes," he recited, and rushed on with an air of desperation: "Ashes to ashes, dust to dust—looking for the resurrection of the body, when—when . . ." His voice failed. Obviously *when the sea shall give up her dead* was not the right phrase for the occasion.

George looked despairingly at Wiki, who came to the rescue with the words "in sure and certain hope of eternal life." Then, quietly but with great feeling, he added, *"Haere e te hoa, ko to tatou kainga nui tena."* Everyone looked puzzled, but the brief ceremony was over. Ezekiel Reed's wedding celebrations had lasted seven days; his funeral had taken seven minutes.

"Reminds me of a prime embarrassin' burial I once witnessed at sea," George confided as he and Wiki watched the four seamen fill in the grave. "When the captain came to the words *We therefore commit his body to the deep,* the burial party tipped up the plank at the gangway rail, just as the good fellows had been trained. But, though they gave it a jiggle, the corpse refused to drop off into the sea. The captain, going red in the face, repeated the words, *We therefore commit his body,* and this time the poor wretches gave the plank a manful shake, but still the corpse remained with us. He was standing up against the upright board for all the world as if he'd come back to life, and the superstitious ones amongst us were beginning to whimper. *To the deep!* roared the captain in a monstrous bellow; the burial party gave the plank a tremendous jerk—and off the corpse sailed."

"Great heavens," said Wiki, feeling glad that the funeral procession was halfway back down the track and out of earshot of this cheerful little yarn.

"It cartwheeled three times before it hit the water," George assured him.

"I'm not surprised!"

"Then we saw this famous great nail sticking out of the plank."

"Which had snagged the canvas shroud and held the corpse in place?"

"Exactly," said George, and smiled benignly, back to his placid self now that the ordeal was over.

The grave was filled in and the dirt patted down. The four seamen joined them, their shovels on their shoulders, grinning broadly, not even trying to pretend they had not overheard the yarn and enjoyed it. "Back to the brig," said George cheerfully, setting himself in motion. He looked up at the sky and observed, "By the time we get there food should be just about to hit the table."

"Not for me," said Wiki. "I'll get you to drop me at the *Annawan*." As she had thanked Rochester for the part he had played in the brief ceremony, Annabelle Reed had put out a hand, and without even looking at him, had gripped his wrist.

To his relief, George nodded without asking for details. Then, just as he started to follow Rochester and the four seamen down the graveyard path, a distant rattle of stone distracted Wiki's attention. He stopped, looked around, and saw a man standing on the ramparts of the prison, looking out to sea. It was Forsythe—the burly figure was unmistakable. Wiki wondered if he was looking for a ship from the exploring expedition, but as he watched, the southerner turned round, and made the same long careful survey of the land. Wiki hesitated, on the verge of going to the prison ruins to see what he was about, but by the time he arrived at the top of the track to the beach, Rochester was out of earshot. When he looked back at the bastion, Lieutenant Forsythe had vanished.

Thirteen

*W*hen Wiki clambered on board the schooner *Annawan*, the crew was at midday dinner, and so the
decks were very quiet. Because it was hot, the off-duty watch was in
the forecastle, and those on duty were in the shadiest spots they
could find while they took a break from their work at the pumps. No
one tried to approach him; instead, he was aware of hostile stares.
Wiki looked around for Hammond so he could announce his arrival, but couldn't see him anywhere, so he headed for the quarterdeck and went down the after house stairs.

When he arrived at the threshold of the captain's cabin, he
paused. He'd forgotten just how great a contrast the after house was
to the brightly sunlit deck—how it was so much more like a Stonington parlor overburdened with furniture than a regular captain's
cabin. Instinctively, he checked the floor where the corpse had lain.

The blood-soaked mat was gone, and the deck boards were clean. Then he saw that Annabelle was hunched in a chair in front of the heating stove. Despite the heat of the day, flames flickered. Perhaps because of that, she hadn't noticed his arrival.

He cleared his throat, and she whirled around in her seat. With a gasp she said, "Wiki!" When he went up to her, she stood up and gripped his wrist again, dragging him close as she hissed, "What was it you recited at Ezekiel's burial?"

It was the very last thing Wiki had expected her to say. He detached his wrist, took a step back, and then said, *"Haere e te hoa, ko to tatou kainga nui tena."*

"What does it mean?"

"Literally, *Go, my old friend, to the eternal abode that awaits us all.*"

Annabelle slumped back in her chair, her eyes huge with horror, and he abruptly remembered that Cajun were reputedly superstitious. "You spoke to Ezekiel's *ghost?*"

He grinned reassuringly, and joked, "I didn't expect him to answer."

However, she was not amused. Instead, she glanced wildly around the room—and something rustled in the darkest corner. It was the same stealthy scraping sound Wiki had heard while he was examining Captain Reed's corpse. Again it reminded him of rats creeping toward the scent of blood. The hairs on the nape of his neck shivered and lifted.

Another furtive scrape. It came from the big covered birdcage. Cautiously, Wiki crept over to it, and lifted a corner of the cover. A round unblinking eye peered back at him. It belonged to a parrot— a large white parrot that shifted about on its perch. In the sardonic fashion peculiar to parrots, the bird revolved its neck so it could study him coldly, first from one side of its head, and then from the other.

When Wiki looked back at Annabelle, she had her eyes squeezed shut. Dropping the cage cover, he went back to her, saying more gently, "I quoted that proverb at the burying ground at the top of the cliff. Even if it worked, there's nothing to be afraid of in here."

"Isn't there?" Her voice shook wildly.

Wiki said carefully, hoping she was not going to succumb to another fit of hysteria, "According to my people's beliefs, by now a bird will be carrying your husband's spirit on his journey to the underworld."

"Ezekiel's spirit is in a *bird*?"

She sounded more horrified than ever. Wiki shrugged helplessly, and excused himself by saying, "It's a common belief in the Pacific, not just in New Zealand."

He saw her shudder, and then she shifted about, groping for a handkerchief to dab at her cheeks. When she looked up there were still tears in her eyes, but somehow she managed a shaky smile. "Wiki, dear Wiki, what are you doing here?"

"I know Lieutenant Forsythe told you I am with the exploring expedition," he said, standing and surveying her with his hands propped on his hips. "A much better question is what are *you* doing here?"

"On this ship?"

"Aye." He paused, watching her tilt her head to one side in the way he remembered so well. Despite the passage of eight years and the terrible events of the day before, she was just as young and beautiful as she had been the week before her wedding.

He said, "Every time I thought of you, I imagined you in pretty gowns, pouring tea from pretty tea sets, prettily entertaining Ezekiel's friends."

"Life was indeed a lot like that," she admitted, and a dimple flickered in one cheek.

"So why in the devil's name did you come on voyage?"

"Because I was bored." Her eyes flashed, and she exclaimed, "Have you any idea what it is like to live in Stonington, Wiki? It is very pretty, the village, yes, but those New Englanders! Not only are they as cold in nature as an undertaker's doorknob, but the womenfolk—they spy, you know. And gossip. All the time, they spied on me."

"But why would they do that?"

"Wiki, you're teasing me," she accused. Her superstitious fright and hysteria had vanished; she was as pert and challenging as he remembered. "Can't you imagine the contrast to my life before?" she demanded.

"To your life in New Orleans?"

"You have no idea of what life is like for a New Orleans belle—the flowers, the passion, the poems and the duels! Life for a belle in New Orleans is perfectly dazzling, while life for a Stonington matron is perfectly drear."

"Then you should have married one of your New Orleans beaux," he said callously.

"Wiki, you are cruel—you were ungallant back then, and I made myself excuses for you because of your youth, but now you are too old to be ungallant."

"Not so." Damn it, he thought, she was flirting with him, and he should have more sense than to allow it; she'd been widowed for less than twenty-four hours. It was indiscreet enough for him to be alone with her, even with the door wide open; it reminded him too much of the week before her wedding.

She leaned forward and commanded softly, "Sit down."

Wiki looked around. There was a big chair close to the lady-chair where she was perched, but he had a strong feeling that it had been Ezekiel Reed's, so he chose one with an upright back which was farther away. While he sat on it, he was conscious that she was watching his every small movement intently.

When he was settled, she said, "You have greatly changed since the age of sixteen—you were a man already then, but now you are even more so." She studied his face with those enormous, rapt eyes. "But very handsome still—and I am so glad you did not tattoo your face as you so often threatened. Your face creases up so beautifully when you smile that I assure you yet again that a tattoo is not necessary. Why do you wear your hair so long?"

"Right after your wedding I gave up the attempt to look like a Yankee," he said. "It didn't make sense any more."

She nodded. "It is a great pity Ezekiel did not get to see you again before he—died. He would have greatly approved."

He said, astonished, "What in God's name makes you think that?"

"He thought it was a huge joke that his great friend William Coffin should have the wonderful effrontery to carry his good-looking half-breed son to Salem, and introduce him to his oh-so-proper Nantucket-born wife and all her neighbors."

Wiki said wryly, "It wasn't such a joke for me."

"Or her, no doubt—but Ezekiel greatly disliked your father's wife, Huldah." Then she demanded, "So what happened to you right after my wedding?"

"I went to college."

"College? What do you mean?"

"My father was furious—because of that waltz." He grinned wryly and said, "You know how Stonington people gossip?"

She pouted her lips. "You're teasing me again."

"No, I'm not." His father had been so furious about that sensational last waltz and the gossip it had caused that when he had sailed off to the Pacific he had left Wiki behind. "And the minute his ship was hull-down on the horizon his wife packed me off to a missionary college in New Hampshire, so I could learn how to convert the poor benighted Indians."

Wiki grinned reminiscently. "But instead I met George Rochester, who'd been sent there in disgrace as well, and the Abnaki Indians converted *us*—they told us yarns and taught us how to hunt. After a few months the authorities found out about it and all hell let loose, so we built a birchbark canoe and paddled off down the Connecticut River."

"Wonderful!" She clapped her hands. "So why can't you understand how tedious it was to pour tea from *pretty* teapots and wear *pretty* gowns in Stonington, when all the time you were having such adventures?"

Wiki smiled, but then said soberly, "Was Ezekiel an unkind husband?"

Her perfect brows flew up. "No, not at all. When he was home he was always generous—but he was too often away. After eight years I was tired of it, so I made up my mind to go on voyage and find romance again."

"Romance—in *sealing*?"

"Mrs. Palmer went a-sealing in this very same schooner, so why shouldn't I?" she demanded, and flipped a hand in a very Gallic gesture.

"Mrs. Palmer sailed on the *Annawan*?" Wiki exclaimed, astounded.

"The voyage didn't go well—but she was proud of it. Everyone praised her valor—including her own husband," Annabelle said resentfully. "Even that fool—that *couyon* Joel Hammond was praiseful. Did you know he was on the *Annawan* at the time?"

Joel Hammond had sailed on the *Annawan* with Palmer? *Good God*, thought Wiki, and said, "What do you mean, the voyage didn't go well?"

"The ship was commandeered by a crowd of wicked convicts. They were on a prison island, just like this one, and those horrid desperadoes made Captain Palmer carry them to the mainland."

"*What?* When was this?"

"They sailed from Stonington in 1832, and came back the following year," she said, and added serenely, "They said they were lucky to get away with their lives, and Ezekiel was able to buy this schooner very cheap because of it."

Wiki deliberated, wondering if there was any documentation of this in the box that still sat on Rochester's desk, and whether this was the kind of thing she had been hunting for. He said, "Why did you try to burn the ship's papers?"

"Why do you ask me that?" she said evasively. "I was just clearing away. The *Swallow* will carry me to Rio de Janeiro—Lieutenant Forsythe has said so—and I must tidy up and pack my things."

"*Forsythe* told you we're going to Rio?"

"Yes—when your ship leaves, I leave with it, so I must make haste to be prepared."

"Have you spoken to Captain Rochester about this?"

"No, but Lieutenant Forsythe offered passage on the *Swallow*—and he is a lieutenant, while Rochester is just a passed midshipman, no?"

"But Rochester's the commander of the ship—he's *Captain* Rochester."

"Only when he is on board the ship, is that not right? That's what Lieutenant Forsythe told me."

Wiki, feeling hopelessly bogged down, said, "It's complicated."

"Well, when I ask *Captain* Rochester for passage he can't possibly refuse because I cannot stay here," she said pertly, "A married woman without a husband, you know, is in a most peculiar position—especially at sea."

Wiki thought that most surely was the truth, and that even if they managed to save the *Annawan*, George would probably have to offer Annabelle passage to Rio out of sheer gallantry, because it wasn't decent to leave her alone with these men. Curiously, he said, "Where were you yesterday when Forsythe and Kingman came on board?"

She frowned. "Wasn't I in this room?"

"Not according to Lieutenant Forsythe."

"Then I must have been in the galley."

Wiki studied her thoughtfully. This helped to explain why she had fled to the galley when her husband had thrown her out of the cabin, but it still seemed an odd place for someone so elevated as the wife of the captain. "Were you alone?"

She shrugged.

"Were you chatting with the cook?"

"No, that is not possible. My husband shipped him in Rio, you know, because our old cook ran away—and there is something wrong with this cook's brains. Ezekiel said that maybe it is because he has had a big bang on the head not so long ago, but myself, I don't even think he has our language—not French, not English; perhaps a little Cajun, but not enough to make any sense. When I heard Ezekiel screaming for another bottle of brandy, that fool of a steward was gossiping on the fo'c'sle deck, so I fetched it myself. Then my husband wished me to stay, so I remained to talk with Lieutenant Forsythe and that horrid Kingman—who made such a crude joke that Ezekiel became very angry, and drove them out with his stick."

Wiki's brows shot up at the mental image. "And they went?" he asked.

"They went," she said expressionlessly. "Then I, too, went. I started to go back to the galley—but instead I went back into the cabin." Her voice was beginning to shake again. "And—and I f-found poor dear Ezekiel lying on the floor with a knife in his back, making a terrible, terrible choking noise, ch-choking on his blood. I tried to turn him over, to sit him up . . . but the b-blood, it made—made him so slippery and heavy. He dropped back and was silent." She shuddered and said, "I don't remember much after that."

"Can you remember why you went back into the cabin?"

"I saw someone by the door to this after house. There had been trouble enough, and I wished to stop more, if I could."

"What!" Wiki said very quickly, "Did you see who it was?"

"The man on the quarterdeck? It was Lieutenant Forsythe, I think," she said, and nodded, her wide gaze earnest on his face. "Yes, of that I am almost sure."

Fourteen

*W*hen Wiki came out onto the quarterdeck, Joel Hammond was striding toward him from somewhere forward, his face dark with suspicion and anger. He said, "What the bloody hell were *you* doing down there?"

Wiki said quietly, "I'm a family friend; I was passing on my sympathies."

"Friend?" Hammond reared back, his expression scandalized. His small eyes looked Wiki up and down. "How can you be? You're a godless Kanaka!"

Wiki remembered that according to Ezekiel Reed's letter Hammond was a Stonington man. However, he had no recollection of meeting him there—but then, he thought, it was highly unlikely that Joel Hammond would have been invited to Ezekiel's wedding, not being of the right social caste. He said stiffly, "Ask Mrs. Reed, if you don't believe me."

Hammond muttered something about Mrs. Reed that didn't sound at all complimentary, and then demanded, "How did you get here? I don't see a boat."

"Captain Rochester dropped me here after the burial. Perhaps you would oblige me by lending me a boat to get to the beach?" Wiki gestured to where the cutter was moored.

For a moment he thought Hammond would refuse, but finally he reluctantly nodded. A boat was lowered and manned, and Wiki jumped down into the stern. It was a relief to see the friendly face of Alphabet Green, who was standing at the steering oar; when Wiki asked jokingly if he could steer, his old acquaintance gave it to him with a mock bow and a grin, taking one of the ordinary pulling oars instead. Accordingly, Wiki was facing forward as they rowed into the cove and was the one who saw the cutter's men first.

They had a small fire going in the shade of a tree, and were busily cooking up a mess of fish. However, two of them plunged co-operatively into the water to hold the boat steady while Wiki handed the steering oar back. Then he clambered out, and helped the cutter's men turn it and push it back into the surf.

The moment the boat had headed off, he said, "Where's Lieutenant Forsythe?"

The six seamen looked at each other and shrugged. "Haven't seen him since the hour after breakfast, when he come around that headland yonder," said one, and pointed at the rocky outcrop that barricaded the way to the beach where the sloop was wrecked.

"Why, what was he doing there?" said Wiki, puzzled.

The men all grinned at each other.

"Spent the night on the *Annawan*, he and the passed midshipman did," said one.

"A-roistering," said another. "It was a wake for Cap'n Reed. And they dropped him off at the wrong beach."

"Lieutenant Forsythe looked the worst for wear I've ever seen 'im," said a third. "Must've got most terrible drunk."

Wiki said, "So where did he go?"

They all jerked their thumbs toward a steep track that straggled up the cliff. "Off a-huntin', I guess," said one, and another confirmed this by saying that the lieutenant had been toting his gun when he left.

Wiki was prepared to guess that Forsythe had taken a bottle, as well. He looked at the fire, a shipshape affair with a wire rack across the top of it, *boucanier* style. They were roasting some fine fish on this, while an assortment of shellfish sat spitting on the outer edges of the coals, alongside a steaming coffeepot.

"Smells good," he observed.

In truth, it was an aroma fit to lure a bear from its lair, so he readily accepted the men's invitation to join them in their feast. Not only was it a long time since breakfast, but he wanted to find out if they would confirm Annabelle's sighting of Forsythe on the quarterdeck just before Ezekiel Reed was murdered. What they told him now, he thought grimly, could condemn Forsythe as a killer—or vindicate him, by backing up his statement that he was hurrying forward at the time.

He didn't rush it, however, instead waiting for an opportunity to broach the subject in a casual kind of way. For a long while he and the men chatted casually, sitting in a companionable circle in the shade of the scrubby tree, sucking fish bones and throwing them to the gulls. It was a peaceful scene. Surf swished rhythmically, lacing the edge of the golden sand with white, and while there was a little puff of cloud clinging to the black and emerald triangular pinnacle that gave Shark Island its name, the sky was otherwise a deep, quiet blue. For these men, as Wiki knew from his own experience, being here was a luxurious respite from their hard life at sea.

Conversation came easily, as Wiki was a seaman who knew the ways of other seamen. Respect was given, and received: He knew they were the pick of the crews of the discovery fleet; and they knew that he had done his apprenticeship in whaleships, which might have been the most disdained of the merchant fleet of New England, but whose captains and officers were famous for training better seamen than any other branch of the trade.

"I hear you were royally entertained by the steward of the *Annawan* yesterday," Wiki observed at last, throwing away the bones of the last succulent fish head. For some reason, he'd noticed, Americans didn't like to eat the heads. If Sua and Tana had been there he would have had to divide up the bounty, but as it was, he had them all to himself.

"Bit too slick, that Jack Winter," said one with his lips pulled down.

"Winter?"

"The fat old steward," said another, and spat to one side. The men were looking at each other with identical expressions of wry amusement. "Gammoned us good, he did," said one. "When Cap'n Reed bid him carry us a bottle of grog, he brung lemon squash, too. Told us to drink up the lemon to take the edge off our thirst, so we'd 'preciate the rum better. But all the time we was working through the lemon, he was helping himself to the grog."

"Gossips worse'n a woman," said a man with a New Bedford accent, his tone disparaging. The other five nodded in agreement. As Wiki was very aware, having spent years in the crowded confines of the forecastle, proper seamen knew that minding one's own business was a virtue, and a buttoned-up lip a distinct asset.

"Did this Jack Winter leave the fo'c'sle deck at all?" Wiki

pursued; he remembered that Annabelle had complained that the steward hadn't responded when Ezekiel had hollered out.

They all laughed. "Stuck to us like a leech so long as there was rum in that bottle."

"What about the men who stayed behind when the boats went off? How many were there?"

The six thought a long moment, and then the New Bedforder said, "Four."

"You're sure?"

"Aye—but not counting the captain, of course."

So the crew of the *Annawan* totaled sixteen, Wiki mused; it was a number that seemed about right for a sealer. The schooner was small enough to be sailed by four, plus the captain, so the twelve extra men meant that two six-man sealing gangs could be put on shore once they arrived on the ground. Coincidentally, it exactly matched the number of crew on the *Swallow* when the cutter was off— George, Wiki himself, Midshipman Keith, the boatswain, the carpenter, the cook, the steward, the gunner, and eight hands. George Rochester had mentioned a complement of seventeen on the *Annawan*, he remembered, but realized that he must have included Annabelle.

He said, "I wonder who those four men were?"

The cutter's men consulted among themselves. One, of course, had been the steward, Jack Winter. But, while they had distinct memories of him, as he had been with them—and their bottle of rum—just about the whole of the time, they were otherwise exasperatingly vague. Because they had sat in the bows, forward of the windlass, they hadn't had much of a view of the deck, not unless they stood up and turned round for any reason.

"What about the man who was working aloft?" one of them prompted.

"He was a Gee," said the New Bedforder, using the whalemen's derogatory term for a Portuguese.

"Aye," said the other. Now that the old whaleman had mentioned it, he, too, remembered seeing a Spanish-looking type in the mizzenmast lower rigging, after he'd stood up and looked to see what Mrs. Reed was making her ruckus about.

Then another seaman reckoned he'd seen the cook come out of the galley—but that had been a lot earlier, and had been just a glimpse because he hadn't been stood up at the time, and no sooner had he glimpsed him than the fellow had vanished, he said.

"He went back into the galley?" Wiki asked.

"Well, I didn't actually see him get back inside," the seaman allowed. "But it stands to reason that he did, don't it, because Mrs. Reed spoke to *someone* in there."

"You mean when you first arrived at the schooner?" said Wiki, puzzled.

"No, no. Well, she was in there when we first boarded," said the seaman. "Not that we knew it, not until she left the galley to go aft to the captain's cabin. But about a half hour later, just after we heard the lieutenant and the midshipman calling out to us and started to turn around to look, I glimpsed her hurrying helter-skelter to the galley. When she got there she called somethin' through the doorway, which proves that the cook was there, don't it? Then she whirled around and ran back to the cabin. A couple of minutes after that, and out of the cabin she burst again, yellin' murder and mayhem, and that's when we stood up for a proper look at what the hell was goin' on."

"And you saw Lieutenant Forsythe and Passed Midshipman Kingman come along the deck?"

"Aye—though they was running back and forth, too, what with all the commotion."

"Did you hear what Mrs. Reed called out to the cook?"

The seaman frowned mightily, but finally shook his head. "Even if I heard it, I reckon it was foreign."

So that accounted for three of the men on board—the steward, the cook, and the man aloft—and seemed to substantiate what Forsythe had said, even if the details were blurred. Wiki pursued, "So who was the fourth man left on board?"

"The bo'sun's mate," said one of the men positively.

"How can you be so sure?"

"He's a big cove, very noticeable. He came out of the sternward end of the forward house when Mr. Hammond called for two boats' crews, with a knife and a hammer in his hands. Another man came out with him, an older feller, and I reckon he was the bo'sun, be-cause he gave the big young feller instructions before he departed."

"And after the boats had left, this man went back into the for-ward house?"

"Aye. And then we heard a lot of hammering. He was working in there, all right."

Wiki said carefully, "Any idea why *two* boats went to the *Swal-low,* when there was only occasion for one?"

There was a bit of a silence, while three of the cutter's men leaned back on their elbows ruminating at the sky through pipe smoke, and the New Bedforder leaned forward to pluck up an oys-ter from the edge of the fire. As he bent over he accidentally broke wind, and everyone laughed, including the culprit himself. Then he said around the carefully slurped hot mouthful, "I don't reckon there's very good feeling on board that there schooner. They could've been glad of the chance to get away for a bit."

"I don't hold with women a-going to sea," said one.

"Never a truer word," agreed another.

"They're powerful unlucky," said another, and they all nodded sagely. "Thank God Cap'n Wilkes don't carry his wife on the *Vin*. Two cap'ns on the quarterdeck be one too many by far."

To Wiki, it was news that the commodore of a U.S. Navy fleet had the option of carrying his wife. He also meditated that Mrs. Wilkes, if present, might have moderated Captain Wilkes's increasingly erratic behavior. However, instead of responding to this, he asked, "So you think Mrs. Reed is to blame for the bad morale on the *Annawan*?"

"Oh aye," said the New Bedforder. "I mean to say, it figures, things bein' the way they are with Hammond. There's not a man on board who likes her, and Hammond in particular. Truth be told, he can't stand the sight or sound of her."

Wiki said, "Does Captain Hammond hold a grudge because he was forced to shift his berth to the forward house, perhaps?"

"Wa-al, according to the steward, he's got a bigger grudge than that," said one.

"An incurable hand for gossip, that man," said the New Bedforder with deep disapproval. "Stewards are ever so, I guess, but Jack Winter really ought to keep a stiller tongue in his head."

"What did Winter tell you?"

"That Mr. Hammond and Mrs. Reed had an understanding once, but then she became the captain's wife."

Wiki said, thunderstruck, "An understanding to be *married*?"

"Aye," said the New Bedforder, and nodded with his mouth pulled down. He spat out one fishbone and picked his teeth with another, his expression disdainful.

"In N'Orleans, he told us," said another. "She met Hammond when he dropped anchor there, and then Cap'n Reed later. Played 'em both like fish, or so I heard, and naturally became affianced to the one what was richer."

"That Jack Winter should keep his mouth buttoned up," said the New Bedforder. "Gossips like an old woman."

As if in emphasis, the clap of a rifle shot echoed from the prison high above, followed by a shout. The cutter's men sat up, turning to stare up the cliff.

"That be the lieutenant," observed one in a tranquil tone, and leaned back on his elbows again.

"Shot a rabbit, d'you reckon?" said another. "That would be a tasty treat."

"I'd fancy a nice young goat, myself," said the New Bedforder.

"Aye, a goat would go good—roasted over a fire with hot stones inside to cook the innards."

"And sprigs of rosemary to make it proper nice."

"Aye," said another wistfully. "My ma used to cook a goat like that."

Wiki grasped his chance to leave. Silently opting out of this culinary conversation, he clambered to his feet and set off up the track.

It was hot away from the shade where they'd been eating, and the gulls flew a long way up in the sky as if to avoid the reflected heat from the sea and sand, but it was good to stretch his legs. Wiki had his head bent as he climbed, his mind moodily turning over the distasteful notion that Annabelle had had a relationship with Joel Hammond. He felt as if she should have told him; it was a jolt to find that she had held back something so important. Perhaps, he thought, the scurrilous gossip wasn't true. The higher he clambered, though, the more uncomfortable the concept became.

Fifteen

*W*hen Wiki surmounted the last traverse toward the fortified walls, he looked up to find that Forsythe was aiming a rifle at him. He stopped, and surveyed the southerner with utter disgust. Forsythe looked like the last three days of a dissipated life and stank even worse, downwind. He was still wearing uniform, but stained white breeches, grimy knee-high boots, and an untied stock did not improve his appearance in the slightest. The fancy claw hammer coat had been discarded somewhere, and his shirtsleeves were rolled up to bare the snake tattoos that coiled from wrist to elbow on each of his brawny forearms.

"Don't shoot me, I'm innocent," Wiki growled, and clambered up the last slope.

Close up, the stink of rum and tobacco was overwhelming. Wiki stepped aside a pace to get into clearer air. "Weren't you jest a little nervous that my finger might twitch on the trigger?" Forsythe queried with a crooked grin. "You wouldn't be the first New Zealander I've shot, you know."

"You've passed up too many good opportunities for me to start worrying now," Wiki said ironically. And there was no point in trying to run away—Forsythe was a superb marksman, even when too drunk for speech.

They were standing where Wiki had glimpsed Forsythe that morning, and the view over golden sands and white-edged surf and sea was stupendous. Wiki could see the *Swallow* bobbing lightly on a tapestry of green and turquoise ripples, and the *Annawan* wallowing with a sick gush of water pouring from her side. The watch was pumping manfully, obviously, but their efforts looked increasingly doomed.

He turned to look about the huge courtyard that fronted the ruined prison. Close up, he could see why Ezekiel Reed had found it so hilarious that the *Peacock* lookouts had taken fright; if the *Annawan* had not been in such dire need of a good navy carpenter, it would have indeed been a capital joke. The cannon that had looked so ferocious from a distance were blotched with age, rust running from where they had been spiked. Judging by the abundant white splatters and blown straw, for many seasons past the gulls had used the fallen-in parts of the redoubt as nesting places. On the far side of the cracked, sun-scorched pavement the seaward wall of the prison reared up, looking even more decrepit than the side that overlooked the burial ground.

Wiki looked at Forsythe again and said, "What *were* you shooting at, anyway?"

Instead of answering, Forsythe said, "Is Zack down on the beach?"

Wiki frowned, because he hadn't given Kingman much thought

at all. "No—I took it for granted that he was with you."

"The silly bastard's asleep somewhere with an empty bottle in his fist, I reckon. I fired the shot to rouse him up."

"Your men are going to be disappointed," Wiki observed dryly. "They're expecting a tender young goat at the very least."

"Have you been pestering those poor bastards?"

"Just passing the time of day," Wiki said. "They settled in very comfortably, down there." Then he looked Forsythe up and down again, and said with distaste, "Didn't you wonder what they would get up to on the beach while you and Zachary Kingman spent the night on the schooner?"

Forsythe looked affronted. "As you noticed, my men are perfectly capable of looking after themselves—and we only went to pay Mrs. Reed our respects, and be a supporting presence during the prayers. How were we to know that the wake was goin' to turn into a goddamned spree?"

Wiki said, "Mrs. Reed informed me that you invited her to sail to Rio on the brig, and read her a lesson on ranking in the U.S. Navy—you explained that George Rochester outranks you only when you're on board his ship, and that you outrank him everywhere else."

Forsythe flushed red with anger, and snapped, "Wa-al, it ain't nothin' but the goddamned truth! And *Annabelle* had no objection to my reassuring company, neither," he said, and leered.

An unexpected rush of hot, jealous rage hit Wiki. Involuntarily, his elbows flexed, and his quivering fists clenched at the level of his bulging biceps. He wanted to yell at Forsythe that Annabelle had virtually accused him of murdering her husband, and that he had questioned the cutter's men in the hope of proving that she had been mistaken. Instead, he turned away to hide his expression, striding off across the courtyard in the direction of the prison entrance.

He heard Forsythe's footsteps, and glanced back to see the southerner following him, rifle hanging loosely from one hand. Then he was through the doorway. It was suddenly much cooler, and very gloomy.

He was in a cavernous stone hall. Corridors leading off to either side were lined with cells, most of them with their bars rusted loose. Ahead, a wide stone staircase wound on and on upward. There was rubbish everywhere—fallen rubble, broken furniture, collapsed racks that had once held firearms. Curious, Wiki went down the left-hand passage and into a few of the cells, where he made an attempt to read the scratched words—names, dates, enigmatic messages—on the walls, all very old and meaningless. There was a chilling sense of . . . *waiting*, a preternatural recognition of the thousands of hours that had been waited out by hundreds of imprisoned men, endless time endured in the numb hope of release or even, maybe, just for an explanation of why they were here.

He returned to the hall, where Forsythe was standing looking around, and said, "What kind of men were incarcerated here—did Captain Reed say?"

"Nope, he did not," Forsythe said. He spat a yellow gob onto the old stone floor. "But I hear that prisons on islands like this are reserved for the worst kind of bastard, on account of it's harder for 'em to escape when surrounded by sea."

So they would've been hardened criminals—or men with the wrong political views. Then Wiki's attention was seized by a big stack of squared timber beams leaning against the highest wall. He went over and hefted one, bracing his feet in a pile of rubbish to do it—and Forsythe fired his gun. The ball whistled past Wiki's thigh. The deafening report sent echoes crashing back and forth in the huge stone space.

Wiki shouted, "What the hell?" Then he saw the snake, headless and writhing beside his right boot, and heard Forsythe's derisive grunt of laughter.

"You oughter take more care," he said. "This island is alive with 'em."

Wiki said nothing, waiting until his heart stopped hammering.

"They don't have snakes in New Zealand, huh?" Forsythe queried on the same sardonic note.

"No," Wiki said shortly. When Forsythe had finished reloading the gun, he nodded at the lengths of lumber and said, "What do you reckon those were for?"

"For gallows trees—and for making triangles for floggin' the poor buggers against."

"What makes you so sure of that?"

"Figures, in a place like this."

He was probably right, Wiki thought. In Sydney Town, in the penal settlement of New South Wales, a flogging triangle was permanently set up beneath the windows of the barracks where the female convicts were held, to wrest the maximum humiliation from the public punishment, and the ground beneath it was eternally sodden with blood. However, balks of timber like these were also used in shipyards.

Looking at them thoughtfully, he said, "When you promised Annabelle that we would carry her to Rio on the *Swallow*, did it occur to you that we might be forced to carry the entire complement of the *Annawan* there?"

"Wa'al, it does look as if that poor bloody schooner is going to sink beneath the waves at any minute." Forsythe paused, staring in the direction of the courtyard, and then said frankly, "Bloody horrible thought, ain't it—I have to admit I dislike the notion of those goddamned sealers boarding the brig for the passage; I've a bad feeling in my gut about it."

Wiki looked at him consideringly. Forsythe had been away from the *Swallow* when the twelve *Annawan* men had boarded, bringing an indefinable sense of menace with them, and yet it was evident that he shared his own instinctive uneasiness. He and the Virginian had regarded each other with animosity since the time Forsythe had confronted him in an inn in Norfolk, and picked a quarrel just because Wiki was squiring a fair-haired southern girl. Yet, in the weeks since then, Wiki had been surprised by how often they shared the same thoughts. He supposed it was because they were both seamen, with similar experiences behind them.

"We could make the *Annawan* seaworthy," he suggested.

"You think we can mend her? Tell me how," Forsythe said scathingly.

"Thinking up a way of getting at that leak isn't easy," Wiki agreed.

Then he watched Forsythe surreptitiously through his thick, lowered lashes, wondering if he would take up the implied challenge. Finally, the southerner shifted from one foot to the other, and said, "We could warp her up onto the beach—lay her on her side alongside the sloop, and use timber from the wreck to replace the damaged planking."

"Careening her on the beach is a good idea, but I'm not sure it would work," said Wiki, remembering what George had said. "The *Annawan* is pretty old, and she's had a lot of hard usage—her timbers might not take the strain. There's a big risk that the planking on the grounded side would give way. I'd rather have her hove down close to where she is, away from the channel but with enough water under her to give her buoyancy."

"Heave her down to what?" demanded Forsythe.

This was indeed a problem, which they set to discussing in workmanlike fashion. The job of heaving down the schooner so that she tipped over on her good side, bringing the damaged side up into the air, would call for two mighty blocks, one at the head of the mainmast, and the other securely fastened to a belaying point outside the ship, plus a heavy cable rove between them, and some kind of capstan at the end. This, as it winched the cable up, would haul the schooner over. Normally, the belaying point was a large heaving post on a wharf, where the winch was sited, too—but obviously that was impossible, here.

"How about a raft?" said Wiki. "We could build one out of those beams, and anchor it up to the good side of the schooner. Fitted out with a post and winch, it would serve as a floating wharf. Maybe we wouldn't even need a capstan on the raft, but could work out a way of using the schooner's own windlass." Once the hole was patched, the schooner could be righted by letting the cable out again—though the ballast would probably have to be shoveled from one side to the other. It wouldn't be easy, but it was possible.

"But hell, a thousand strokes an hour means a bloody big leak. I'll give it more thought," Forsythe interrupted impatiently as Wiki opened his mouth to object. "But right now I'm a damn sight more interested in finding Zack. Tell the truth," he said, his eyes sliding away, "I'm starting to get bloody worried."

"When did you see him last?"

"On the beach where they dumped us—up over by the wreck." Then Forsythe grimaced and said, "I think so, anyways. Maybe I'm wrong. I was pretty drunk, and I guess I just assumed he was with me. But when I come to he wasn't there, and when I got round to where the cutter is anchored, he wasn't there, neither, so I figure he's passed out someplace on this island." His tone was careless, but his stance betrayed inner tension.

Wiki, frowning as he remembered that the cutter's men hadn't mentioned Kingman at all, went restlessly outside to stare at the cove where the two vessels were anchored. On the *Annawan* both whaleboats were back in their davits. He looked inland, but the graveyard of the prison was as empty as when he had left it, and the summit of the island was deserted, too.

"How can you be sure he's not still on board the schooner?" he asked.

Forsythe had followed him, but his attention was elsewhere. Instead of replying, he muttered, "Don't make a sound." Then he lifted his rifle, squinting down the barrel at a clump of bush midway down the cliff. Wiki saw the goat just as the southerner squeezed the trigger. Again, the shot set up echoes.

The animal dropped stone dead on the spot, which was nothing less than expected. Forsythe plunged down the path to claim the prize, and then stopped, looking about alertly. As Wiki arrived he dived headfirst into a copse, looking very much like an animal himself, and backed out with a bleating kid in his fist.

His other hand moved to the empty scabbard at the back of his belt, and groped about a bit while an expression of puzzlement crossed his face. Then he looked at Wiki. "Gotta knife?"

Silently, Wiki opened his jackknife and handed it to him. The bleating abruptly stopped. "And you reckon I don't look after my men," Forsythe snorted derisively.

Then, heaving the she-goat's carcass onto his shoulders with a fine disregard for his best shirt, he set off for the beach and the cutter. The men crowded around, highly delighted with the result of their skipper's little hunting trip, but Forsythe cut the congratulations short by barking at them to get the cutter under way for the schooner.

"So you think Passed Midshipman Kingman might be there after all?" Wiki queried.

"Doubt it," Forsythe said, his tone nonchalant. "Won't hurt to make certain sure, though."

Still his manner was elaborately careless, but his bloodshot eyes avoided Wiki's as they made their way to the stern of the *Annawan*. The instant the cutter had sheered to, he stood up and bawled, "Halloa! Ship ahoy, there!"

Joel Hammond arrived at the taffrail, where he stood surveying them with his fingers hooked into his belt. "You've forgotten something," he observed.

"Aye," agreed Forsythe, and waited in obvious expectation of seeing his missing second-in-command lounge up to the rail. Instead, Hammond handed down a long object wrapped in a rag, saying through his strange thin smile, "I assume you still want it."

It was the knife, Wiki realized—the murder weapon. He had forgotten Forsythe asking for it.

Forsythe reached up, took it, and said gruffly, "What about the mat?"

"The mat?"

"The one where the corpse was lying."

"You didn't ask about that."

"Wa'al, I'm asking now."

"It was soaked with blood, and no good any more, so we used it for a winding sheet to save wasting canvas."

Forsythe grimaced, and then said, "Seen anything of Zack Kingman?"

Hammond shrugged. "Ain't he on the brig?" he said without interest, and terminated the conversation by stepping back from the rail.

"Let's get there," said Forsythe to his men.

As soon as the cutter was under way again, he handed the tiller to Wiki, and then set to unwrapping the killing knife. Wiki looked away, concentrating on getting the cutter on course, but then the quality of Forsythe's stunned silence got through to him.

When he looked at him, the southerner silently handed him the knife, and took over the tiller again. Wiki studied the weapon with growing puzzlement, turning it over and over. Whoever had given it to Joel Hammond hadn't bothered to clean it—there was a blob of dried blood where the blade met the handle. He touched the clot with a fingertip, and frowned. Under the crust redness gleamed, still moist.

Then Forsythe said in a hoarse mutter that sounded scared as well as angry, "That's *my* goddamned knife. I had it with me right up until the time I went on board the schooner for the wake, I swear—so there's no way it could've been used to kill Reed. If Hammond reckons that's the murder weapon, he's telling a deliberate lie—but why?"

Sixteen

*O*nce on board the brig, Forsythe went forward in search of news of Kingman, while Wiki headed down the stairs to the saloon, where he found George Rochester seated at the table, a coffeepot in front of him, still going through the box of the *Annawan*'s papers.

Wiki said, "Passed Midshipman Kingman's missing. Forsythe hasn't seen him since the wake."

"He isn't on the schooner?"

"I didn't see him, and when we called by just now, Joel Hammond said he isn't there."

Rochester frowned. "What about the camp?"

Wiki shook his head. "I've talked to the cutter's men, and they haven't seen him, either. Forsythe has gone to the fo'c'sle to see if any of the *Swallow* men have heard any news."

"Maybe he's run away—but that does seem odd." Then Rochester said, "What have you got there?"

Wiki handed him the knife, and watched him touch the rust-colored crust where the blade met the handle and then contemplate his red fingertip. He said, "Strange."

"Aye," Wiki agreed. "Joel Hammond reckons it's the same one that killed Captain Reed. He gave it to us just a few minutes ago, telling us it was the knife that was taken out of his corpse."

"That can't be right! *That* knife was hauled out of Reed's chest this time yesterday, so this *can't* be the same weapon, because the blood is too fresh."

"Worse still," said Wiki; "*this* knife is Forsythe's—he recognized it instantly, and swears yet again that he was not the killer."

"Dear God." There was a long silence and then George said slowly, "What do you reckon about Hammond's chances of being the murderer?"

"He was away from the schooner when it happened."

"So who *was* on board at the time?"

"According to the cutter's men, there were four of the schooner's crew there—the steward, the bo'sun's mate, a South American seaman, and the cook. The steward was with them all the time, but they didn't keep track of the other three—and Annabelle Reed told me she changed her mind about going into the galley because she glimpsed someone on the quarterdeck, so it does seem that someone went there via the between-decks area."

"Did she recognize the man she saw?"

Wiki said grimly, "She's almost certain it was Forsythe—or so she says."

Again, they both looked at the bloodstained knife. "Oh God," said Rochester, and shut his eyes. When he opened them he demanded, "Does she have any reason for thinking Forsythe would want to kill her husband?"

"She said she ran back to the cabin because there'd been enough quarreling already, and she wanted to prevent more unpleasantness."

"I suppose Captain Reed might have called him back—Forsythe is the kind to respond to a challenge."

"And the murderer was extremely powerful," Wiki said grimly.

And with a rumble of hurried boot steps Lieutenant Forsythe arrived down the companionway. His face was flushed, his expression baffled and angry. "Zack ain't anywhere here—no one's seen him since we left the brig last evening."

Rochester tapped his fingers on the table, frowning. "When did you see him last?"

"The last time I can remember for sure was on board the *Annawan*. For a long time I thought they dumped him on the beach the same time as me, but then I wasn't so certain. But he ain't on the schooner, and he ain't here on the brig, so he *must* be on the goddamned island."

The steward came in, placed the steaming coffeepot on the table, and went back into the pantry. Forsythe grabbed it, filled a mug, and drank deeply without seeming to notice that it was scalding hot. His brooding stare was fixed on the knife.

Wiki looked at it, too, and said, "Tell us again what happened yesterday after Captain Reed threw you and Kingman out of the cabin."

"Oh, for God's sake! How many times do I have to repeat it? It's simple enough for even a half-breed—" Forsythe, catching Rochester's icy expression, stopped. "Look, he was the one who attacked us, not us who attacked him! He came at us in a drunken fury, whistling his goddamned stick around his head! We got out in a hurry, and neither of us went back in, I swear. When Annabelle came flying out the first time, we was near enough to hear the old man call her all kinds of god-damned bitches, but only just. Then she headed for the galley on one side of the deck, while we headed for the fo'c'sle deck on the other."

"How close to the galley did she get?"

"What?" He scowled. "Pretty close, I think. I wasn't looking."

"Did you hear her say anything to the cook?"

"For God's *sake*—" Then the southerner caught himself. "Now that I think of it, maybe she did," he said with a frown.

"Did you hear what she said?"

Forsythe struggled to remember, but then he shook his head. "Nope."

"Did you see anything that might account for her changing her mind and running back to the cabin?"

"All we wanted was to get the cutter away and get back to the brig, and that was all that was on our minds. We was calling out to the cutter's men, and they was getting themselves to their feet and calling back to us. We didn't even think of checking on her until she come bustin' out yellin' blue murder. *That* made us turn around pretty bloody quick, but till then we wasn't interested. Ask Zack Kingman, if you don't believe me."

"You didn't see the cook on the quarterdeck?"

"What? No, I didn't. What the hell would *he* be doing there?"

"What about the seaman who was aloft? Or the bo'sun's mate?"

"No, I tell you, no! What the bloody hell is this all about?"

"Mrs. Reed says she turned back because she glimpsed a man by the after house, and she thinks it could have been you."

"*What?*" Forsythe stared. Then he put down the mug so fast the remaining coffee splattered the table. "My God," he said numbly. "I really do have to find Zack."

And with that he was gone, yelling for the cutter's men to get under way again.

Seventeen

*D*usk fell, marking the passing of twenty-four hours since any of the men on the brig had last seen Zachary Kingman. Within minutes of the departure of the cutter, a boat had been lowered in the charge of the brig's boatswain with five hands to help search the island, and since then everyone had been waiting nervously for their return. The searchers had taken food and drink with them, but because they'd come back as soon as they found Kingman, their absence felt ominous.

On the quarterdeck George shifted uneasily as he stared at the island. "I keep on thinking he's fallen somewhere and broken his leg."

"Worse, he could be dead," Wiki said somberly.

"Aye," said George, and sighed. "Necks break as easily as legs."

George was looking tired and strained, Wiki thought, and said, "Go below. I'll take the deck till Midshipman Keith's watch."

"You'll let me know at once if there's any news?"

"Of course."

It was very quiet after Rochester had gone. After a while, feeling in need of companionship, Wiki was about to head forward to where he'd spied Sua and Tana on lookout, but was interrupted by the arrival of Midshipman Keith.

"Is it change of watch already?" said Wiki.

His tone was amiable, because he liked the lad. Until Keith had tapped on the stateroom door the first night, he had felt grave reservations about sharing accommodations with a callow officer cadet, something that the sight of the lad's white, apprehensive face as he peered around the doorway had done nothing to diminish. But then he'd said, "Come in, I won't bite you," and Keith's expression had been so peculiar that Wiki had demanded an explanation. And he'd got one—Keith had quite candidly described his friend's dire warnings about sharing accommodations with a notorious cannibal. They had both roared with laughter, and had got along famously ever since.

Too, Wiki liked Constant Keith's insatiable appetite for maritime learning, plus his determination to advance his naval career by absorbing as much of the technical and theoretical aspects of seafaring as was humanly possible, so that when he finally stood in front of an examining board of senior officers he'd pass the test with flying colors, thus earning the right to call himself a passed midshipman. If all of his dreams came true, he would not only come out as top of his class, like his hero, Captain Rochester, but he would be given the command of a fine small navy vessel, like Captain Rochester, too—and the key to this, he was firmly convinced, was Wiki Coffin. He was positive that Wiki Coffin was the most talented seaman on the breast of the briny wave, and so constantly prodded him for reminiscences and tips—which created a bit of a problem for Wiki. At the beginning of this voyage he had felt that he was really quite young at the age of twenty-four, but ever since he'd started sharing a stateroom with Midshipman Keith, he had felt quite remarkably old. He'd occasionally contemplated asking the seventeen-year-old lad to call him "Wiki," instead of "sir," or "Mr. Coffin," but had then decided that it would make him feel even more like the ancient mariner.

Now, Wiki said, "I don't mind taking the deck, if you want a watch below."

"There's no need, sir—I'll probably stay up all night," said Constant Keith, and joined Wiki at the rail. He stared out over the black, shimmering water, and said, "I keep on wishing I was out there with the searchers. It's hardest of all to do nothing."

"Aye," said Wiki. The men on the island had lit torches, and dots of flaring light wound to and fro beneath the deserted, snake-infested fort. A cool wind had sprung up, and gooseflesh rose on Wiki's bare arms as he watched the little fires pass back and forth across the blackness.

"I don't even *like* him much," Keith said in his candid way. "But I'd give a great deal to see him right now. Is that unusual, do you think, Mr. Coffin?"

Wiki shook his head, because he knew exactly how the lad felt. No one—apart from Forsythe—liked Zachary Kingman, but he was a shipmate, one of *theirs*. Without him, their force was diminished.

There was a bit of a silence, and then Keith said with passion, "I don't *like* this place. I mean, it is beautiful, and—and peaceful. On the surface it looks like the kind of island paradise that young coves picture when they dream of running off to sea. But it has nasty undercurrents. Maybe that's because I brood a lot about those privateers that haunt this coast, and how they drove the captain of that sloop into sailing her right up the beach. That would take a lot of courage—and you know, Mr. Coffin, if I had been that sloop's master I don't believe I would have even *thought* of doing such a thing."

"Improvisation is the soul of seamanship," Wiki pronounced in his most grandly instructive manner. Then, more informally, he went on, "That's often the best thing to do when a ship runs aground—run the bow ashore with the last of the ship's momentum. Many men have saved their lives by running along the bowsprit and jumping onto land. Because the sloop was run right up the beach, the sailors were able to dash into the trees and then up the cliff to get away from the pirates—assuming they were hot on their heels."

"But what if that captain had been no good at it—this improvisation that's the soul of seamanship?"

"It's a good idea to get into the way of it by thinking up emergencies and then working out how you would deal with them. For instance," Wiki went on pensively, "imagine that your ship has struck a hole in her bottom when you're a long way from port, and you have to fix the leak without dock machinery."

Midshipman Keith might have been irritatingly youthful, but he certainly wasn't stupid. "Like the *Annawan?*"

"Aye. Can you think of any way we could get her hove down so we can fix the leak?"

"You mean, like careening?"

"Aye—but without the heaving posts and heaving blocks and so forth that ship carpenters use to do the job in port."

There was a pause while the lad thought about it, and then, typically, he angled for another of Wiki's yarns. "Have you had any experience of heaving down a ship at sea, sir?"

"Aye," Wiki said. "On a whaleship, of course—whalemen being natural improvisers," he added with a grin. "Not only is it anathema to whaling skippers to ask foreigners for help, but they're afraid it will cost them money."

"Sir, I would be highly gratified if you would be kind enough to tell me about it."

"We were on the Callao ground—off Ecuador, the roughest whaling ground in the whole eastern Pacific, cutting in a big whale in a storm, and as we brought in the whale's head, the ship strained her timbers. She didn't broach, but her planking started, and soon she began to leak. The captain didn't think it was much of a problem, so we cruised on for whales regardless, but then all at once it dawned on him that we were putting more time and energy into pumping ship than we were into the whale hunt, so he decided to put away for Callao to get her fixed. However, another gale came along, and the leak increased, and he realized we weren't going to make it. If he hadn't been a whaling master, he would have made preparations to abandon ship, but instead he set out to fix her himself, in the open sea. We lowered all five boats, offloaded what heavy stuff we could into them, and shifted what was left in the holds until she leaned over far enough for us to get at the gaping strakes."

Midshipman Keith's mouth was hanging open. "But if the wind had suddenly gusted while the ship was lying over?"

"I'm here to tell the tale because the weather had calmed down by then."

It had been uncommonly nerve-wracking, though, Wiki remembered. The knowledge that any reasonably sized comber would have filled and sunk the helpless ship in an instant had weighed heavily on the minds of all—even, no doubt, on the mind of the captain, though Wiki didn't recollect him betraying much concern.

"How did you fix the leak?"

"Went over the side on lines and caulked the gaps. Then we shifted the barrels in the hold until she was back on an even keel, unloaded the whaleboats and brought them in—and sailed back to the whaling ground to get on with the cruise."

"Jesus," Midshipman Keith said reverently.

"Aye," agreed Wiki, and then said in his best pedantic manner, "It also demonstrates that there are three requirements for heaving down. What are they?"

"Well, judging by your yarn—and you're a first-rate story-teller, I assure you, Mr. Coffin!—the first is to lighten the load, and the second, move the remaining contents of the ship so she heels far enough over to get at the leak and fix it."

"And the third requirement is calm water, preferably in a sheltered bay. Well, there's twenty tons of loose ballast in the *Annawan* that I happen to know about. Too, her holds are almost empty. She's lying in sheltered water, so we have a reasonably ideal situation. But how do we make sure that she doesn't overset—and, even if we manage that, and get the hole patched, how do we get her back on an even keel again?"

Keith was squinting alertly, looking remarkably like a terrier that had found a rabbit in a hole. "We'd need stout lines—"

But he was interrupted. George Rochester materialized beside them. He cast Midshipman Keith only a glance before turning to Wiki and saying quickly, "Any news?"

Wiki shook his head, knowing that if a boat had come to the brig George would have heard, but that he couldn't help the question.

George sighed, and then said, "There's a fresh pot of coffee on the table, if you're interested."

Wiki, who was always interested in fresh coffee, went below to the empty saloon. As promised, there was a steaming pot on a tray, next to the box of *Annawan* papers. Sitting down after pouring a mug, Wiki opened it and took the schooner's crew list out of the special slot in the lid.

The original crew, he saw, had signed articles in New London, Connecticut, where the paper had been officially stamped. He counted down the list. Sixteen names, two crossed out with the words "Run in Rio," marked beside them. Two more—Robert Festin and Pedro da Silva—had been added, and the crosses they had made were witnessed by a Rio de Janeiro customs house officer. Festin, Wiki deduced, was the cook, and da Silva had replaced the good-for-nothing New Jerseyman greenhand that Ezekiel Reed had described in his letter; maybe he was the Spanish-looking type who had been aloft in the mizzen rigging about the time that Ezekiel Reed was killed. The steward, as the cutter's men had said, was named Jack Winter. The boatswain's name was Folger, and his assistant—the boatswain's mate, who had been on board when Reed was knifed—was Bill Boyd. Interestingly, both hailed from the same town—Tiverton, Rhode Island.

Wiki had a notebook stowed in the bookcase he had hung at the foot of his berth. Fetching it, he sat down again and copied down the names of the current crew of the *Annawan*—cook, steward, boatswain, boatswain's mate, ten seamen, and the officers, Joel Hammond and Isaac Hunt—and when he'd finished, he counted them again. Sixteen, definitely. When Rochester had said *seventeen*, he had been including the captain's widow. Though Wiki had known it all along, to have it confirmed was a strange relief.

After he got to bed, however, he dreamed about seventeen *Annawan* men coming on board the *Swallow*. One of them was the ghost of Ezekiel Reed, grinning like a maniac, and counting an enormous hoard of silver.

Eighteen

*W*iki's eyes blinked open at eight bells, four in the morning. With the habit of seven sea-going years, he had woken at the time for change of watch, four in the morning, which in this equatorial latitude felt like the middle of the night.

He could hear Midshipman Keith's breathing, and realized the lad had come in without disturbing him. Wiki didn't move for quite a while, lying there listening to the quiet noises above his head, hearing a man hailing the cook in a low voice as he came out on deck, and then the distant clattering as the cook chopped kindling to start the fire in his stove. There'd been no news from shore, he knew, because he would have woken at once if the boat or the cutter had returned. Then he thought about heaving down the schooner and getting her fixed . . . so that Rochester would not be forced to take the *Annawan* hands on board. His plan for a raft would work, he was certain of it. Much, however, depended on how badly the schooner was damaged. And the way she was taking in water . . .

Wiki moved decisively, though he swung over the side of the bunk with due care and attention. Midshipman Keith slept in such a gangling fashion that more often than not his long, bony shins and feet stuck out from his berth, posing a hazard for the unwary. Over the first couple of days of sharing the stateroom Wiki had regularly collided with those shins as he'd got up in the morning. Today, however, the lad's eyes were open, blinking sleepily, and his feet were drawn into his own territory.

"I'm going for a swim," Wiki said. "Would you to bring a boat over to the *Annawan* in about twenty minutes? I'd be obliged if you'd meet me there."

Midshipman Keith looked puzzled, but nodded and repeated the instruction word for word, as all good young officers were taught. Wiki went into the saloon, and then padded up the companionway as naked as he had slept. After looking about at the rising sun, the mist rising off the crest of the island, and the *Annawan* lying heavily at her anchors, he jumped up onto the rail, braced himself, and launched himself into the sea in a long, smooth dive.

The water, surprisingly cold, closed about his head and gurgled in his ears. The world turned green. Wiki lifted his head to check his direction, shook back his hair, and then struck out for the schooner. The sun was rising fast, in the precipitate way the sun moved at the equator, and soon he could see his long shadow rippling along the sand below. The water was as glassy as a millpond, and so clear that he could see the astounding violet color of a half-open clam on a coral ridge, three fathoms below. Pink and orange sea anemones waved their tentacles, while crabs and shrimp crawled among them. Multicolored fish flicked back and forth at the edge of his vision. The flow of the cool current across his skin was like silk.

Then all at once the world changed color. Wiki had entered the channel where the *Annawan* had run afoul. Here, the water was deeper and darker. The current was stronger, and had changed direction so that it now flowed in the direction of the mouth of the cove, heading out to the open sea. The little sea anemones were replaced with great stands of waving kelp, which grew out of rock, not sand. The water was not nearly as friendly.

Wiki abruptly became aware that something had joined him in the water. His consciousness was full of the foreboding presence of something heavy enough to be inanimate, but which nevertheless felt alive and dangerous. When he lifted his head, he saw that the *Annawan* was right ahead, just a few yards away. So that was the weight in his mind, he thought. There was no movement at the rail or in the rigging. He swam right up to the schooner, took a deep breath, dived, and began to swim slowly along the starboard side, searching for the damaged part of the hull.

He found a hole within minutes—*a* hole, because it was not the one that had been fothered with the thrummed sail. It was as he had feared—the coral reef had done a lot more damage than the crew of the *Annawan* had expected. Wiki rose to the surface, breathed slowly until he had refreshed his lungs, took in another deep breath, and dived again.

Slowly, taking his time, he inspected the whole starboard side, underwater. Even though he rose frequently for air, there was no sound from the schooner. In the before-breakfast quiet, no one had yet looked over the rail. Wiki found the hole that had been fothered, and studied it in detail, comparing the damage to what he remembered from seeing inside the hold. Then he looked at the rest of the strake, finding it so badly started that fothering the second hole would make little difference. It was little wonder, he thought, that the schooner was taking on so much water. However, if the vessel could be hove down, the damage was certainly not too severe to be fixed.

Then he was at the bow. When he rose for air, he was under the martingale chains. Holding his nose and swallowing, he cleared his ears. Above, he could hear the cook chopping kindling, making the same domestic sounds he had heard on the *Swallow* when he'd left the brig. It felt homelike, but when he dived again, preparing to inspect the larboard side of the hull, the sense of a threat close at hand became almost overwhelming. There was a lot more kelp on this side—because of the landward current, which was stronger here, he supposed. Perhaps, he thought, that was what was weighing on his unconscious mind so much. Nevertheless, he came up for another breath much more quickly than he'd intended.

When he looked around, it was to see the boat from the *Swallow* about twenty yards away, a reassuring sight. Down again he dived—and came face-to-face with a man who was standing on the floor of the sea.

The man was grinning. It was the huge inhuman grin that shocked Wiki the most. Then the current surged. The kelp waved, and the man's head flopped forward, closing the obscene smirk. It was the body of Zachary Kingman, his throat slit deeply from ear to ear. As Wiki watched the current surged, the head flopped back, and Kingman grinned again. Wiki tried to scream—bubbles streamed from his lips. He surged to the surface in a panic, and floated there panting, while his heart thundered madly in his ears. His sight was blurred with red. When it cleared he could see Midshipman Keith's boat, oars stirring the sea while Sua and Tana leaned far over, studying something intently. One of them called out in Samoan, but Wiki's ears were full of water. Taking courage from the fact that he was not alone, Wiki sucked in a huge gasp of air, and dived again.

And the sense of something huge and living and ferocious nudged horribly at his consciousness again. It was the ghastliness of the body that affected him so—Kingman's body, he told himself, and with a thrust of legs and arms swam up to the corpse. The eyes were gone already, the lips and nose nibbled away. Kingman, who had been as thin as a mummy in life, now looked like a skeleton already, his floating garments pulled hard against his bones by the current. That he was wearing uniform made the sight still more grotesque.

A rope tied his shinbones to a heavy grindstone, which kept the cadaver standing upright in the bottom of the channel—and the knife that had presumably been used to cut the rope had been casually jammed into his thigh. Wiki grabbed it, and hauled it out, clenching his throat so he wouldn't be sick. It was a long skinning knife with a pointed blade. He bent and sawed at the rope with the blade, which was so blunt he managed only to fray it—and a huge force slammed past his bent back and seized Kingman's body in enormous jaws that were rimmed with jagged teeth. Then it shook the cadaver with brute force, breaking the shreds of the line that held its prize to the bottom of the sea.

Wiki had just one appalled glimpse of the shark's oyster-dead eye as the great creature writhed and vanished, parts of the corpse dangling out of each side of its jaws. Kelp sucked and waved frantically in its wake. Every muscle in Wiki's body spasmed—he surged to the surface and kept on going, scrambling up the straking of the schooner without knowing he was going to do it, to arrive on the deck without the slightest idea of how he had got there. Then he stood still, shaking too much to take a single step, water streaming off his long hair and his chest and shoulders and down his naked loins and legs to pool on the planks.

He was still holding the skinning knife. That was his first conscious thought. Then, as the red haze that blurred his sight cleared, he saw Annabelle. She was standing in the doorway of the after house, her mouth gaping wide open with shock, her dark eyes huge in the whiteness of her face. She was half the ship away from him, but he could have sworn he heard her gasp. Then she turned and disappeared. He could hear her running down the stairs.

The air was full of the ghastly scent of . . . burning feathers. Wiki identified the stench only because of the sight of all the dead chickens lying on the planks about a bloodied chopping block. That was how Mrs. Coffin's cook used to prepare a hen for dinner—she had been a stout, practical woman, who would grab a fowl, chop off its head, and then singe its feathers to make the plucking easier.

Then Wiki saw a short, squat, heavyset man standing by the block, holding a bloody hatchet in one hand. He must be the cook—Robert Festin, Wiki remembered. In the other fist he clutched—a bird, but not a hen. It was a parrot—the parrot that had been in the captain's cabin. Its head and breast were horridly burned, blackened and seeping red; its eyes were dead, burned out to blindness like spark holes burned into a rug. Then Wiki saw it move, and realized the bird was still alive. For a moment he thought he would vomit.

The cook—Festin?—was staring at him, openmouthed. Then, as Wiki watched, the cook's eyes flickered about the otherwise empty deck. Festin looked back at him, and then moved abruptly, thrusting the feebly pulsing parrot at him, saying something urgent in an incomprehensible gabble of sounds. Wiki stared, immobile, wondering what it all meant. Then he heard Sua calling out in Samoan from below the rail. Blessedly, this time he heard and understood him—he was telling him to get into the boat. When he looked down at the boat the oarsmen were standing in the bottom, all gaping up, Midshipman Keith in the stern sheets; all their faces were shocked.

The paralysis fled away. When the cook thrust the weakly struggling bird at him again, Wiki grasped it, clutched it to his chest, turned, and jumped down into the boat. He landed awkwardly, but without falling into the water, because Tana and Sua grabbed him and held him steady. He had dropped the knife, but it hadn't fallen into the water, either. Instead, it dropped into the bottom of the boat.

"My God," Midshipman Keith said in a scared, shocked voice as the boat pulled away. "Did—did you see that—that monstrous shark? We—we saw it carry a body away, and we—we thought it was you, Mr. Coffin! Are you all right? Are you hurt? Mr. Coffin," he insisted, his voice shaking.

Sua and Tana were saying the same things, but in their own language. Wiki opened his mouth to tell them all that he was perfectly fine, but the words wouldn't come. So he sat silently on the middle thwart and shivered, clutching the poor burned parrot to his chest.

Nineteen

The saloon of the *Swallow* was very crowded. Dressed, but still shivering with shock, Wiki sat on the bench at the foot of the saloon table, his hands tightly clasped around his warm mug. Stoker, the steward, was clucking agitatedly as he tenderly applied strips of thin wet cloth to the burned parrot, which was perched miserably on the back of Rochester's chair. It looked extremely odd, festooned with ribbons of torn fabric which were draped from the top of its head, the whole dripping freely as Stoker gently squeezed more water onto it from a soaked flannel. Every now and then he put a finger under the poor blistered, blackened beak that protruded from the draperies, lifting it to dribble water inside. The saloon was full of the stink of wet, burned feathers.

The cutter and boat had returned to the brig in response to the signals that had been set to recall the men who had been searching the island all night, and George had called all hands, and briefly broken the news. Now the men were gathered in traumatized huddles about the decks, aghast that their efforts to find Zachary Kingman had been so doomed to failure. While it was officially Constant Keith's watch on deck, Captain Rochester had decided it would be both unfair and unwise to have him there right now, when the men were so confused and upset, so, after ordering a ration of rum to be given out, he'd put the boatswain, who was a very steady and experienced old fellow, in charge.

Now, Midshipman Keith was hunkered on the bench on the starboard side of the table, his gangly body crammed into a corner. Rochester was sitting opposite; he had swung a leg over the end of the larboard bench near the stairs, and was ready to go up at an instant's notice. Forsythe was slumped on the starboard bench next to Midshipman Keith, his bloodshot eyes glazed and unseeing, his weathered face so bleached of its usual color that old fighting scars stood out on his chin and cheeks. Nobody had liked Zachary Kingman, but somehow that made the sight of Forsythe's grief more terrible, not less.

He looked bleakly at Wiki, and said hoarsely, "You're the one who found him?"

"Aye—when I was swimming."

"So he drowned?"

Wiki swallowed, and then said, "His feet had been tied to a grindstone, and he'd been dropped into the sea."

"*What?* Oh, Jesus, so they murdered *him*, too." Forsythe rubbed a broad hand over his cheeks, scrubbing away wetness, and then said shakily, "Do you reckon the poor bastard was alive when they dropped him over?"

"His throat was cut first." When Wiki lifted his coffee mug his teeth knocked against the rim. He might have spent the last seven years a-whaling—a hard trade that created hard men—but, as tough as he might have become over those seven years, he knew he was going to be haunted for the rest of his life by the ghastly memory of the wide grin that had opened and closed as Zack Kingman's head flopped back and forth.

"Oh, *Christ*." Forsythe's eyes were squeezed tight.

Wiki said quietly, "I found a knife, too—though I don't believe it's the knife that killed him. Evidently it had been used to cut the length of rope that tied him to the grindstone."

Without describing where he had found it, he produced the knife he had plucked out of Kingman's dead thigh. They all stared at it. There were rust spots on the blade, and the handle was rough. Salt water didn't account for this—it was a long time since this knife had been cleaned, honed, and oiled.

Wiki looked up at Forsythe and said, "It's blunt. When I was trying to cut him free from the grindstone I had to saw at the rope. That's why I don't think this was the knife that was used to cut his throat." Then he added deliberately, "It's not sharp enough—not like *your* knife."

"What the *hell* do you mean?"

"When Hammond gave you *your* knife, he said it was the one that had been pulled out of Captain Reed, and yet it had blood on it that was reasonably fresh. I think *your* knife was the one that was used to cut Zachary Kingman's throat."

"*My* knife—*my* goddamned knife?" Forsythe shouted. His face flooded with red, and then went white again.

"Aye," said Wiki, indicating the sealing knife on the table. "And I think that *this* knife is the one that killed Ezekiel Reed. It mightn't be sharp enough to cut a man's throat, but the point's sturdy enough to stab a man—and I believe this is the handle I saw sticking out of Reed's back. Also, I'm not sure that your knife is long enough to go right through a man's chest, while this one is. We can compare them to make sure, but I have a strong feeling that your knife was switched with the one that killed Captain Reed."

Rochester got up from the table and fetched Forsythe's knife, and they laid them side by side. The skinning knife was a good three inches longer than Forsythe's knife, and slenderer in the blade. While it was not nearly as well maintained as his, it still looked lethal.

Forsythe said, "You haven't told me where you found him."

"Off the larboard bow of the *Annawan*, in amongst kelp in a deep part of the channel. Though the grindstone had been tied to his ankles to weigh him down, with time the seaward current would have dragged his body away. However, I got there first."

"Where is it?" the southerner demanded. "I want to be the one to sew his shroud."

It was traditional for the dead man's best friend to put the last stitch through his nose, Wiki winced. "A shark—a huge shark came before I could cut him free."

"A shark?" Forsythe echoed blankly.

"Aye. When I hunkered down to cut the rope, a shark charged from behind, grabbed the body, and tore it away. If I hadn't ducked down at that precise moment," Wiki said, his voice beginning to shake again, "he'd have got me. Instead, he swam off with Zachary Kingman's body in his jaws."

"Oh, *Christ*," said Forsythe. He pushed his hand over his big craggy face again, and then looked at Wiki and demanded, "What the hell were you doing there, anyway?"

Wiki said, "I was checking the damage in the hull of the *Annawan*."

There was a blank pause as they all stared at him. George said, "What did you find?"

"There's a lot of damage. The straking is started and splintered, and there are two holes, not one—but it's mostly all in one plank. If she was careened, we could fix her."

Forsythe exclaimed, "We fix her so the bastard who slit Zack's throat can sail free?"

"It's better than having an unknown killer on board during the passage to Rio."

Forsythe nodded grimly. "That's a very good point."

George Rochester suggested, "We could carry the *Annawan* crew to the expedition fleet, and hand over the problem to Wilkes. He could hold an inquiry."

There was another silence while everyone contemplated this unpleasant prospect, and then Midshipman Keith piped up, "Why don't we try to catch the foul murderer ourselves?"

They all stared at the lad, and he blushed, but said gamely, "Mr. Coffin could do it."

"That's true," Forsythe exclaimed, and rounded on Wiki. "You're supposed to be a goddamned sleuth—you've got that paper from the sheriff of Portsmouth deputizing you to be an agent of law and order on the high seas, right?"

"But I have no authority on board the *Annawan*—you know what Joel Hammond is like!" Wiki objected. The derisive words *godless Kanaka* were ringing in his head.

"You can find murderers; you've done it before," Forsythe urged. "Now find this one—for me, for Zack!"

When Wiki looked at George Rochester, his friend had his head tilted in deep thought. Then, he nodded encouragingly, so Wiki turned to Forsythe and took a deep breath. Then he managed to say, remarkably steadily, he thought, "So you wouldn't object if I asked you some questions right now?"

"Go ahead," said Forsythe grimly.

"You were the last of us to see him alive. Can you remember where?"

"Of *course* I can bloody well remember!" Then Forsythe's aggressive stare faltered, and he said, "No, I can't. That's a lie, because I was drunk. I was *bloody* drunk," he mourned, staring down at the table. "I was so drunk I thought he was with me when they dumped me on the beach, and for a long time I was quite certain the poor bastard was on the island, too. So," he said, looking up at Wiki again, "that means the last time I saw Zack was on the foredeck of the schooner."

"Can you tell me anything about the boat's crew that carried you to the beach?"

"I'm not even sure I was awake."

"That doesn't make it very easy for me," Wiki pointed out.

"It wasn't supposed to be goddamned easy!"

George Rochester said in placatory tones, "Why don't you start from the beginning—from the time when you left the *Swallow*?"

"Wa'al, as you know, the cutter's men came and fetched me, and then dropped Zack and me off at the schooner before headin' back to the beach."

"Was the coffin open for viewing?"

"It was set on the carpenter's bench, and it didn't have a lid on yet, so men could take the opportunity to say farewell if they wanted. I can't say I took more than a glance, just enough to see that the body was all wrapped up in a rug, the way Hammond said. I guess," Forsythe added on a ghoulish note, "the rug was dark on account of it being the one he'd bled all over. Then I headed to the after house to pay Annabelle—Mrs. Reed—my respects."

And to hand her an assurance that the *Swallow* would carry her to Rio, Wiki thought moodily. "Was Zachary Kingman there?"

"Nope, Zack was on the forward deck at the time."

Biting back jealousy, Wiki said, "Did you escort Annabelle Reed to the wake?"

"Nope. A dark-looking fellow came and fetched her from the cabin when it was time for the prayers. They seemed to know each other well."

Alphabet Green, thought Wiki. "And after the prayers were over?"

"She went back to the after house. Then the steward started handing out the grog."

"Was Joel Hammond there all the time?"

"He headed off after he'd finished the Bible reading, and I didn't see him again."

"While the men were drinking? Didn't you think that was odd?"

"Didn't bother to think about it at all, tell the truth."

"Did all the hands take part in the spree?"

"Nope. There was some what went into the fo'c'sle instead."

"So who stayed?"

"Look, I don't know these men—they're strangers to me. And I got bloody drunk," Forsythe said again, this time defiantly. "I've never in my life got drunk so hard and fast."

"What about Zachary Kingman?"

"Aye, he was in the same condition." Forsythe paused, then said, "How do you reckon it happened?"

Wiki hesitated. Then he said, "According to where I found him, he was dropped off the foredeck, probably over the rail behind the galley. If it was there that his throat was cut, the galley would have hidden it from anyone on the open deck."

Forsythe's eyes went flat and dead, and Wiki suddenly felt some sympathy for the murderer if the southerner ever caught up with him. "In God's name, *why*?" he demanded. "Why would anyone want to cut the throat of a poor harmless silly bastard like Zack?"

Wiki paused, and then said very carefully, "It might have been so you wouldn't have an alibi for the time that Ezekiel Reed was murdered."

"*What!*"

"Zachary Kingman would have backed you up in everything you said about going forward after Reed had thrown you out of the cabin, and not going back to the quarterdeck until you heard his wife screaming, but now he can't." Wiki paused, and then said bleakly, "If Hammond keeps on claiming that Reed was killed with your knife, it's not going to look good."

"You think those bastards are trying to pin Reed's murder on me?" Forsythe exclaimed. "And that's why poor Zack was killed?"

Wiki nodded grimly. The men stared at him in shocked silence. Then George shifted uneasily and said, "What about Mrs. Reed? Is she part of this conspiracy?"

"Bloody good point!" Forsythe snapped. "When I saw her the night of the wake she said nothin' at all about glimpsing me goin' back into the cabin—and yet she tells you about it the next god-damned day, right after the captain is buried. That sounds kinda convenient to me!"

Wiki said uncomfortably, "That's true—and if she sticks to that story it's now your word against hers."

"And what do *you* reckon? Is her word more believable than mine?"

Wiki chose his words carefully. "Right at the start I did think that you might have pulled a knife after getting into a brawl with Captain Reed. Too, it took muscle to shove a knife all the way through his chest and out the other side—and you have plenty of that. But no, I don't believe you killed him. It has to be one of those who stayed behind on the schooner when the two boats came over to the *Swallow*."

Said Forsythe sardonically, "Wa'al, that's a huge relief. Can I ask the reason I'm off the suspect list?"

"Captain Reed was stabbed in the back—which isn't your style."

"And thankee for the kind compliment," Forsythe said in the same ironic tone. Then he slammed his fists on the table, and used them to lunge to his feet. "I'm off," he announced.

George Rochester blinked, but said mildly, "Can I ask where?"

"I'm off to build a raft," said Forsythe grimly. "Because if we take the *Annawan* men to the expedition fleet, and Hammond and Mrs. Reed repeat their goddamned lies to Wilkes, he'll have me hanging from the yardarm of the *Vincennes* before the next sun sets."

Twenty

*A*s the sound of Forsythe's boot steps retreated on the deck above, George Rochester thoughtfully studied his mug of cold coffee. Finally, he said, "I'll hand the deck back to you, Constant, if you don't mind. Wiki, if you would join me in my cabin?"

Midshipman Keith wriggled out of the cramped space along the bench, and then scampered up the companionway. Rochester transferred his gaze to the steward, who was still fussing over the parrot. Wondering if he would ever get his chair back, he demanded, "Don't you think the poor wretched creature should be put out of its misery?"

"Oh no, sir," Stoker earnestly replied. "A regimen of salt butter admixed with pepper would set him up a treat, and in time even his poor blind eyes will heal."

Rochester said, thunderstruck, "Pepper—for *birds?*"

"My father was a higler, sir," the steward informed him, "and my mother a henwife. Pepper, whether cayenne or black, was their strong resource in a crisis of the poultry kind. Strengthens the innards, they used to say. For hen lice flowers of sulfur in lard is the remedy, but I doubt we have that problem, the lice all being scorched to death, as it were."

"You consider parrots *poultry?*"

"Well, sir, taking into account that he has a beak, sir, and feathers, though sadly damaged, I do reckon this parrot is pretty close to being kin with hens. You have to remember, sir, that though hens are certainly more useful than parrots, they belong to the same kingdom of birds. What would really set this poor fellow up," said the steward, his tone becoming confidential, "is a gruel of fine cornmeal in milk."

"Milk?" exclaimed George. "Where the devil can we get milk? *Good God,*" he muttered, and then, more loudly, "Do leave your higlering, there's a good fellow, and brew us a good pot of hot coffee and break out my dress uniform." After he and Wiki had settled in his cabin, he said in a hushed voice, "What the devil is a *higler,* do you reckon?"

Wiki, from his customary seat on the sofa, said, "A man who peddles eggs."

"Good God, the things you know, my lad. But how do you reckon the parrot got burned in the first place?"

Wiki shook his head. The memory of the strange little cook thrusting the horribly damaged bird at him was vivid, along with the stink of burned feathers, but he could think of no explanation. Instead, he said, "What are you up to, *e hoa?*"

"I'm going to rig myself up in the full pomp and glory of an officer of the U.S. Navy, and we're going together to the *Annawan.* The sooner you get your questions asked and answered, the better."

"You really think wearing uniform will make a difference?" said Wiki dubiously. Fine uniforms had never made any difference to him—but if George was going to go aboard in full formal fig, he supposed he would have to break out his best broadcloth.

"Absolutely, my dear fellow. Wilkes would be the first to assure you that a few yards of gold lace and a flourish of a cocked hat can work miracles."

Wiki rose to go and shift his own clothes, taking this as a hint to do so, but Stoker arrived with a pot of steaming coffee, and Rochester signed to him to stay. The steward set to rattling drawers in and out and slamming locker doors, and like magic George's dress uniform materialized on his berth, everything already starched and ironed. As George had often observed, Stoker was a *gem*.

Then, with the final slam of a door, Stoker was gone. Stepping out of his trousers to reveal a pair of well-muscled, remarkably hairy legs, George pulled on white pantaloons, saying as he buttoned them up, "Now, what's this about a raft?"

Wiki, having drunk his coffee, was slumped into his favorite thinking position with his forearms along his thighs and his hands at rest between his knees, scowling at the carpet between his feet. He cast a look up at George, who was smoothing down his shirt and tying his black stock, preparatory to putting on the close-fitting, single-breasted white vest, and said, "When I was looking for Forsythe on the island yesterday, I found him up at the prison—which truly is a ruin—and inside the main building we found a big pile of heavy beams, which would make first-rate material for a raft to careen the schooner against."

George was silent a moment, absorbed in the fiddly job of doing up the row of little gold buttons that ran down the front of the vest. Then he said, "How's my stock?" The one small looking glass the brig boasted was infamously spotted, the result of years at sea.

"Looks fine to me," said Wiki after a cursory glance.

"As if I could trust you," George derided, and then asked, "Enough to make a raft that's big enough for the job?"

"Aye," said Wiki, and nodded.

"I'd already gathered that you're very keen to get the *Annawan* hove down," Rochester observed; "but the raft is a new idea."

Wiki said, "I don't think the schooner's timbers would stand her being beached, but with a raft anchored tight up to her side, and fitted out with heaving posts, she could be hove down with water under her bottom. If well anchored, it would prevent her getting overset and sinking. The raft will make it a lot easier to get her righted, too, once the broken plank is replaced and caulked tight—all we'll have to do is let the cable out again. And we happen to know about twenty tons of loose copper ballast, which could be shoveled from one side to the other to help the process along."

George picked up his blue dress coat and shook it out. Light from the stern windows twinkled brightly on thirty-two gold buttons—nine down each swooping lapel, one on each side of the stand-up collar, three on each cuff, and three on each of the two pocket flaps in the tails of the coat—and several expensive yards of half-inch gold lace.

Squinting as he inspected the coat for grease spots, he said, "You certainly do seem to have it all worked out—but I have to confess it gives me a problem."

"How so?" said Wiki with foreboding.

Rochester hollered for Stoker, who came in and held the coat while he shoved his right arm into the sleeve. "Wilkes should be informed as soon as possible that we've lost a man—an officer, damn it!" His left arm went into the other sleeve, and the coat was lifted over his shoulders. It was so close-fitting that it took the concerted efforts of both the wearer and the steward to get him into it.

Wiki objected, "But Forsythe is right, you know."

"You agree with his gloomy prognostications of being hanged from the yardarm?"

"I most certainly do. If Joel Hammond persists in his claim that the knife hauled out of Reed was Forsythe's, and if Annabelle Reed repeats her assertion that she'd glimpsed Forsythe on the quarter-deck just before she discovered her husband's murdered body, a court-martial could very easily end up that way."

"It hasn't occurred to you that Forsythe might, in fact, be guilty?"

"He's not," Wiki said with perfect sureness. "I honestly don't think he knifed Ezekiel Reed, and I'm damn sure he's not capable of killing Kingman, drunk or sober. And if you did set sail for the fleet, what would you do about the *Annawan* crew?"

"If I followed regulations, I'd take all seventeen on board, and carry them to safety. In fact, if I don't, Wilkes is likely to have my guts for a bandanna."

Seventeen. It was that indefinably threatening number again. Wiki involuntarily exclaimed, "But at least one of them is a murderer—who would happily stand by and watch as Forsythe was hanged for his crime!"

George paused, first fastening his belt, and then waiting as the steward fussily arranged the gold epaulette on his right shoulder. "In that case," he said, "we must keep our fingers crossed that you get some useful evidence from questioning the crew, and find the murderer—or murderers—first."

"And if I can't?"

George sighed deeply. "Then we'll stay and get the schooner fixed—if we can."

Thank God, thought Wiki. Then, he said very soberly, "You have no idea what a relief it is that you're coming with me to the *Annawan.*"

"Glad to be of assistance, old chap. Hand me that letter of authority from the sheriff of Portsmouth, and I'll smooth your path with everything in my power." And Captain Rochester, his gold-mounted cut-and-thrust sword tied to his belt, picked up his gold-trimmed cocked hat, and headed out of the cabin and up the companionway.

Wiki hesitated a moment, and then went to his stateroom to fetch the letter of authority. Rochester didn't have to wait very long. Figuring it was hopeless to even try to match George's brilliant appearance, Wiki didn't bother to shift out of his workaday dungarees into anything more formal.

Twenty-one

*A*fter they arrived on the deck of the schooner, Wiki stopped and looked around, vividly reminded of his precipitate arrival early that morning, though the scene was very different. Joel Hammond was on the waist deck talking to the men on watch, who were huddled in a sullen group about the pumps. He turned and walked up, his small eyes wary.

"To what do I owe the honor?" he demanded.

"It's an official call, I regret to say," said Rochester.

Hammond paused, but then demonstrated that he was shrewder than he looked, because he said, "Any sign of your midshipman?"

"There's been an accident."

"An accident—to your officer?"

"I'm afraid so. Mr. Coffin needs to ask some questions of your men."

"What?" For the first time, Joel Hammond looked properly at Wiki, his expression a mixture of puzzlement and disdain. "What right has *he* got to question my men?" he exclaimed, and George Rochester produced Wiki's authorization from the sheriff's department of the town of Portsmouth, Virginia.

It was a grand parchment affair, now much creased, but still highly embellished with the town's seal, a scarlet ribbon that was beginning to fray, the coat of arms of the port, and a number of impressive signatures. Wiki watched the Stonington man's face become wooden as he read the flowing script that authorized the bearer, William Coffin, Jr., to act on behalf of the sheriff's department, and demanded from the reader whatever cooperation and assistance that the said William Coffin, Jr., might request.

Usually, as men read it, their expressions became first astounded, and then impressed, even if unwillingly so. Hammond, however, looked more aggressive than ever. Flicking the heavy sheet back at Captain Rochester, he snapped, "I can tell you all that's necessary. The last I saw of Midshipman Kingman was when he was passed out in the bottom of one of the boats. Apparently he couldn't handle his liquor. I don't allow such offensive sights on board my ships, and so I gave orders for him to be taken to the beach where his men were camped."

That, thought Wiki, was a change from yesterday afternoon, when Hammond had insinuated that Kingman was back on the *Swallow*.

Rochester said, "Well, he didn't get there."

Hammond shrugged. "I didn't see him go—I don't know what it's like on your smart little navy brig, Captain Rochester, but on this here schooner when I give an order I know damn sure without looking that it's going to be obeyed. They probably dumped him off by the wreck, and left him to make his own way to the next cove—or get himself back to the brig, if that was what he wanted. Sounds like he went somewhere on the island to sleep it off—and who knows where that might be?" Then he added derisively, "Your sheriff's deputy here mightn't know it, but I am sure you can explain to him, Captain, that going off somewhere private to sleep off a debauch is a common story with seamen."

Rochester snapped, "We know for a fact, sir, that that is *not* what happened." He paused, and then said grimly, "Midshipman Kingman's body was found this morning."

Hammond's hands shifted uneasily on his belt. He muttered, "I'm sorry to hear that. How did he die? Did he fall?"

"His throat was cut."

"What?" Joel Hammond recoiled, and stammered, "Who d-did it?"

"That, sir, is what Mr. Coffin has been deputized to find out. So, I repeat my request for you to allow him to go about his legitimate business of questioning your men."

Hammond, looking shaken, said, "Show me that paper again."

This time, he read the parchment more slowly, and folded it carefully before handing it back. He nodded at Wiki, saying curtly, "Do as you will. If any of the men give you trouble, send someone to me, and I'll make goddamned sure they think twice about being difficult."

Wiki inclined his head, but before he headed forward to ask his first questions, he said curiously, "So where were you while your boat was taken off to the beach?"

"Minding my own goddamned business in what passes as my stateroom—and the mate, Isaac Hunt, was there, too. It was only decent that some kind of prayerful service should be held for Captain Reed, despite the debased nature of the deceased." Hammond went on resentfully, "The Bible bids the servant to be faithful unto death—though I guess that you, bein' nothing but an unbaptized heathen, don't know such holy truths. But after the service was held I didn't reckon I was a servant no more, so I chose to stay no longer."

"You left the men to it?" queried Rochester, still nettled by that comment about his smart navy brig, and disliking the reference to unbaptized heathens, too. "Even though they were making free with the ship's grog?"

"Who told you that, sir? Because it's a goddamned lie! The captain's widow herself supplied grog to be given out after the prayers, that bein' the custom in her family, and her cousin arranged it with the steward, at her request."

That was usual enough, Wiki supposed. At home in the Bay of Islands the *tangihanga* funeral ceremony always included a feast, as well as long speeches and much wailing. However, he also knew the ways of seamen with grog, so was not surprised when Rochester said with a frown, "But you didn't stay to make sure the spree didn't get out of hand?"

"I allow neither the grape nor the barley to pass my lips, Captain; nor do I choose to witness the degradation of others. However, we did inspect the deck at regular intervals—which is how I found your officer in my boat."

"You're a *temperance* man?" Wiki exclaimed, stunned.

"I've signed the Pledge, and am proud of it, and Isaac Hunt's with me on that."

Good God, Wiki thought. Suddenly he knew why Ezekiel Reed had been so delighted to see Forsythe and Kingman when they'd first arrived. It must have been a refreshing change to have some drinking company on board.

"And," Hammond went on, "that was their last goddamned spree. The ship's grog's gone overboard—the whole goddamned lot. As the good book tells those who are wise enough to listen, wine is a mockery, and strong drink is a raging."

No wonder the watch was looking sullen, Wiki meditated, and with a nod he took himself off to find Boyd and the steward, and ask which of them had hauled the knife out of Captain Reed's back and what had happened to it after that.

Twenty-two

*O*n his way to the sternward part of the forward house, where he expected to find those two men, Wiki had to circle around the hatch that led to the holds and the between-decks area. To his surprise, a head popped out of it as he passed, and he recognized the cook, Robert Festin. First a beaky nose materialized, then a wide, thick torso, and after that short, spindly legs came into view. Then Festin stepped up onto the deck. He had a small molasses barrel on his shoulder, the spigot turned upward, evidently fetched from the storage area.

He gave Wiki a broad, friendly smile, but Wiki remembered that he was supposed to be too addled in the brains for speech, so instead of pausing to cross-examine him he kept on walking, saying casually, "*Kia ora*—good day to you."

"*Kuwai,*" said the cook brightly in return.

Wiki froze, midstep. He turned and said huskily, "*What* did you say?"

"*Kuwai*," said the cook, his smile becoming uncertain.

"You speak *te reo Maori*!" Back in the Bay of Islands, *kuwai* was a word for *shark*—and who knew where the strange little man had voyaged?

Looking puzzled, Festin shook his head. He opened his mouth, but then closed it again as his eyes focused beyond Wiki's shoulder, and his expression became guarded. Wiki turned swiftly, but it was only Alphabet, carrying a coil of rope over one shoulder.

"An exciting conversation?" Alphabet inquired.

Instead of answering, Wiki said to Festin, "What did you say back to me after I said *kia ora* to you?"

The cook's tortured frown was painful to watch. His mouth opened, shut, opened again, and then he said very awkwardly, "Good-day-to-you."

"No, you said *kuwai*."

"*Kway! Kway!*" exclaimed Festin, light dawning. "Good-day-to-you."

Wiki was surprised how disappointed he felt. "Damn it," he said to Green. "For a wild moment I thought we had a language— my language!—in common, because when he said *kway* I thought I heard *kuwai*, which is one of our words for *shark*."

Alphabet looked at Festin, shook his head, and said, "He doesn't talk—doesn't even understand what we say, most times, so I expect it's just a meaningless noise."

"I know," said Wiki, and sighed. "Festin's one of the four *Annawan* hands who was on board when Ezekiel was killed, and could maybe tell me something important—but I'm not even sure where he was. The cutter's men tell me that he left the galley, but I don't know where he went, or even whether he returned."

"Have you tried asking him? Maybe his mind is improving."

"That's a point," said Wiki. He turned to the cook, and said, "Where were you when Captain Reed was killed?"

"Hein?"

Wiki lifted his hands, while Alphabet grinned. Then, just as Wiki was about to walk away, Robert Festin said, *"Pantree."*

"Pantry?"

"Aye, aye, *pantree.*"

Alphabet shook his head. "I wouldn't bet that he means the pantry. The steward is very jealous of his domain, and there would be hell to pay if Festin invaded it."

"But the cutter's men say the steward was with them the whole time, and so the opportunity was there—if for some reason Festin wanted to go to the pantry."

Alphabet Green looked unconvinced, but he said, "Some of the men reckon they've heard him stammer words that sound like Cajun, so I could try him, if you like."

"Why not," said Wiki, and the Cajun turned to Festin. *"Allons parler,"* he said, and when he had the cook's attention, rapped out, "Where you at *avant-hier, hein?"*

"Pantree," said the cook blankly.

Wiki wryly observed, "Your luck is no better than mine."

"Couyon, that one," Alphabet agreed.

"Couyon means *stupid?"* Wiki remembered Annabelle using the word.

"Also damaged in the head," said Alphabet, and produced a stream of speech that included the sentence "Don't make the *misère* with me," but was otherwise incomprehensible, apart from the one word *galley,* repeated many times.

When Green finally silenced, Festin blinked warily and said, *"Gallee."*

"Dit mon la vérité?"

"Gallee."

"Fait pas une esquandal, peeshwank," Green said in a warning tone.

Festin spread his hands wide, and repeated, *"Gallee."*

Alphabet shrugged, and turned to Wiki, who had been listening with fascination. "He says he was in the galley."

It was such an anticlimax that Wiki almost laughed. Then Alphabet Green said, "What was that about a shark?"

Wiki quenched a shiver, and said, "Festin was watching when I was attacked by a shark while swimming this morning, and when he said the word *kuwai*—which is one of our words for *shark*—I thought he was asking me about it."

"A *shark*?" Alphabet exclaimed. "Where was it?"

Wiki said, "Cruising along the larboard side of the schooner."

Looking alarmed, Green went round the back of the galley shed to the rail, and looked down into the sea. "Don't worry, it's gone," Wiki said, joining him. Then he looked down at the deck. This was where, according to his theory, Kingman's throat had been cut. The blood must have spurted out violently. However, there were no stains on the scrubbed boards.

Alphabet said, "You look grim. What's the problem?"

"Passed Midshipman Kingman is dead. I found his body in the water—down there, right below us—this morning."

Alphabet Green looked over the rail. *"There?"*

"Aye," Wiki said grimly.

"So where's his body now?"

"The shark carried it off." Wiki's mouth had gone dry, and he swallowed.

Alphabet said, "Are you all right? You don't look too good."

"It was—a shock. It was a very big shark, and I was in the water at the time."

"But you saw the body?"

"Aye," Wiki said. He swallowed again and added, "His throat had been cut."

Alphabet shut his eyes, wincing. "Jesus. You're sure?"

"I had a good long look at the body before the shark carried it off, and I assure you I did not *imagine* that his throat had been cut," Wiki said very evenly. He gripped the warm, dry wood of the rail and stared down at the place in the rippling water where he had blundered into the ghastly corpse. Just beneath the dark surface leathery kelp waved to and fro, and it was impossible to see the bottom.

Then he turned and looked about the foredeck, envisaging the night of the wake, and how crowded the shadows would have seemed as the seamen jostled for their liquor, and the babble of voices as everyone relaxed after Hammond and Hunt left. He looked at Alphabet and said, "His throat was cut with Lieutenant Forsythe's knife—which was stolen from his belt sometime during the spree. After everyone else had headed off elsewhere, the thief grabbed Zachary Kingman, cut his throat, tied his feet to a grindstone, and tipped him over this rail—right here."

Alphabet, frowning deeply, was casting rapid glances about the foredeck himself. "The lieutenant's knife? Are you sure?"

"Aye. Do you remember the names of the men who took part in the spree?"

Without a pause for thought, Alphabet shook his head. "Sorry, I can't help you—I wasn't here. But if it was done with Forsythe's knife, it sure sounds to me as if the lieutenant is the most likely murderer."

Wiki shifted, feeling most perplexed. Ignoring the last part of what Alphabet had said, he said, "But I was told that you attended the wake."

"Of course I attended the wake," the other said shortly. "But the service was on the afterdeck."

"You didn't come to the foredeck for the spree? After all, it was Annabelle who supplied the grog," he added, remembering that Alphabet had organized it with the steward.

Alphabet's mouth compressed, and he repeated, "I wasn't here."

"So where were you?"

"In the after house with Annabelle."

"What?"

"I escorted her there after the prayers were finished, and—and she was too upset for me to leave her. She needed company—my supporting presence."

"But surely you didn't stay in the after house all night?"

"But I did," confessed Alphabet, his gaze sliding away from Wiki's puzzled stare. "I slept in Ezekiel's stateroom. But for God's sake, don't tell anyone. Hammond would have my guts for a bandanna if he knew."

There was a shout from the quarterdeck—Hammond himself, summoning the watch for an important announcement. Alphabet muttered distractedly, "What the hell is he on about now?"

Wiki opened his mouth to tell him about his strange appointment as a sheriff's deputy; that Hammond would be following up his promise to instruct the men to cooperate in the inquiry. Before he could utter a word, however, Alphabet Green turned on his heel and left.

Twenty-three

*W*iki walked back round the galley shed to its open door, which faced aft. Like the galley on the brig *Swallow*, it was surprisingly spacious inside. There was a large windowlike aperture facing the foredeck, which could be closed with a shutter but was open now, letting in plenty of light. Evidently the food was handed out to the crew through this, because there was a bench just inside with a couple of high stools handy, making a pleasant place to sit when the sun was shining in. Too, when the schooner was in icy waters and the window was shut, this would be the warmest spot on board. Wiki thought now that he could understand why Annabelle used this room as a refuge—she was the last person to worry about the proprieties of the captain's wife sunning herself in the galley, he mused.

Huge pots and pans hung from one wall, along with great forks, knives, and ladles. Ten headless hens dangled by their feet from hooks set into another wall, while the back quarter of the shed was taken up by an enormous iron stove. Festin was crouched in front of this, raking out the grate and expostulating in his unintelligible tongue. Evidently the fire he had lit that morning had gone out, much to his fury. When he saw Wiki he stood up and waved his arms about in dramatic fashion—it was somebody's else's fault, his expression plainly said, and once he found out who the culprit was, that man would be very sorry.

Frowning, remembering the stench that had pervaded the schooner when he'd come on board this morning, Wiki hunkered down by the open fire door of the stove, opening his jackknife to pry around in the ash and cinders Festin had raked out. The blade hooked on something which dangled when he lifted the knife—a blackened scrap of cloth.

Squinting at it, he said over his shoulder, "Do you have a sieve—a strainer?"

Receiving nothing but blank silence in return, he stood up, searched the wall of cooking tools, came up with what he wanted, and then, ignoring Festin's horrified exclamations, emptied the grate into the sieve, and shook it over a pan.

The result was some more scraps of fabric, and one button, all of which Wiki took over to the window for close inspection. It had been a shirt, he thought—a striped blue and white shirt of the kind that seamen bought by the dozen from dry goods stores in port, or even from the slop chest—the ship's store of goods for sale. The button, however, was unusual. The heat had shrunk and warped it, but when he sniffed there was a distinct smell of scorched animal bone. It had been a piece of antler, he thought.

There were stains as well as scorch and ash on the disintegrating bits of cloth. Kingman's neck would have spouted blood like a hosepipe, soaking his killer's sleeve—maybe the entire shirt. It was easy to imagine the shirt being so sodden with blood that when it was thrown into the galley fire it eventually quenched the flames— though not before the garment was almost entirely destroyed. Again, Wiki remembered the ghastly stink that had pervaded the decks, now realizing that it had been due to more than burning feathers. Had the killer seized the chance to get rid of the blood-soaked evidence while Festin had been busy fetching the poultry from the coops and chopping off their heads? It seemed very likely.

So who had been the owner of that common seaman's shirt with an unusual antler button—the man who had knifed Zack Kingman? It seemed logical that it was the same man who had killed Ezekiel Reed, which meant it had to be one of the four *Annawan* men who had remained behind on the schooner. Putting the button in his pocket, Wiki set off again for the sternward end of the forward house, leaving Festin to clean up the mess.

Just as in the after house, a short companionway led down from the sternward entrance of the forward house to a passage, but here, instead of staterooms, there was a boatswain's locker to one side, and a steward's pantry directly opposite. There was a closed door at the end of the corridor—which led to the berth shared by Hammond and the mate, Wiki surmised.

The boatswain's locker was neatly stacked with barrels, ropes, paint and tackle, while the pantry was furnished with shelves of plates, platters, mugs, and bowls, a dry sink, and a spirit stove for heating water and coffee. Both rooms were occupied, with a man— presumably Boyd—overhauling gear in the boatswain's locker, while Jack Winter was rattling cutlery in the pantry. Both had their backs turned as they worked, and neither heard Wiki arrive, so instead of accosting them right away he walked up the short passage as far as the shut door. Then he turned to face the way he had come. From where he stood, looking along the short passage and up the stairway, he could just glimpse the fore hatch—the one from which Festin had emerged with the little keg of molasses.

Rousing himself from deep thought, he walked to the boatswain's locker and tapped on the open door. Then, when the man still didn't respond, he reached out and touched him lightly on the shoulder of his plain blue frock shirt.

Boyd swiveled, startled, and then stared at him silently with rather protuberant blue eyes. Unlike most of the men on the schooner, he was clean-shaven. Past his burly shoulder Wiki could see a neat array of carpentering, blacksmithing, and coopering equipment. A cooper's wheel stood in a corner, complete with grindstone. Another grindstone stood in a rack, with two empty spaces next to it. One gap would be for the stone that was in the wheel right now, Wiki guessed—but where was the other?

He said sharply, without preamble, "Where's the other grindstone?"

"What?" Boyd frowned, and turned and looked at the rack. "Some bastard's borrowed it without permission," he exclaimed in a loud, hoarse voice.

"Do you think you'll get it back?"

"I'll make bloody sure I do!" His protruding eyes became suspicious. "Who the hell are you to ask questions?" he demanded—but before Wiki could answer, an older man came hurrying down the stairs.

This, as Wiki immediately found out, was Boyd's superior, the boatswain, Folger. A weather-beaten, scarred, and heavily graybearded fellow, he had two fingers missing from each of his hands. "You be polite to Mr. Coffin," he sharply scolded his assistant.

"Captain Hammond has been tellin' us that he's none other than a sheriff's deputy from Portsmouth, Virginia, and that we are to give him all our cooperation, so you be careful what you say to him." Then he turned to Wiki, and said anxiously, "Bill couldn't be nothin' to do with the murder of Captain Reed, sir—he was overhauling this locker the whole of that afternoon."

Wiki glanced sideways at Boyd, who was listening stolidly, and said, "But how can you be sure of that?"

"If you could've seen the state of the locker after dinner, and compare it with the way I found it when I got back from the *Swallow*, sir, it would be as plain as the nose on your face that Boyd followed my instructions to the letter, and didn't have the time for nothin' else."

Wondering why Folger was so patently eager to clear Bill Boyd of suspicion, Wiki said, "Have you been a sealer for long, Mr. Folger?"

"Many years," said the boatswain, and looked ruefully at his maimed hands. "I started in the good old days, when there was money to be made, but this is all I have to remember it by. Sealing's how Captain Reed founded his fortune—did you know that? He discovered a new rookery back in the days when a shrewd man could get five dollars for a prime skin in the Canton market, and that was only the start of his luck. He made a lot of sealers rich," Folger confessed, "and we was hoping he'd do the same for us."

"*We?*" Wiki echoed.

"There's eight experienced sealers on board of this here schooner," Folger said, and went on to reveal that Bill Boyd was one of that select group.

Wiki, feeling more intrigued than ever, said, "Bill and who else?"

One, to Wiki's great surprise, was the steward, Jack Winter, who by now was openly listening, and who confirmed that they'd all held high hopes that this voyage would do well, on account of Captain Reed's great reputation.

"Then it's most unfortunate for you that Captain Reed is dead," observed Wiki.

"Aye," said Folger glumly. "Horrible business, horrible. I do hope you catch the wicked murderer, sir."

Wiki looked at Boyd and said, "Did you see anyone go into the pantry the afternoon Captain Reed was murdered?"

"Not after Jack went a-drinkin' and a-gossipin' with them hands from the cutter," Boyd returned at once. "Spent the whole confounded afternoon having hisself a good time on the fo'c'sle deck while everyone else was working."

His malicious tone got an immediate response from the steward, who cried, "That's a damn lie! I wasn't drinking—or only just enough to be sociable, and it was on the orders of Captain Reed himself, so it's not right to infer I was slacking!"

Wiki said, "What about the wake?"

He was immediately aware that the boatswain looked alarmed at the sudden turn of the questioning, but the steward answered readily enough, "Mrs. Reed requested me to issue grog after the prayers was done with, and sent the bottles forward, so that's just what I done."

"Did you serve a lot of grog to Passed Midshipman Kingman?"

Jack Winter's stare wavered guiltily. He said in a lower voice, "Aye, Mr. Coffin, I did."

"Even though he got very intoxicated?"

"Mrs. Reed's request was for me to be hospitable, and so I didn't see it was up to me to stop him from drinking hisself so drunk."

"Where was he when you saw him last?"

The steward paused. It was as if he and Boyd communicated

silently, and then Jack Winter said, "He was asleep in the captain's boat. It was hangin' in the davits, and when Bill looked he was a-lying in the bottom, dead drunk, so he called me, and I looked, too."

Folger scratched his ear and said, "May I inquire why you're asking, sir?"

"There's been another killing. We found Midshipman Kingman's body this morning."

"Another murder?" When he saw Wiki's nod, he said softly, "Oh, my lord."

"Were you at the wake?"

"Not after the prayers—and Bill wasn't there, neither. We was both in the fo'c'sle."

Boyd's loud voice broke in. "You're forgetting that he knows I spied the midshipman a-lying drunk in the bottom of the cap'n's boat."

"Well, we both inspected the decks now and then," Folger said quickly. "Seeing as there was a spree on the foredeck, and the ship sinking under our feet."

"So you saw him in the boat, too?"

Folger looked down, and mutely shook his head.

"When was the last time *you* saw Midshipman Kingman?"

"During one of the inspections of the deck I took special note of him, on account of he'd got into a quarrel with his lieutenant."

Wiki exclaimed, *"What?"*

"He'd set up a game of four-card monte, and his lieutenant didn't like it."

Wiki frowned. Zachary Kingman was known to be addicted to gambling, but Forsythe was a gambler, too. He said, "Why was Lieutenant Forsythe upset about it?"

"The midshipman was winning all the men's money, and the hands were a-grumbling about it, on account of they reckoned he was cheating, and so they complained to his lieutenant, tellin' him to put a stop to it, threatening that otherwise there'd be a row. He was angry with the midshipman already, for some reason, and so he agreed it wasn't polite, and ordered him to give the money back, but had to shake him around a bit to make him obey."

My God, thought Wiki—here was another motive for Kingman's murder. Four-card monte was the most popular form of gambling in most ports of the Pacific, and also the fastest way to lose your money. If Folger told Captain Wilkes about this during an inquiry, Forsythe was doomed to hang, for sure. Swinging round to the steward, he demanded, "Why did you go out of your way to get our officers drunk?"

Winter's eyes bulged, and he expostulated, "I didn't intend for *anyone* to get drunk! It was a goddamned wake—a serious business!"

"I don't think Cap'n Reed would've minded if you did," observed Boyd unexpectedly, and let out a raucous laugh.

"Hush, Bill," said Folger. He sounded nervous.

Wiki looked thoughtfully from Folger to Boyd and back again, and then said to Boyd, "You laid out his corpse, I hear."

"He just built the coffin," Folger interrupted quickly. "Didn't do no more than that."

"So who put the body in the coffin?"

Folger looked at Boyd, and the younger man said, "I did. But Jack here had already sewed up the body in that rug what was a-soaking with his own gore. Disgustin', I call it. Bloody un-Christian."

Jack Winter exclaimed, "I don't think it Christian any more than you do! But when I asked Captain Hammond for a piece of old canvas for a winding sheet he bid me use the mat to save expense. Not only was it bloody mean—if you'll excuse my biblical language, Mr. Coffin—but it turned a nasty job into a dirty one. You ask Captain Hammond, and if he speaks the truth, he'll tell you that's the way it come about, and 'twasn't nothin' to do with me."

"What about the knife?"

"What knife?"

"The murder weapon. When I inspected the body," Wiki elaborated with rapidly ebbing patience, "there was a knife in his back."

"Well, there wasn't no knife when I saw it," said the steward sulkily. "Just a gash in his back, and a hole in his front, and his shirt all soaked with gore."

Wiki exclaimed, "So who the devil took it out?"

"Not Bill," said Folger instantly.

"Not Bill nor me, because the knife was already gone," the steward said righteously. "You'll have to ask Captain Hammond how it got out and where it went."

"I'll do that," said Wiki grimly, and turned on his heel.

Twenty-four

*O*ut on deck, the noon sun was hot and bright, and Wiki was amazed how little time had passed since his dreadful swim at dawn. He went to the rail, and looked out at the bay where the *Swallow* floated serenely, and then turned to look at the beach, to find it ornamented with the glitter of George Rochester's uniform. Wiki blinked, feeling very startled, wondering why George had left the schooner. Then he saw that Rochester was conferring with Forsythe, whose men were swarming over the wreck of the sloop. It was a hopeful sign, he thought. George, having established Wiki's credentials on the schooner, was thinking over the proposition of building a raft and getting the *Annawan* hove down and repaired.

When Wiki turned to survey the decks again, his attention was caught by a furtive movement. Someone, he realized, was doing his best to keep out of his sight—a Spanish-looking type, wearing a loose striped red and white shirt over tight black pantaloons, the waist of the shirt cinched in with a broad, brass-studded belt. Having a very strong feeling that this was the character the cutter's men had described coming down from the mizzen rigging about the time that Captain Reed was killed, Wiki approached him with intent.

When this stylish figure saw Wiki coming toward him he started like a spurred horse, and moved decisively in a different direction—which confirmed to Wiki that this was indeed one of the men he most wanted to question. Pursuing him determinedly, he finally cornered him by the taffrail. *"Hola, "* he said, and the seaman stopped trying to get away.

Remembering the name in the crew list, Wiki checked, "Da Silva, right? Pedro da Silva? Didn't you join this ship in Rio?"

"Senhor." The bloodshot eyes were slipping in every direction to avoid Wiki's stare. Though he bravely shoved out his chest by cramping in his buttocks and clasping his hands tightly behind his back, he was so obviously nervous he looked as culpable as sin.

Wiki contemplated him for a long silent moment, something that didn't ease the man's jittery state. Then he asked in Portuguese, "Did you ship out to avoid conscription into the army?"

"No, *senhor*! Never!" Pedro protested, but still refused to meet Wiki's stare.

"Because if that is the case, it might explain your guilty look."

"Guilty?" Pedro jumped a foot with fright. "I am guilty of nothing, sir, nothing!"

"Yet you are trying to avoid me—why?"

The seaman wavered, and then said uneasily, "I do not wish to appear before an official court of inquiry, sir. It would not be good—for my reputation."

"But why should you be called up to give evidence—unless you saw something of importance?" The seaman was silent, and

Wiki pursued, "You could be the man whose evidence is the means of apprehending a vicious killer."

"Oh," said the Portuguese seaman, and obviously wavered, impressed by the possible importance of his role.

"So what *did* you see from aloft, that afternoon that Captain Reed was killed?"

There was a long, suspenseful silence, while Pedro's dark eyes slid from side to side, but then he said boldly, "I did see a great deal. One sees much from there."

"Perhaps what you saw will prevent more murders in the future." Wiki paused, and then said reassuringly, "Just tell me what you saw that afternoon, right from the beginning."

It was as if he had turned on a faucet. Pedro suddenly became garrulous, the words hurrying out of his mouth and his sentences tumbling over each other; it was as if he had been anxious to tell someone about it, but hadn't had the courage until now.

"The cutter arrived at about the same time as the two boats," he described. "I saw the two officers talk with Mr. Hammond, and then Captain Reed came out and they went into the cabin with him. Soon after that I saw the steward come out. He took a bottle to the seamen on the fo'c'sle deck, and I saw him sit down with them. Later still, I saw the captain and your two officers come out, and stand talking—I think they were arguing. The captain was yelling for more brandy, and I saw the captain's wife bring it to him. Then Mr. Hammond called for two boats' crews to go to the navy brig, but I am not one of those, you understand. Instead of going to the *Swallow*, I stayed aloft. After the boats had gone away, they all went into the cabin; then after a while I saw the two navy officers come out. They were in a hurry. I saw the captain's wife come running out after the two officers from the navy ship, but she did not join them. She ran to the galley; then she ran back to the cabin; then she ran out again, screaming. That was when I came down from the rigging to see what she was screaming about."

"When she ran to the galley, did you see anyone else on the quarterdeck?"

To Wiki's surprise, Pedro nodded without even troubling to think.

"Who was it?"

"I can't tell you, because it was only a glimpse—a movement, you understand. The man was either very short, or bent low down. Then he was gone. It happened very quickly, and my attention was on Mrs. Reed."

"Did you hear her call out to the cook?"

"To the man in the galley?"

"Aye," said Wiki, thinking that this was the first confirmation he had had that there was a man in the galley at the time, because the cutter's men had been so unsure of it.

"She did say something to him," Pedro said. "But I did not know the words. It was in a different language, perhaps."

Wiki hesitated, and then said, "Do you remember the kind of sound the words made?"

Pedro shook his head, but then to Wiki's surprise he laughed, saying, "When she called out it reminded me of the call of an owl— *tu-whit-tu-woo*."

Wiki's brows shot up. "What happened next?"

"Next, Mrs. Reed turned around and ran back to the after house. Down she ran, then back she came, screaming. Then everyone was running to the quarterdeck all at once and you came on board. I did not know then that you are an officer of the law, or I would have spoken to you right away," he added importantly, just as if he expected Wiki to have forgotten that only minutes before he'd been doing his damnedest to avoid being questioned.

Wiki said, "You can't remember anything else—what the man you glimpsed was wearing, for instance?"

Pedro shook his head.

"Were you at the wake?"

"But of course! Our captain was dead, and it was the right thing to do."

"And you played monte with the midshipman?"

Pedro went back to looking nervous, blustering, "Is that something wrong?"

"Perhaps you lost all your money."

"His lieutenant made him give it back."

"Who else was playing?"

The seaman hesitated, but then rattled off a short list of names that did not include the steward, Boyd, Folger, or the cook. Wiki said, "Did they all lose their money to the midshipman?"

"He was cheating, we think."

"But they all got their money back?"

"Aye, sir. Your lieutenant made sure of that."

"So what happened afterward?"

"Most went into the fo'c'sle, as it was no longer fun, you understand."

"What about yourself?"

Pedro shrugged. "I stayed to have a small drink. Then Captain Hammond came out and ordered me to go to masthead lookout."

So, coincidentally, he was in the same vantage point where he'd been when Ezekiel Reed was knifed. Wiki said, "What else did you notice about our midshipman?"

"He and your lieutenant were very, very drunk, and they were still very angry with each other, I think. Then the midshipman went and lay down in the captain's boat."

"You saw him from aloft?"

"He was directly below me. I saw people come and look at him—the boatswain's mate, the steward, and then Captain Hammond. After they had gone away he got up and jumped out of the boat again. Some men came and lowered the boat, but he was not there. They pulled to the beach after putting your lieutenant in the bottom. After that I was off duty, so I went to my berth."

"Did you see where the midshipman went after he got out of the boat?"

"Aye, sir. After he jumped out of the boat he staggered off to the after house, heading for the captain's cabin."

"Is that so?" said Wiki slowly.

Twenty-five

*T*he door at the top of the short companionway
to the captain's cabin was clipped open, so that
as Wiki descended the stairs Annabelle was in plain view. Again she
was sitting in an armchair by the stove. This time, however, the fire
wasn't lit. When she heard Wiki's step she turned in the chair,
looked up, and gasped, "Oh Wiki, you've come!"

"Aye," he said, and when he stepped right into the room he
stood up and rushed to him as if she were desperate for reassurance.
He held her, feeling the different ways her trembling body pressed
hard against his. Looking down at her, he saw that the black hair
was the same, shining like silk, falling in wings from a center parting and braided into the tender nape of her neck. Without volition,
his hand cradled the back of her glossy head.

He wasn't even sure she felt it, because she pulled away, and settled back in her chair. "Please sit," she said, in the formal way she adopted every now and then. He looked around, and took the seat he'd used before.

She said, "Captain Rochester tells me you are now a sheriff."

"A deputy," he corrected, and added wryly, "I didn't apply for the position. The sheriff of Portsmouth felt frustrated because he couldn't follow a murderer onto the exploring expedition, and so he delivered a document to Captain Wilkes appointing me his proxy."

"And did you find that murderer?"

Wiki nodded.

"So that makes you a most important person."

Wiki couldn't find an answer to that—he didn't agree, but he could hardly make the investigation more difficult by saying so. So instead, he gave her a self-deprecating smile.

"Now you understand the situation," he suggested, "you don't mind if I ask you some questions?"

"Only if I can do the same," she said pertly.

He laughed with surprise. "What do you mean?"

"For every question you ask, I can ask you one of my own. Isn't that a fair trade?"

"I'm not sure that's the usual procedure."

"But that is the condition I set," she said. Her eyes were dancing with sudden mischief, but he nodded. *Damn it,* he thought, *we're flirting again.*

He said, "Me first?"

"You are the important one," she said saucily, "so of course you go first."

"How did Ezekiel find out that the sloop was wrecked on Shark Island?"

"Shark Island?"

"Ilha Tubarão."

"Is that what this island is called?"

"Aye," said Wiki, and added severely, "Now I have answered two of your questions, and you haven't answered even one of mine." He repeated, "Who told Ezekiel the sloop *Hero* was lying here?"

She shrugged, and said, "Ezekiel would never discuss his business affairs with a woman, even a woman who was his wife."

"Annabelle, that is not an answer!"

"All I can tell you is that he went on shore at Rio, and came back very angry. He had learned that the sloop had been wrecked, and while he was away the cook and a seaman had run off. Next day, my husband received Festin and another seaman called da Silva on board, and we weighed anchor, and sailed for this coast. I didn't go on shore at all," she said resentfully. "This I did not expect when I made up my mind to go to sea."

"I've already told you that coming on a sealing voyage was a crazy idea."

She shrugged elaborately, looking very Gallic, and said, "What does it matter? This voyage turned out to be not for sealing."

"He gave up the sealing idea because the *Hero* had been wrecked?"

"Of course. He wished to come and salvage it."

Wiki watched her through his lashes as he insinuated, "I wouldn't have thought the sloop valuable enough to be worth the trouble."

She waved an eloquently dismissive hand. "I don't know about value. All I know is that the captain of the *Hero* ran the sloop ashore in order to escape some pirates."

"So what happened after you arrived here?"

"That *couyon*, Joel Hammond, he sailed the schooner over a rock, so she got a hole in her bottom. There was a great fuss with canvas and ropes as the men tried to stop the leak, and then Ezekiel came back from shore rubbing his hands together, and after that he drank a great deal of brandy."

Remembering something Forsythe had said, Wiki checked, "As if he were celebrating?"

"And as if he were angry, too. He was pleased about finding the wreck, but furious when he found that the *Annawan* was no longer fit to go to sea. Every now and then he said he would send for one of his captains to come to the rescue, but mostly he was too drunk for anyone to guess what was going on in his head. I did not know until I came on voyage how much my husband drank. He was a different person at home. At home he was generous and attentive. At sea he was so . . . so unloving."

She leaned closer, so that Wiki was suddenly aware of her scent. The movement lifted her breasts in the confines of her low bodice.

She said, "You have asked me four questions, and I have only asked you two."

Wiki thought back, and realized she was right, so he waited.

"So why did you come on deck . . . the way you did this morning?"

"I'd been swimming."

"But—*met tes fesse a l'aire?*"

"I prefer to swim naked—and that's two questions," he said.

She bridled. "Perhaps you think it is clever to come out of the water like some kind of—of primitive sea god."

He smiled wryly, and said, "No insult was intended."

"But your buttocks are tattooed! In—in great, bold spirals. Is that the custom in your country?"

He thought about it. "In my *iwi*—my tribe," he corrected.

"So you have been back to your home since you saw me last?"

"Oh aye," he said. Getting home had been his chief aim after he and George Rochester had run away from the college in Dartmouth. He'd shipped on a whaleship because that was the most direct way of getting to the Bay of Islands. When the ship had sailed in the wrong direction, he had solved the problem by deserting at the next landfall and joining another ship that was going the right way. "I've been back twice," he said.

"And your people were glad to see you?"

"Of course. I had many wonderful tales to tell," he said dryly. "And because of that I was a person of importance."

"And you got your—*tes fesses*—tattooed." She leaned forward again and whispered, "Did it hurt?"

It had hurt like hell. On other islands in the Pacific, tattoos were tapped into the surface of the skin with special combs, which was painful enough, but in New Zealand the patterns were carved with a chisel as if the living flesh were wood. By the time his buttocks had healed, sitting down had become an unaccustomed luxury.

However, Wiki merely smiled, and said, "Do you realize how many more questions you have asked of me than I have asked of you?"

"Those don't count, because you never answered the first question properly."

"Which one was that?"

"Why did you rush up the side of the ship onto the deck?"

"Because I was attacked by a shark."

"A *shark*?" For a moment he thought she would dash up to deck and go to the rail, like her cousin, and he said, "It's gone." Then he leaned forward, coming closer, breathing in her scent, resting his forearms along his thighs as he watched the subtle changes in her expression, and said, "Now it's my turn."

She pouted, and waited.

"How did the parrot get burned?"

"It was an accident. It flew into the cabin stove all by itself."

"It escaped from its cage?"

"No, I took it out. I opened the door and grabbed it."

"But why?"

She exclaimed passionately, "You told me that Ezekiel's ghost was in a bird, and I knew it was *that* bird—and I couldn't bear it. Can you even start to imagine what it was like? Once, that bird was my special pet, but now every time the poor creature stirred on its perch I knew it was possessed!"

Dear God, thought Wiki, what nightmares had he inadvertently triggered?

He said, wincing, "So what did you do?"

"I took it out of the cage to take it on deck and throw it over the railing—but it escaped; it struggled away from me, and flew into the fire. It fell to the floor and I thought it was dead. But it started floundering about—it was horrible, *horrible*! I heard Robert Festin killing hens for dinner—and when I looked he was chopping off their heads, so I wished him to chop off the parrot's head, too, because it had to be put out of its terrible pain. He will cook it with to-morrow's stew—and why not? Those *couyons* of sailors won't notice it."

Wiki grimaced. Then he said, "Did Captain Rochester tell you about Passed Midshipman Kingman?"

She looked puzzled. "That horrid skinny man who made that very crude joke about the convent where I was educated? What should I know about him?"

"He was murdered the night of the wake."

"Murdered?"

"Aye—and the last anyone saw of him, he was staggering to-ward the after house."

"What? But why would he come here?"

Her voice had become shrill, verging on hysteria, so he said in a more gentle tone, "He knew that you had supplied the liquor for the spree, so maybe he wanted more. If he did come in here, though, you might have been the last person to see him alive."

"But I tell you I didn't see him!" she cried.

"Perhaps he wanted to see Alphabet?"

She blinked, looking confused, and demanded, "Who told you Alphabet was here?"

Wiki felt puzzled. "He did—Alphabet did. He said he slept in Ezekiel's stateroom because you were so upset."

"Oh." She bit her lip, blinking hard as if more tears were threatening. "He gave me his arm to escort me, yes, when I came back after the prayers, and I was crying, of course, but I don't know why he told you that; he went off with the boat that took your officers to the beach, I think, and after I had finished crying I slept remarkably well."

"So you didn't hear anything unusual?" he asked.

She frowned, and said, "I heard the boat being lowered, and after that it was quiet. I went to sleep, but then I was woken by a bump against the wall."

"A bump?"

"Yes. Just one bump, and maybe I heard footsteps, too. Later, I was woken again by a splash—or maybe it was the boat returning—and then I went back to sleep and did not wake up until morning."

"A bump?" Wiki looked around. "In here?"

"No, no. Outside, on the deck—up there."

He stood up and headed for the stairs, hearing the rustle of skirts as Annabelle hurried after him. When they arrived on deck, he looked at her queryingly, and she pointed toward the larboard side of the after house.

He strode around the corner. Sun bounced up from the rippling water, forcing him to squint, and it was hot in the sheltered space between the wall of the after house and the larboard rail. He turned as Annabelle came up alongside him, and she said, "The noise came from here. A bump, and sometime after that, a splash."

Wiki looked down, and his heart seemed to freeze. Though someone had tried to scrub it away, there was a wide, dark stain on the planks.

Twenty-six

When Wiki returned to deck, George was still standing by the wreck, and so he dived over the rail and swam to the beach. As he walked out of the surf, Rochester came to meet him. For some moments his friend said nothing, instead frowning and watching assessingly as Wiki took off his shirt and trousers, wrung them out, and put them on again.

Then he said, "Are you all right?"

"Aye," said Wiki. As a matter of fact, he felt magnificent.

"You weren't worried about sharks?"

Wiki blinked, and turned and looked at the sparkling stretch of water he'd just swum across. The thought of shark attack hadn't even occurred to him.

Rochester gave up waiting for an answer, and led the way to the wreck, which looked different, Forsythe and his men having taken away a great deal of the cordage. Feeling awkward because of the odd quality of George's silence, Wiki said, "Thank you for establishing my credentials—you must have done a good job on Joel Hammond, because he ordered his men to cooperate."

"So what did you find out?"

"The cook was definitely in the galley at the time Ezekiel Reed was killed—and when I had a look around in there, I found that someone had burned some clothing in the fire. There was very little left, but enough to guess it was a bloodstained shirt."

"Any particular kind of shirt?"

"All I could tell was that it had been one of those common blue and white striped ones that find a good market with seamen—though it did have an unusual deer horn button."

Wiki dug around in his pocket and handed it to George, who turned it over in his fingers. Then he handed it back, and said, "So you reckon the man who killed Kingman got rid of his bloodstained shirt in the galley fire—because he was handy to the galley already?"

Wiki hesitated, and then said quietly, "Zachary Kingman wasn't killed at the back of the galley, as I'd thought—he was killed on the larboard side of the after house."

Silently, without meeting George's penetrating stare, he remembered the bloodstain on the planks at the sheltered side of the after house. His vision had grayed, and Annabelle had taken hold of him because she thought he was going to faint. He remembered the grip of her hands, and how she had hurried him back to the after house; he remembered her shutting the door to her stateroom, and how she had trembled as she explored the texture of his spiral tattoos. She had been frantic for him; what happened had been unstoppable.

George prompted in his clear, cut-glass accents, "How did you find that out?"

Abruptly brought back to the present, Wiki said, "Pedro da Silva—the seaman who was aloft at the time Captain Reed was killed—was also aloft during the spree that followed the prayers. He said that after Hammond had given the order to take him to the beach, Kingman woke up and stumbled off to the after house, and so they took Forsythe, instead. Then I found a big stain on the planks on the larboard side of the deck."

"But his body was anchored by the bow, you said."

"The current must have dragged it there." Wiki hesitated, looked around, lowered his voice, and said, "Where's Forsythe?"

"He and his men are up at the fort, sizing up those beams. Why?"

"Apparently he and Kingman had a quarrel during the spree; Kingman was cheating at cards, and Forsythe had to shake him around a bit before he would give back the money."

Rochester whistled. "That's bad."

"And da Silva saw someone on the quarterdeck just before Annabelle ran back into the after house and found her husband dead."

"Did he recognize him?"

"No—but he described him as burly, and either very short or bent low down."

"That fits a number of men as well as Forsythe."

"Aye," said Wiki. "The cook is short and squat, and the bo'sun's mate is heavyset."

"What about Annabelle Reed? Does she still reckon that it was Forsythe she saw on the quarterdeck?"

Wiki was silent, realizing that he had completely forgotten to check. Acutely aware that Rochester's frown was deepening as he studied his face, Wiki turned away, pretending to contemplate the pleasant scene. In the uncomfortable silence gulls screeched, circling the afternoon sun. Then he saw that Forsythe was heading their way down the cliff.

Rochester set off to meet the lieutenant, but then abruptly stopped a dozen yards up the trail. When Wiki caught up with him, he was bent like a heron to look at the ground.

George straightened, and said, "Something has been dragged along this track."

"Aye," said Wiki. "I noticed those ruts the day of Reed's burial. I thought they might have been made by construction stones."

"For the fort? They seem too recent for that. And do they lead upward or down?"

"I've no idea," said Wiki, and crouched down to look. As expected, the marks in the dust and stone meant little. Shaking his head, he pushed himself to his feet.

The movement disturbed a bird. It burst out of the scrub and soared straight up into the sky, circling in the air directly above the patch where it had been roosting. When Wiki tipped up his head to follow it with his eyes, he was unsighted by the bright sun directly behind it, so that for an instant the bird was a black beckoning flicker against a kaleidoscope of color.

The circling bird cawed a challenge. Back home in New Zealand, it would have been a potent omen. With a fine disregard for snakes Wiki pushed through thorny bushes toward the place where the bird had risen, tripped on something, and nearly measured his length in the scrub. As the bird cawed again in the sky right above, he recovered his balance with a few running steps, and went back to see what had caught his foot.

It was a spar of timber, about five feet long and four inches in diameter, roughly rounded, evidently cast aside there when it had finished serving its purpose. Wiki picked it up, tested its weight and heft, and then whirled it around his shoulders, swinging it from hand to hand, closing and unclosing his fists as its balance shifted. It was a skill he thought he'd forgotten. For a moment memories of childhood days were as vivid as the sun and sand of Shark Island—he could almost hear the voice of the warrior elder who had coached the village boys in hand-to-hand combat, and see his fiercely handsome tattooed face.

"What's that?" said George.

"It was the shaft of an oar, I think," said Wiki, balancing the spar on his palms and then sighting down its length. A dense, strong, finely grained hardwood, it was surprisingly rigid—because of the way it had seasoned as it lay in the sun, he supposed, as it was ash, which was usually more flexible. He braced his legs, whirled it powerfully a few more times, and then peered along it again, taking great pleasure in the way it maintained its straightness.

When he looked down at the ground where the spar had lain, he found that the bird had left two feathers behind—long, primary feathers, deep blue-black rimmed with white and with white shafts. This was another omen. Carefully, he put them in his shirt pocket. Then, carrying the staff over one shoulder, he made his way back to the track.

Forsythe, arriving, said, "What the hell are you going to do with that?"

"I'm going to make myself a *taiaha*." Wiki enjoyed saying the aggressive word with its long vowels, and wondered if Forsythe, who had once hired himself out as a mercenary to a Maori chief, and had led a musket-armed *taua*—war party—in a massacre of enemy warriors who were armed just with traditional weapons, knew what a *taiaha* was.

Apparently he did. "Don't see the point," he said. "The best damn war club in the world ain't nothin' better than a broom straw when seen down the barrel of a gun."

"Nevertheless," said Wiki, but didn't bother to finish the sentence, which would have pointed out that there was little honor in killing a man with a gun. Instead, he thought about how alive the spar had felt in his hands as he whirled it, luxuriating in its promise of deadly strength. Already abundantly blessed by omens, his *taiaha*-in-the-making needed no justification from him.

Forsythe said, "Have you picked Zack's murderer, yet?"

Wiki shook his head. The southerner was looking a lot better, he thought; immersing himself in hard work had done Forsythe good.

"What about the knives? Have you sorted out how they switched my knife for the one that killed the old man?"

"The steward, who was the one who sewed Captain Reed up in the rug they used for a winding sheet, says the knife had been removed from the body before he arrived."

George said unexpectedly, "Hammond informed me that he was the one who had taken it out—he freely admitted setting a boot on the dead man's back and yanking out the blade."

"Strong stomach," said Wiki with distaste.

"Well, he's a sealer—even if he'd make a better horse jockey, according to popular opinion—so must be naturally cold-blooded."

"So what did he do with the knife after that?" Forsythe demanded.

"He says he wrapped it up and put it away in the bo'sun's locker."

"Then someone must have got a hold of it there."

Rochester said, "Why have you come back?"

"There's some hoisting tackle in the hold of the wreck that could be useful."

Forsythe led the way back down to the beach, with Rochester just behind him, and Wiki, having shouldered his spar, tailing at the rear. They clambered up the plank to the deck, and then down to the hold. As Forsythe had said, hoisting tackle had been dumped at the bottom of the hatch, in a tangle of stout ropes and heavy blocks. While he sorted through it, Rochester went over to another corner, evidently having glimpsed something in a stray shaft of light. He dipped down, and came back with a big silver coin in his hand, which he bounced.

Forsythe said, "What's that?"

"A Chilean dollar," George said, and handed it to him. Then he said pensively, "I've been wondering about those privateers—and what happened to the cargo."

"Cargo?" Forsythe's expression became alert. He looked from George to Wiki, and said, "What do you know that I don't?"

They told him about Reed's letter and the hundred thousand in specie, and he whistled, impressed. "That's a hell of a haul. The revolution could do with that kind of cash, I'm sure."

"Indeed," George agreed, and then added, "*If* the privateers got it."

"What do you mean?"

"The captain of the sloop might have run her up on the beach so that he and the crew could get the bullion out of the hold before the insurgents caught up with them. Somebody certainly hoisted something out," Rochester observed, indicating the tackle.

Wiki said slowly, "It struck me all along as very odd that Captain Reed should break the sealing season to come north after hearing the news in Rio. It doesn't make sense for him to come to salvage the sloop, because it's an almost worthless wreck. But if someone from the crew told him they had managed to hide the bullion, he would have sailed here as fast as he could, before someone else—like the privateers—beat him to it."

Forsythe said, "How do we know Reed got here in time to save it?"

"You told me yourself that he behaved as if he had something to celebrate."

"By God, that's right!" the Virginian exclaimed. "So you reckon he was all excited and in a holiday mood on account of he'd found the bullion?"

"It sounds very likely—so what did he do with the silver after he found it?" Rochester asked. He led the way back up to deck.

"Hid it on the schooner?" said Forsythe. He was staring at the *Annawan*, which was still spewing water down her side, but was lower in the water than ever.

"A hundred thousand silver dollars take up a lot of room," Wiki objected. "My father once carried specie to Canton, and it was stowed one thousand coins to a box—which in this case means a lot of boxes, and no small weight. Yet there's nothing much at all in the holds of the *Annawan*—just casks of salt and the freshwater tank. Though I didn't look in the lazaretto," he allowed, thinking of the small hold beneath the captain's cabin, traditionally the place where the captain's personal trade goods were stored.

"She'd be fearfully down by the stern if it had been stowed there, though," Rochester objected. "Too, Joel Hammond would be taking much greater pains to keep her pumped out if he had any idea that when the ship sinks a heap of bullion goes with her. If the crew of the *Annawan* had carried out such an interesting task as retrieving a lot of heavy boxes from a hiding place, surely at least one of them would have gossiped about it. And there are those interesting ruts in the track that goes up to the fort."

"You reckon they hauled the boxes up there, and hid them somewhere in the prison?" queried Forsythe. Rochester nodded, and the southerner's thick lips pursed in and out as he deliberated. "I didn't see anything significant while I was hunting for poor Zack," he said at last; "but I wasn't looking for anything like that.

Hell of a haul to get it up there, though. How many was there in the sloop's crew?"

"Eight," said Wiki. "Two bunked in the after cabin, and six in the fo'c'sle."

"Eight could manage it," said Forsythe, and headed down the plank for the track.

Zigzagging up the slope was strongly reminiscent of the morning of Reed's burial—the same dust burst up from around Wiki's feet, and the same thorny branches snagged at his legs. As they passed by the archway to the graveyard he could see the piled dirt of Reed's grave, and the place under the tree where Rochester had struggled to adapt the ritual for burial at sea for an interment on land. The path straggled on for about twenty yards past the gate, ending in a battered wall with a diagonal flight of stone steps that led up to the great, sunbaked forecourt of the ruined prison.

In contrast to the way Wiki had seen it last, it was a hive of activity. The cutter's men had hauled out all the big balks of timber, and were devising tackle to lower the beams down to the beach. After handing them the ropes and blocks he had been carrying, Forsythe led the way into the cavernous hall. Just as before, it was abruptly cooler as Wiki passed over the threshold. "Hmm," said George, looking up and round and about, and contemplatively stroking his fluffy fair sideburns. "I hadn't realized it would be quite so spacious."

"I could've told you that," said Wiki, feeling beaten before they even started. They explored all the corridors and cells of the ground floor, figuring that the boxes of big silver coins would have been too heavy to carry up or down stairs easily. The same sense of endless endurance assailed Wiki at every turn, and he was the first to abandon the search. Forsythe was the most obstinate, but even he gave up in the end, joining Wiki and George in the yawning entrance hall after a fruitless hour of poking around in dismal dungeons.

"It must be someplace else," Forsythe decided. "Though I think I covered the whole damn island in the hunt for poor Zack."

Rochester asked, "Do you remember seeing anything that had been recently disturbed?"

"Only that hole they was a-diggin' for Reed's coffin."

George sighed heavily, looked up at the sun, and said, "I have to get back to the brig, so I'll borrow the cutter, if I may. Then I'll get them to drop me at the *Annawan* on their way back to the cove."

Forsythe nodded, but said as they set off down the track to the camp set up by the cutter's men, "What's happening on the *Annawan?*"

"When Joel Hammond wanted to know what the hell you and your men were doing on the wreck—which, as he pointed out, belongs to Captain Reed's heir, and not to the goddamned navy—I explained that we hope to careen his schooner and fix her for him. Naturally, he's delighted. He issued an invitation to supper so that we can discuss our plans in detail."

As they sailed to the brig in the cutter, Wiki thought that George was unusually quiet. Every time he looked around at him, his friend was studying his face, and there was a definite coolness in his demeanor. Surely, Wiki thought uncomfortably, he hadn't guessed— surely it wouldn't be possible for even such a close friend to read his mind so easily.

As they clambered back on board the brig, he broke the silence with forced lightness. "It's excellent news that Joel Hammond is so pleased that we're to fix the *Annawan, e hoa,*" he said, and added, "I'll dress more properly, this time."

"You're not coming with me." Rochester's gaze was steady. "I'll take Midshipman Keith along, and would be obliged if you would take care of the brig while we're away. In fact," he deliberately elaborated, "I'll put you in charge the entire time that we are working on the *Annawan*. Lieutenant Forsythe will be supervising the raft-building gang, and I'll give young Keith the job of overseeing the work on the ship. Until the job is finished, I would prefer you not to leave the brig at all."

And with a guilty, uncomfortable knot in his gut, Wiki realized that George had guessed very accurately what had happened in Annabelle's stateroom that afternoon, and was coldly furious about it.

Twenty-seven

*I*n the captain's cabin of the *Annawan*, the atmosphere was convivial. Joel Hammond, as delighted as any other shipmaster whose command was on the verge of foundering and who'd been handed a reprieve, had personally ushered Rochester into the cabin, where the massive furniture was hauled around to make room for company. Now, they were seated around the table, Midshipman Keith on one side, Rochester on the other, and Mrs. Reed at the foot, while Joel Hammond presided at the head.

The steward paraded around serving a snack of succulent little salt pork dumplings, along with saucers of molasses for dipping. Hammond had defied expectations in that a Madeira wine was being poured—and such a remarkably fine one that George was glad it hadn't gone overboard with the grog.

He leaned back in his chair as he sipped, thoughtfully observing his hostess. If he'd felt any doubts at all about what Wiki had done that afternoon, they had been thoroughly dispelled the instant he'd entered this room. One of the few advantages of the dog's life of a junior midshipman was that a fellow quickly learned to sum up his shipmates, and sort out the likely lads from the potential mischief makers by studying the way they spoke, acted, and looked—and Annabelle Reed had the same catlike, complacent, slumberous look that Wiki had worn as he'd waded out of the sea. Too, as Rochester had come into the cabin she had smiled brilliantly with her eyes focused beyond him, and when Midshipman Keith had hove into sight instead of the man she expected to see, her face had gone blank, just the way Wiki had looked when Rochester had brutally informed him that he was confined to barracks for the duration.

Annabelle Reed had covered up quickly by chattering vivaciously about Rio de Janeiro, and what she would do when she got there; evidently the massive furniture that surrounded the table would furnish a house in that city. Joel Hammond, though he cast her a brooding look every now and then, didn't even pretend to be listening. Midshipman Keith, on the other hand, was hanging on her every word. He was dipping and eating freely, and his wine glass wasn't neglected, either, but otherwise the silly young salt could scarcely wrest his yearning gaze off their hostess—and watchable she was indeed, George allowed. Despite his innate good taste and the beautiful manners instilled by the grandparents who'd raised him after he was orphaned, he couldn't help thinking of feather beds and rumpled linen every time those enormous, languorous, lambent eyes slid sideways in his direction.

But goddamn it, he thought, it was still impossible to understand why Wiki had done something so stupidly dangerous, no matter how she'd enticed him. Men were men, particularly at sea, and when the gossip ran around jealousies would arise, and there would be absolute hell to pay. Rochester vividly remembered a cruise as a junior cadet when one of the master's mates had smuggled a girl on board. The captain, when he found out about it, had paraded the woman in front of all the men, and roared at her that she would either service none of them, or else she would service them all. George, like the girl, had been shocked—but had also quickly seen the sense in what the old man had bawled.

Belatedly, he became aware that Mrs. Reed had run to a stop, and silence had descended. Looking at Hammond, he said, "I hear that you sailed on the *Annawan* when Nathaniel Palmer was in command."

"This is my third cruise in the unlucky old tub."

George was surprised. "You were on that 1829 exploring expedition, too?"

Hammond let out a grunt of sour laughter. "If you can call it that. We didn't discover a goddamned thing."

George said mildly, "I did hear that there was a lot of desertion, and that Palmer was forced to abandon the voyage because he was so short of hands."

At that, the Connecticut man flicked an inimical look at Jack Winter, who was clearing the table ready for the next course, and George remembered that the steward had been in the list of eight experienced sealers on board that Wiki had given him. Then Hammond said flatly, "I wouldn't go so far as to call it 'desertion.' In my opinion it was nothing more or less than goddamned *mutiny*."

George blinked with surprise. "You consider desertion a form of mutiny?"

"When one of the sealing gangs threatens to take over the ship if the captain don't steer in a certain direction, I consider it mutiny."

George Rochester thought that it sounded worse than mutiny—close to piracy, in fact. The steward's plump face was expressionless.

He picked up the last plate and left the cabin. George listened to the sound of his footsteps going forward, and then asked, "Who were the troublemakers?"

"That goddamned po-faced steward was one of them, and I can name the boatswain, Folger, too, along with his assistant, Boyd, plus a few others. Though they just numbered eight, they turned the entire crew against the captain. There's something so *blind* about a certain kind of sealing man," Hammond said with angry passion. "All he can think of is killing seals and filling the holds with skins. It's a kinda religion with him—he has this childish belief that if the ship keeps on a-going no matter what the weather throws at 'em, they'll blunder across a rich new sealing ground. So he gets bloody minded if it turns out that the captain has something else in mind."

"Something like discovery?"

"Unless it's the discovery of seal rookeries, aye." Hammond paused, and then said, "It was just the same on the 1832 voyage of the *Annawan*, and it was the same goddamned party of men what created mischief."

George frowned. "But why would Captain Palmer ship the same set of men who gave him such trouble on the 1829 venture?"

"That's because he *did* intend to go sealing that time, and it's bloody hard to find willing and experienced sealers these days. But he was askin' for trouble, of course, and he got it. They forced him to abandon the voyage yet again, on the grounds that he wasn't sailing where they wanted."

"But surely it wasn't his fault that the schooner was taken over by desperate convicts?"

"Was that what you heard—that the schooner was overtaken by desperate men? Well, it ain't quite the truth," Hammond bit out as Jack Winter came back down the stairs. "Let it be my privilege to set you right—that Nat was *pleased* to carry 'em to the mainland, being as they'd fought on the same side when he was sailing for Simón Bolívar."

George was too astounded for words. Palmer had sailed for the revolutionary—and had carried the convicts willingly? Because they'd been comrades in arms? They had been *political* prisoners? This was a whole new aspect of the affair. He wondered what Wiki would make of it.

Then, he was distracted from this revelation. Winter had set down a great baking dish of some kind of pie with a golden top that smelled like heaven. Without meaning to, George sniffed luxuriously, and his stomach rumbled.

"And if we'd stayed in South America we'd have made a goddamned fortune, because those men we rescued was influential in the new government," Hammond went on moodily, oblivious of the pie. "But no, those goddamned sealers were determined to either go sealing or go home. I won't stand behavior like that," he said with a snap.

He glanced at Annabelle Reed, his expression aggressive, and then looked back at Rochester and said, "I know exactly where I'll take this ship once she's fit for sea—and it ain't no sealing ground, believe you me. That ain't no way to make a fortune, and if those sealers don't like it, they can leave the ship the first moment I choose—in Rio."

George felt extremely curious. So Hammond had definite plans for the schooner, even though the *Annawan* did not belong to him? He wondered what Annabelle Reed—who, as her husband's heir, owned the *Annawan* now—thought of such highhanded tactics. However, she didn't seem to be listening. Instead, she watched the steward as he set out plates, her expression brooding.

George murmured, "I have to admit I've heard tales of sealers getting wonderful rich."

"There was a time when an eight-man gang could take twenty thousand skins in just one four-month season," Hammond agreed. "But that was thirty years ago! Sealers who were carrying skins to market by the thousand back then are glad to sail in with a few dozen these days. It's their own goddamned fault, you know, because they worked against the natural way of the Lord. Anyone with a brain in his head could see that it only makes sense to leave a few seals alive so they can breed some more, but instead in their blind avarice they killed every single one. They tore out the goddamned tree to get at the fruit! They didn't care about wiping out the seals right down to the last little pup because they reckoned there was always another beach or island to discover. But they've run out of time—all the beaches and islands have been discovered and all the seals are gone. It's God's judgment on them, and it's exactly what they damn well deserve."

He wiped sweat off his face, and gulped at his glass of water. Joel Hammond, Rochester mused, was as obsessive in his own way as the sealers were in theirs. Judging by his expression, Jack Winter would have liked to argue, but he didn't have the right to open his mouth so instead he cut into the golden crust of the pie.

Steam curled out, carrying an aroma that made George's mouth water. He nodded thanks as a heaped plate was set in front of him, and then said tentatively, "So what are you going to do once the schooner is seaworthy again?"

"I'm staying on the coast, that's what—and I'm going to make the kind of money what sealers can't even dream of. Perhaps I haven't told you yet that when Captain Palmer was sailing for General Bolívar, I was with him as first mate?"

George, though suitably amazed, said nothing; he'd taken his first mouthful of the pie, and his mind was focused on the delicious sensation. As far as he could tell, both the bottom crust and the top were made of grated potato, while the middle layer was packed with succulent pieces of chicken. Evidently the whole concoction had been soaked in the gravy that the chicken had been stewed in, and then baked in the oven until the potato was as redolent with flavor as the meat. George's rich and social grandparents had kept the most famous table in Boston, but he'd never in all his life tasted anything half as delectable as this.

Then he noticed that Annabelle Reed was poking fastidiously about her plate and eating scarcely a morsel. He wondered what was wrong with the woman's appetite. By contrast, young Keith was gulping down his pie at a truly remarkable rate. With the expertise of hungry young midshipmen all over the seven seas, his obvious aim was to get it firmly packed down and then be first in line for another helping. However, he managed to say around an enormous mouthful, "If you sailed in the service of the great Bolívar, sir, you must've had some wonderful adventures on this coast."

"Aye," agreed Hammond, looking indulgent.

"And marvelous yarns to relate," Keith went on, though indistinctly, because he'd engulfed another huge forkful.

"Tales of treasure," Hammond informed him. In contrast to his harsh moodiness of a couple of minutes earlier, he sounded so genial that Rochester kept his mouth shut, masticating instead. Not only was young Keith doing a good job of keeping the new captain of the *Annawan* both talkative and happy, but George, like Midshipman Keith, reckoned he could do justice to another portion.

"True tales, sir?"

"True as I'm sitting here. There's one particular remarkable fine tale—of Spanish silver and a thieving shipmaster."

"Would you do us the favor of relating it, sir?"

"Why not? It happened back in 1823, when Bolívar's troops were marching on the town of Lima, and Bolívar learned from his spies that the Spanish merchants had put the bullion from the town treasury onto the ship *Mary Dear*, commanded by a man by the name of William Thompson. According to the way we was told it, Thompson's instructions were to keep his offing until he heard the outcome of the battle. If the city held out, he was to return the bullion, and if the Spanish were defeated, he was to take the treasure to Panama."

"Captain Thompson must have had a wonderful reputation for honesty, sir."

"Silver tongue, more like," grunted Hammond. "Anyway, once Bolívar heard of it, he hired Captain Nat to chase down and capture the *Mary Dear*. It would've made our fortunes in prize money if we'd managed it. Damn it, though, Thompson got away. Our intelligence was wrong, and we chased in the wrong goddamned direction."

"So what happened to the bullion, sir?"

"Thompson stole it—sailed off with it."

"Good God, sir, did he? So what did the Spanish do about that?"

"Chased him down and caught him up, but couldn't take him without a terrific battle. Everyone on the *Mary Dear* was killed save Thompson and his mate, but when they seized the ship they found the bullion wasn't there any more—it was gone! Thompson had buried it on an island instead of delivering it at Panama the way he was supposed to. Then he and the mate escaped from the Spanish and got to the Galápagos, where they was rescued by none other than Captain Nat and me."

"And they revealed the secret of where they'd buried the treasure?"

"Nope. They died of fever."

"What a blow, sir!"

"Aye," said Hammond, nodding. "But I have a damn good idea of where it is."

George had trouble to stop himself from shaking his head in wonder. He'd come across a lot of dreamers in his time, Wilkes and his vision of discovering Antarctica being a prime example, but in his humble estimation this fellow had all the others beat hollow. Hammond might deride the sealers for their misguided faith in some to-be-discovered sealing ground, but at least their dreams were firmly based on past experience, while anyone who thought a pirate would bury his loot instead of spending it on riotous living was horribly deluded. George also wondered how Thompson and his mate had escaped the Spanish. This, he mused, was a huge great hole in the yarn.

Keith, however, was not nearly so cynical. "That's the best tale I ever heard, sir," he said, and then added candidly, "And the best sea pie I ever ate, too."

By some miracle George Rochester had finished first. He leaned back so that Jack Winter could serve him more pie, and could have sworn he heard the steward mutter, "Foreign muck, not fit for civilized stomachs."

Ignoring this, he said to Hammond, "Should we make plans about heaving the schooner down? Time is of the essence, you know!"

"That it is," Joel Hammond said, abruptly brought to business. He shoveled in the rest of his pie and then signed to Jack Winter to clear the dishes away. That done, he told him to summon the two boatswains and the *Swallow*'s carpenter, who were eating with the men forward and then looked at Annabelle, saying coldly, "If you don't mind——?"

The gentlemen stood up and looked at her expectantly, while she looked uncertainly back at them. While it was evident she understood that it was time for her to leave the table, George judged from the rather lost look on her face that she had no idea where to go. He waited for her to disappear into one of the staterooms that were sited either side of the corridor at the bottom of the companionway, but to his surprise she went up onto deck. As he sat down again, he wondered where she was headed. Surely not the galley, he thought, but could hear her footsteps going forward.

Then Folger and the *Swallow*'s boatswain and carpenter arrived, ready and eager to share their professional expertise, and the conversation settled down into a great deal of wise talk about warping the schooner into shallower water, rafts, and anchors, and heaving tackle. The two boatswains consulted the carpenter, and grave opinions given, until finally, after four hours of intense discussion, they'd all come to the conclusion that it could be done within two weeks if the weather stayed fair.

Said Hammond, "We'll start discharging the after house first thing in the morning."

George murmured, "So soon?"

"You'll take Mrs. Reed on board the *Swallow*?"

"I'm afraid not," said George very firmly. "Our accommodations are extremely limited."

"She can have a tent on the beach," Hammond decided. "And when the ship's seaworthy, I'll move in here. It's my right—I'm the *captain* of this goddamned ship!"

Twenty-eight

*A*s George's boat pulled toward the brig he could hear singing. The sea was like black silk shot with luminescence, drops of water glowing blue as they fell from the blades of the oars. Two baritone voices echoed in harmony from the deck of the *Swallow*, joined in counterpoint by a third voice from the rigging aloft, the effect magical in the starlit night. George silently shook his head. If Forsythe had been on board this musical performance would have been considered a flogging offense: not only was the trio singing in Samoan, but chanteying was forbidden in the U.S. Navy.

As the boat clicked against the side, the singing stopped. Wiki met George at the rail, still carrying his ashwood pole. *"E hoa?"* he said. His grin was just a trifle uncertain.

George stood in silence for a long moment, his hands lightly clasped behind the seat of his white dress trousers, surveying him very thoughtfully, indeed. He treasured being Wiki Coffin's friend—having such an unusual and colorful friend made him feel colorful and exotic himself. Most of the time, however, they weren't even aware of their different backgrounds—because they had shared so many adventures, George supposed. With so many experiences in common, they often knew without trying what the other was thinking; at times they laughed together before other people even saw the joke. Every now and then, though, George was aware of a cultural gulf, and he was experiencing one of those troubling moments now.

Then his glance fell on the ashwood spar, and he realized with professional interest that Wiki had been working on his *taiaha*—what George thought of as a spear. Much had been accomplished in just a short time—the width of the shaft had been trimmed to half of the original diameter, and the two ends, one curved to a teardrop-shaped point and the other flat and paddlelike, had been roughed out.

He exclaimed, "It looks like a weapon already!"

"The shape was already there in the wood," Wiki said modestly. That was the nature of his people's craft—their carvers looked for the shape that was already there, instead of forcing the wood, bone, or stone to yield to their will. However, as George knew from long association, the singing had helped the work along, too.

Then Wiki held the *taiaha* poised in his hands, turned it swiftly end to end, sighted down the shaft, and whirled it around his shoulders. Looking at Rochester, he challenged, "You have your pretty cut-and-thrust sword. Try to put a dent in my carcass."

George studied him, vividly aware of what a contrast they made—that right now, the cultural difference between them was a chasm. He, Captain Rochester, commander of the U.S. brig *Swallow,* was a glitteringly formal figure in dress uniform. Wiki, the native linguister, was barefooted and bare-chested, his long black hair trailing over his shoulders, his *taiaha*-in-the-making held vertically before him with the tonguelike point upward, the epitome of a warrior from the far-off Pacific.

Rochester mused that Wiki had also put him in a deucedly difficult position. If he drew his sword, it would be a contest between sharp metal and dull wood, and despite being extremely cross with him right now, he didn't want to wound his best shipmate. If they'd been alone it could have been dismissed as a joke, but the hands on duty were watching, joined by more men who were trickling out of the forecastle. So George grinned evilly, tossed his hat aside, whipped out his fancy sword, and flourished it.

Up came the *taiaha*, held diagonally across Wiki's body. Rochester smoothly lunged and thrust—to find his sword easily parried by a swift push of the wood. He attacked more seriously, but each time his blade was jerked aside. Then Wiki moved in for his first attack, and George found to his surprise that the spear-shaped end of the *taiaha*, which he'd been taking great pains to avoid, was just for jabbing and feinting, while the broad paddle-shaped other end was the business part of the weapon. Indeed, he realized, it wasn't a spear at all, but much more like that greatly feared two-handed traditional weapon of the English peasant, the quarterstaff. George dodged the blow by the skin of his teeth, ran back a couple of paces, and then came forward with a great deal more caution.

The men on deck were starting to urge them on, caught up in the unusual competition. Slowly, they circled each other. After feinting twice, Wiki lunged forward again—and again George only narrowly missed being rapped. However, he noticed that when Wiki was on the verge of a pounce, the toes of his leading foot clenched for a better grip on the deck.

Thinking about it, he lunged and thrust, watched Wiki dance

back on the balls of his feet, and then saw those feet flatten as Wiki stepped forward again. The pointed tip of the *taiaha* passed his face in another feint, and then the *taiaha* was reversed with a quick flourish. The toes clenched, George swayed back and ducked forward in one smooth motion, the *taiaha* passed through empty air—and when George straightened his sword was resting on Wiki's shoulder.

The men gave a round of cheers, led lustily by Midshipman Keith. "Well done," said Wiki. He grinned widely as they shook hands, and George suddenly wondered if he hoped that the duel had settled their differences, and they could return to being comrades again. However, he said nothing. Wiki stowed his *taiaha*-in-the-making in the galley, where he'd screwed hooks on the wall behind the huge iron stove, so that the heat and smoke would harden the wood. Then Rochester led the way to the saloon, where he silently shed his coat.

"Well, *e hoa?*" said Wiki, sitting down.

"They'll be discharging the schooner before breakfast."

Wiki frowned down at the coffee he was pouring. "Isn't that rather premature?"

"Joel Hammond can't wait to turn Mrs. Reed out of the captain's cabin."

Wiki's expression became troubled. When he didn't speak, George went on, "Hammond had interesting things to say about the eight old sealers on board—that on that exploring voyage they talked the rest of the seamen into forcing Palmer to turn back home because he searched for scientific discoveries instead of new sealing grounds. Then he went on to tell me that on the next voyage, the 1832 one, the *Annawan* wasn't overcome by convicts—that Palmer was rescuing them."

"It was *Palmer's* idea to set them free?"

"Aye. It seems that the convicts were Palmer's comrades in

arms during Bolívar's campaign—that they were political prisoners and not criminals at all."

"And he gave up the sealing venture to do it?"

"Aye. I guess there were old loyalties involved."

"Well, that surely is a new view," Wiki marveled.

"Hammond also went on at length about the blind greed of sealers, how they have chopped down the tree to get at the fruit and so on and so forth, and that it's the judgment of God that there are no seal rookeries left to find. Now that he has the *Annawan* he has no intention of sealing, he said."

"But the schooner isn't his!"

"I had a job to stop from pointing that out to him myself, old chap. Jack Winter, who was serving out the food as Hammond was carrying on, didn't like what he was hearing one bit, either. Don't you reckon it's strange that the *steward* should be one of that eight-strong gang? I can see him fomenting rebellion, but camping out on a rock-bound, ice-ridden seal rookery? No."

Midshipman Keith came out of the stateroom at that moment, having changed into workaday dungarees, and said brightly, "Uncommon tasty grub they gave us, don't you reckon, sir? I do confess I could do justice to another big chunk of that chicken stew pie."

"After the way you stuffed your stomach, my lad," said George sternly, "you should be ashamed of yourself."

"And that was a capital Madeira too, don't you think, sir?" said Keith, unabashed.

"Madeira?" said Wiki.

"Hammond didn't throw it overboard with the grog," said George. Then he went on musingly, "Soon it won't be possible for Festin to do any cooking on board the schooner, and it's not feasible to shift the schooner's galley on shore because the stove is too heavy to lower into a whaleboat. So I'm toying with the idea of bringing him aboard the *Swallow*—he could take over our galley and do the cooking for all, freeing up our man for other work. It would be easy enough to carry meals to the men on the beach."

Keith exclaimed, "What a wonderful idea, sir!"

"I'll discuss it with Hammond first thing in the morning," George decided, and with his face split wide in a gratified grin, Midshipman Keith headed off up the stairs to take charge of the deck.

"Something odd, though," George ruminated. "The lady didn't seem partial to it."

"Partial to what?" said Wiki.

"Festin's chicken stew pie. She took a nibble or two, but otherwise just pushed it around with her fork."

Wiki grimaced. "That's because she thought it was parrot."

"Parrot?"

George turned and looked at the burned parrot, which was still perched on the back of his chair. Its innards were back to functioning, he noticed, because there were droppings in amongst the dripped water on the seat.

He looked at Wiki again and urged, "Explain yourself."

"When Annabelle gave the parrot to Festin she expected him to kill it and add it to the pot. Instead, he gave the parrot to me—but she doesn't know that."

"I wonder what parrot tastes like?"

"No doubt that's what she was wondering while she pushed her pie about," said Wiki. "So what plan *does* Hammond have for the schooner after she's fixed?"

"Treasure hunting."

"You're joking."

"Ask young Keith, if you don't believe me. Hammond told him a farfetched tale about the merchants of Lima entrusting the contents of the town treasury to a devious skipper who buried it instead

223

of carrying it to Panama the way he'd been instructed. The boy fairly lapped it up. You've been overtaken as the best tale-spinner of his acquaintance, I'm afraid."

"You mean Joel Hammond told the story of the *Mary Dear?*"

"You've heard it already?"

"*E hoa,* I thought everyone in the world had heard it already."

"Good God, you never fail to surprise me. But is it true?"

"It could be, I suppose—but Hammond can't be serious, surely. If that bullion from the Lima treasury really was buried, it's bound to have been dug up since. After all, people have been hunting for it for fifteen years now." Frowning, Wiki went on, "What did Annabelle say about this plan to take the schooner treasure-hunting?"

"Nothing. Not a word."

"She just sat tamely and allowed him to make these farfetched plans involving the schooner, even though the *Annawan* belongs to her?"

"Aye. She seemed to be under his thumb altogether. When Hammond decided to get down to business and discuss the technicalities of heaving down, he virtually ordered her to leave the table, and she obeyed even though she didn't seem to have anywhere to go."

Wiki's expression became intensely worried. After a pause during which he was obviously choosing words, he said, "I'd like to be there when the schooner is being unloaded—not just because of the bullion, but to see which of the *Annawan* hands has a stock of blue-striped shirts."

George shook his head without an instant's hesitation. "No," he said decisively. "You will stop on board of the brig."

Twenty-nine

$\mathcal{G}$eorge Rochester went over to the *Annawan* at daybreak, to find the men laboring at the pumps with new enthusiasm, freeing her up for warping out of the deep channel where she was trapped. He sought out Hammond to discuss the matter of the cook, got his agreement, and then headed to the bay where Forsythe and the cutter's men were camped.

To his surprise and pleasure, he found that every last balk of timber had been lowered to the beach, and that the cutter's men had set with gusto to the job of connecting them together to make a sturdy raft. Typically, Forsythe had claimed territory: The largest U.S. flag the *Swallow* possessed was now flying grandly from the tall flagpole on the forecourt of the ruined prison, a signal to all those who passed the island, and privateers in particular, that Americans were in possession.

Rochester headed back to the schooner, to find that a kedge anchor had been lodged in shallower water twenty yards closer to the beach, and the stout hawser that was secured to this had been attached to the windlass. Orders, shouted by Hammond and echoed by Midshipman Keith, rattled back and forth as hands worked manfully at the windlass to winch the hawser in, shortening it so that the schooner was heaved up to the kedge. For some time it didn't seem as if the waterlogged old box would move, but then, inch by inch, the hull groaned and yielded. By noon the *Annawan* was anchored exactly where the carpenter wanted her to be, out of the deep, fast-moving current but still with water under her keel.

Bags and barrels of provisions were coming out of the between-decks area, swayed into boats, and sent over to the *Swallow*. Robert Festin, looking confused and uncomprehending, accompanied the first load, clinging to the side of the boat and looking extremely white-faced. At the same time, there was a great commotion in the after house as massive furniture was heaved around. The big saloon table was manhandled up the companionway with a lot of cursing and shouting, and then dumped over the rail to float upside down, forming a makeshift raft. Buoyed with empty barrels lashed along its sides, it was towed ashore by a line, while a couple of men aboard plied long poles in a vigorous effort to keep it from upsetting.

First to go were the heavy drapes that had covered the bulkheads. Bundled onto the raft, they went off to shore, where a couple of other men were erecting a frame for a tent. No sooner was it covered with one of the curtains than Annabelle Reed, looking flushed and ruffled, was hustled off to the beach. Then the rest of the furniture came up. Most of the great wardrobes and dressers had to be taken apart, but still the pieces were being carried up the companionway at a tremendous pace.

The *Annawan* was being unloaded faster than anyone could have imagined. Soon the captain's cabin was cleared, and the trapdoor to the lazaretto—the captain's private hold in the stern—was opened, and Captain Reed's personal store of trade goods was heaved up to be taken on shore, too. Rochester, watching interestedly, saw a stream of the usual kind of things—kegs of tobacco and bales of cloth, plus crates of the goods like scissors, clocks, folding combs, and mirrors that were colloquially known as "Yankee notions," and which found a ready market all about the Atlantic and Pacific.

There was not a single silver coin amongst the lot, so George Rochester went on shore to cast an eye over what had been dropped on the beach. Annabelle Reed was sitting on a lady chair just inside the opening of her tent, trunks and baskets scattered around her feet. Bizarrely, someone had propped a tall vase of painted feathers on one side of the entrance, making a strange contrast to the live birds that cawed and circled in the air overhead. They were angry, it seemed, by having been evicted from the shrub that grew luxuriantly nearby, and which provided some shade. She'd made no attempt to unpack, but instead was moodily watching the frenetic activity in the bay.

Rochester directed men into collecting up bric-a-brac as it was dropped without ceremony from the floating table. Lacking any kind of direction from their owner, who seemed utterly uninterested in the fate of her chattels, they piled it up on a dry patch of grass. George opened trunks and dressers, but found nothing but clothes and table linen. Then, the last of the furniture having been stacked, the gang set off a decent distance to erect two big tents for the seamen of the *Annawan*, and a smaller one for Hammond and his first mate.

George watched them go, and then approached Annabelle. She was still perched on the low chair, her head bent in deep thought, but when she sensed his presence she looked up. George watched the black-fringed eyes focus, and then she demanded without any preamble, "Where's Wiki Coffin?"

"I've put him in charge of the brig while we're working on the schooner."

"But why?"

"There is the ever-present danger of privateers," he said smoothly.

"Oh," she said, and looked down while she thought. Then her lashes lifted again and she said, "Have you finished with my husband's box of papers?"

George shook his head. He had no intention of returning it to her, because he didn't trust her not to burn the lot before the Brazilian authorities had a chance to check the certificates.

"But it's mine and I need it!"

"Why?" George inquired. His tone was light, but he was studying her alertly.

"My husband's personal papers are in the box, as well as the ones for the ship—and I'm his widow, so I need them, don't you see?"

George kept silent, and after a moment she tilted her head on one side, looked up at him appealingly, and said, "Why won't you allow me to move onto the *Swallow*?"

"The quarters are cramped; you would be very uncomfortable there."

She pouted, and said, "Who is going to watch over me at night?"

"Why do you need someone to watch?" She was no more at risk on shore than she was on the schooner, George thought—except, perhaps, for snakes. There was a barrel just inside the tent that was filled with the knives, clubs, muskets, and pistols that had hung from the wall of the after house. He poked around in it, making a lot of noise but finding no silver coins, and then, straightening, he said to her, "Do you know how to load a gun?"

To his surprise, she laughed. "Didn't Wiki tell you that I am fisher folk—Cajun? Captain Rochester, I could load a gun and shoot a copperhead before I could even talk."

"Perhaps you should carry a couple of pistols."

"Perhaps." She looked around vaguely and said, "There will be a belt with holsters somewhere. I could wear that, I suppose."

"Do that," said Rochester encouragingly. The shadows were growing long, and in the distance a plume of smoke wisped from the chimney of the *Swallow*'s galley. Midshipman Keith and the carpenter's gang had already returned on board, and the boatswain and his men were waiting at the edge of the surf. It was time to get back to the brig.

"I'm starving," Annabelle complained. "Where's our cook? The *peeshwank* hasn't even started a fire yet."

"Robert Festin's on the *Swallow*," Rochester said. "It seemed more efficient for him to take over our galley and prepare food for all."

She brightened. "So we eat on board the *Swallow*?"

George shook his head. "No, it's easier to bring the cooked food out to the beach."

"Like a picnic?"

She pronounced the word *picnic* in a very foreign way, *peek-neek*. George said easily, "Picnics are fun, I am told." The cutter's men certainly enjoyed them, he thought.

He turned to take his leave, and she called out anxiously, "But how about you and your men—don't you picnic, too?"

"No," he said. "The crew of the *Swallow* will eat on board the brig." Without looking at her again, he left her and walked down to the boat.

As they pulled for the brig they passed the floating table, which was heading shoreward yet again, this time loaded high with a great mixture of clutter, evidently from tidying up the last of the paraphernalia in the captain's cabin. Though it was obviously unstable, it was plain that the men who were poling it couldn't have cared less. When the top of the heap teetered dangerously, they simply stood back and let the bulk of it thunder overboard instead of attempting to save it. The heavier pieces fell to the bottom at once, leaving a whirl of clothing and pieces of occasional furniture.

An empty birdcage floated by. George bent down, scooped it up, and dropped it into the bottom of the boat. Now, he thought with great satisfaction, he would get his chair back; he would sit in his rightful place at the saloon table while he tried out the first, doubtlessly ambrosial, meal cooked by Festin on the brig. They had killed a couple of the hogs from the *Annawan*, and he looked forward eagerly to fragrant roast pork.

Instead, Midshipman Keith met him at the rail, his expression utterly tragic. "Nothing went right for him," he mourned. "The stove heats to the wrong temperature, and has an oven that's not quite the right size. The firewood sparks too much, the tormentor is nothing like the right size and shape, and everything is crooked, or bent, or not clean enough, or stowed in the wrong place. Now, the great cook is in tears."

George blinked. "What's a *tormentor?*"

"A kind of big fork," said Wiki, arriving up alongside Constant Keith, and confirmed the sad news. Robert Festin, the famous creator of succulent salt pork dumplings and truly magnificent chicken stew pie, had dashed all their wonderful expectations by burning the anticipated roast.

Thirty

*S*ua said in Samoan, "Did you see Sekatoa's red arse?"

Wiki looked at him consideringly. The two Samoans were sitting cross-legged on the deck of the *Swallow* in the shade of the foremast, chatting while Wiki worked on his *taiaha*. It was toward the end of their watch below—their four hours' off duty—and Sua, as usual, was harping on about the great white pointer, *mango taniwha*, which had attacked Wiki and carried off Kingman's corpse while he, Sua, was watching. It had made a strong impression on him, and over the ten intervening days he had convinced himself that the shark was none other than the great Sekatoa, the shark spirit of Tonga.

"No," said Wiki. "I did not see his red arse. And why should he be in the Atlantic?"

"Maatu, the chief of Niuatoputapu, has the right to call on him whenever he feels the need," Sua informed him. "His people throw some kava root in the sea, and first the remoras—Sekatoa's *matapule* assistants—come, and then Maatu's people send the remoras away with a message; then a small shark comes, perhaps one of your *kuwai*, and they give him a message, too, and send him away; then a bigger shark comes; and so it goes until at last Sekatoa himself arrives and asks what Maatu desires."

"But Niuatoputapu is a Tongan island, and there aren't even any *Tongans* here, let alone any chiefs by the name of Maatu, just you sorry Samoans, *e hoa ma*, my friends."

However, as he worked on his *taiaha*, from the corner of his eye Wiki could see Sua rocking back and forth as he wound himself up into a yarn-spinning frame of mind, and resignedly realized that yet another tale of Sekatoa was on the way.

"Did you know of the time that Samoan ghosts stole the mountain from Niuafo'ou?"

Wiki had been to the Tongan island of Niuafo'ou. He stood up and sighted down the *taiaha*, which was now unmistakably a weapon—and a viciously beautiful weapon, too. The *rau*, the flat striking blade, had been hardened by smoking and heating to the smoothness of a hatchet, and because he and George practiced every evening, the shaft was highly polished by the constant rubbing of his hands. The nightly contest had become so lively that George used an ordinary ship's cutlass instead of risking his dress sword, and the whole crew watched with great excitement. Undoubtedly, bets were laid. Wiki's skill with the *taiaha* had improved beyond bounds, but George's swordsmanship had come along amazingly, too, and so they were very evenly matched.

Wiki sat down again, and said, "There is no mountain on Niuafo'ou."

"That's because the Samoan ghosts stole it," Sua informed him.

"Ah, why didn't I guess?" said Wiki sardonically. "Why did they want it?"

"They wanted to take it to Samoa, but Sekatoa saw what they were doing. It was at night, of course, as Samoan ghosts cannot stand the light of the sun, so he decided to trick them. First he sent his *matapules* in the form of roosters, to crow as if it were dawn."

"So the ghosts took fright and dropped it?"

"Not yet. They simply pulled faster, telling each other, 'Hurry, it is almost morning.' So Sekatoa decided to handle the problem himself. He swam up to the ghosts and showed them his red arse— *mata tuungaiku* in Tongan—and they were so alarmed that they dropped the mountain, and it became the island of Tafahi."

"The ghosts thought his red arse was the sun?"

"Aye."

Wiki said firmly, "I did not see any red arse. And, furthermore, it is time you two relieved the lookouts aloft, *e hoa ma*."

After they had gone, he concentrated on the teardrop-shaped end of his *taiaha*. He had carved it into a stylized head with slanted eyes and a long protruding tongue, which he was now engraving with elaborate curves and whorls. A sennit collar had been twisted about its neck, and into this Wiki had braided the feathers of the bird that had led him to the staff, along with long tufts of his own black hair. This was designed to distract the enemy by being flicked across his eyes.

"*Ko te rakau na Hapai*," Wiki sang as he wielded the tip of his knife:

Ko te rakau na Toa
Ko te rakau na Tu, Tu-ka-riti, Tu-ka-nguha.
This is the weapon of the Ancestors,

This is the weapon of the Warriors,
This is the weapon of Tu, furious Tu, raging Tu.

Tu was *Tumatauenga*, the ancestor-guardian of war. The verse was not meant to be a song, not really—it was supposed to be a chant, a *karakia*, but Wiki sang it because he was feeling so good about the way his *taiaha* was progressing. Secretly he was not even sure he used the right words—there were *karakia* to be used by children, others for laymen like himself, and still more reserved to elders and *tohunga*, priests. Perhaps, he thought, he was being unwittingly presumptuous, but still the words sounded right in his head, and he felt happy about them.

The sun reached its zenith in the sky as the song trailed into silence. It was hot, the sun sparkling fiercely on the rippling surface of the water. Aloft, the two Samoans were silent. A plume of smoke wafted up to the paling sky from the galley chimney, and a redolent steam was drifting out of the door. Wiki went inside and reached over the stove to stow the *taiaha* back on its hooks until it was time for his match with Rochester that evening. Then he lifted the lid of one of the two great caldrons to peer at the bubbling contents. *"Ka pai,"* he said to Festin. *"Oligen, yo*. It smells good."

"Bloody good," agreed the cook.

Over the past ten days Festin had come along by leaps and bounds, and not just in the quality of his cooking. He still had trouble forming sentences, but obviously the bang he had taken on his head was mending. Disconcertingly, the English words he adopted most easily were profane—learned from Forsythe, whom Festin greatly admired—but he also seemed fascinated with *te reo*, Wiki's native language, and had readily picked up a few phrases.

In turn, Wiki was beginning to get a grasp of Festin's strange dialect—something that, oddly, was helped along by memories of the months in New Hampshire when he and George played truant to sit about the campfires of the Indians they were supposed to be converting, because a number of the words the strange little man used were very close to Abnaki—such as the word for greeting, *kway*. The rest seemed to be based on some ancient French provincial dialect, so Wiki theorized that he had originally hailed from one of the remote maritime communities of Nova Scotia or Labrador. How Festin had got to Rio de Janeiro—or, indeed, how he had been hit on the head—was still a mystery, however.

Otherwise, all Wiki had learned was that Festin loathed everyone on the *Annawan,* Jack Winter in particular, and was absolutely delighted to be on board the *Swallow.* The only place he would have preferred to be was in the camp the cutter's men had set up in the cove on the other side of the headland. "Forsythe bloody good skipper," he said, nodding toward the *Annawan,* where the southerner could be heard roaring at someone who had got in his way. Though Forsythe would have shot him out of hand if he'd even begun to guess it, Robert Festin had fallen madly in love with the big Virginian.

"What about Captain Reed?" Wiki asked, amused.

"Bad skipper, drunk-all-the-time skipper," was the reply. As Festin went on to convey, whoever had murdered Reed should be heartily congratulated.

"If that's the case," Wiki said dryly, "it's a pity you didn't see the murderer from the galley so you could pat him on the back yourself."

"*Hein?*" said Festin. "Galley, not the bloody pantry, galley yes, pantry no." Then he spat over the rail, which—as Wiki knew very well, indeed—was his way of telling him that the conversation was over. Wiki loped to the foremast, and clambered aloft to have a look at what was happening on the *Annawan* and the beach.

Over the past days the scene had greatly changed. The raft had been built, complete with heaving post, blocks, belaying points, and a simple capstan, and had been towed around the headland. From where Wiki perched in the topgallant crosstrees, he could see the *Annawan* men anchoring her up to the schooner's larboard side. Above their laboring forms, the *Annawan* was floating high. She'd been completely discharged all the way from the salt in the holds to the sea chests in the forecastle—though not, unfortunately, with any sign of Reed's bullion. The freshwater tank had been pumped out, and a framework had been set up in the hold so that the loose copper dross ballast could be easily shoveled from one side to the other, and a gang was now at work on that.

According to what Rochester had told him at breakfast, this early afternoon they would begin to heave the schooner down, and there was every sign for optimism that the job would go well. Perhaps the repair would be so simple and straightforward that the schooner would be floating and seaworthy again within four more days—which, for Wiki, was a matter for concern as well as celebration. While it would be a great relief to sail off on the *Swallow*, he was no wiser about what had happened to the silver, or any closer to the solution to the murders. Confined to the brig, he had not had a chance to investigate, he thought moodily.

Looking on the bright side, the parrot was very much better. Stoker had been delighted when George had carried the birdcage on board, announcing as he popped the parrot inside that recovery was now a virtual certainty. Now the cage hung from a hook in a corner of the saloon, its occupant almost perky, turning its head from side to side as if it were trying to see out of its poor blind eyes. As soon as the bird was well enough Wiki intended to give it to Annabelle so she could release it herself, and rid herself of superstitious fears. Even though it was blind, poor creature, surely it would manage to survive in the island scrub—and Stoker, that scion of higlers and henwives, was confident that with time the scales would fall off its eyes and it would see as well as ever.

Then the sleepy progress of Wiki's thoughts was rudely interrupted by a yell from Sua, who was poised precariously in the highest truck of the mainmast rigging, while the entire mast trembled under his weight as he waved. He was pointing toward the open sea, while Tana, farther down the same mast, was gesturing at the cutter, which was hurrying to the brig.

A sail could just be discerned beyond the big headland that barred the way to the open sea. Despite the distance Wiki recognized the craft instantly—the little 96-ton schooner *Flying Fish,* the smallest vessel of the United States Exploring Expedition. George should be pleased, he thought, because he had a lot in common with Samuel Knox, the commander of the *Flying Fish.* The son and grandson of Boston pilots and a ten-year navy veteran who had seen service in both the Pacific and the Mediterranean, Knox, like George, had been given the command even though he was just a passed midshipman.

The schooner hove to and fired a gun for a pilot. Simultaneously, the cutter arrived at the side of the brig, Forsythe, who was steering, looking extremely irritated at being sent away when the excitement of finally heaving the schooner over onto her good side was almost nigh. Rochester, he informed Wiki, was busy overseeing a cable rove from the masthead, and sent a message begging Wiki to do him the favor of going out in the cutter to greet Knox in his place, while one of the cutter's men looked after the *Swallow.*

The New Bedforder came on board, and after giving him some advice and a few instructions, Wiki took a flying leap into the boat—in the nick of time, for Forsythe, being in a temper and in a hurry, had got under way already. Not unexpectedly, in view of this, the run out to the *Flying Fish* was an exciting one. Beneath their keel multicolored outcrops of coral fled away at a perilous rate, and the cutter leaned far over under a full press of sail. Then they came round the headland and the *Flying Fish* lay directly ahead.

Wiki studied her with interest as they raced toward her. About seventy feet long, as lean and low as a greyhound and with an abundance of fore-and-aft sail, the *Flying Fish* was a pretty sight. In her earlier life she had been a dashing New York pilot boat, and she looked every inch the part. She was flying a number of signals as well as the Stars and Stripes.

"What the hell is he trying to tell us?" Forsythe asked.

"I haven't a notion," said Wiki. "Could it be some kind of emergency?"

"Beats me," said Forsythe as they sheered up to the vessel. "It ain't like Knox to carry on like this."

The mystery was solved when Lawrence J. Smith, the pompous, self-righteous, prating little lieutenant who had made both their lives miserable when he was second-in-command of the *Swallow*, hove up to the rail with a complacent smirk.

Forsythe muttered, "What the devil have we done to deserve this?"

Wiki grimaced but said nothing. There was no hope of mistaken identification—not only was the *Flying Fish* just a fraction higher out of the water than the cutter, but the little schooner had hardly any bulwarks.

Forsythe said with a pleasant smile, "What the bloody hell are *you* doing here, Lieutenant?"

"You may call me 'captain,'" Smith said smugly. "And welcome aboard my ship."

"What happened to Sam Knox?"

"Captain Wilkes transferred him to the *Porpoise* and gave me the *Flying Fish*."

"I wonder what sin that poor bastard Knox has committed," said Forsythe sotto voce, and stepped up and over the side, Wiki behind him. A boatswain piped in proper navy style, but, while Forsythe returned the salutes of the two seamen standing at attention, he didn't bother to do Smith the same favor.

"Well, sir?" he said intimidatingly.

"I was given the mission of bringing the *Flying Fish* here," Smith sniffed. "On account of Wiki Coffin's failure to report back in good season."

Recognizing Wiki's presence, he enunciated, "Wiremu," and nodded. Wiki, blank-faced, nodded back. He'd almost forgotten Lieutenant Smith's irritating insistence on calling him by the Maori version of his English name as if he had some proprietary right to do so.

"Where *is* Passed Midshipman Rochester?" the self-important little man demanded now. "Alive? Well?"

"*Captain* Rochester is alive, well, and busy," said Wiki, emphasizing the first word only a little.

"That he'd suffered a severe accident was the very least we expected when so much time passed by with no sign of him," Smith sniffed. It sounded, Wiki thought, as if he'd been hoping for the worst.

Forsythe interrupted, "You got some kind of emergency on board?" He jerked his chin at the assortment of flags.

"Just infamous bad luck, sir!"

Knowing Lieutenant Smith the way they both did, they did not feel any great surprise to learn that his bad luck was due to his own mismanagement. Instead of following the course that Rochester had laid down before he'd left the fleet, Smith had called onto the coast to rewater, and there lost two men—one of them the ship's cook—from fever; then four more when they'd run away; then another when he'd fallen overboard and drowned.

Thus, under his guiding hand, the schooner's original complement of fifteen had been reduced to eight. Not only was it an emergency, according to Lawrence J. Smith, but it had greatly retarded the schooner's progress. Wiki wondered why he hadn't returned to the fleet to report this dismal sequence of events, but then realized that Smith was reluctant to confess his failure to Captain Wilkes.

The recital finally over, Smith demanded that two of the cutter's crew come on board to help him get the schooner into the cove. Forsythe flatly refused, but—without consulting Wiki first—offered Wiki's services to take the helm while he, in the cutter, led the way. Then he sailed with his characteristic dash and flair through the myriad obstacles, with no consideration whatsoever for whatever difficulties Wiki might be experiencing. Luckily the *Flying Fish* was swift and agile, particularly when close to the wind.

Coming around the headland, Wiki found a view that was very different from when he had left the cove. Now the great bulk of the *Annawan*'s hull rose high, so she looked very much like a half-beached whale—the *Annawan*, he realized with a surge of triumph, had been successfully hove down! A flimsy platform of planks and barrels was being floated out beneath the exposed side of the hove-down schooner, and by the time the anchor of the *Flying Fish* was dropped, a line was being thrown over the rail with the carpenter dangling from the end to examine the damage.

Unsurprisingly, George Rochester came on board the *Flying Fish* in a highly celebratory mood. Over she'd gone without the slightest hitch, he blithely reported after the briefest of salutes—a steady haul on the cable and over she'd rolled, as gentle as a little lamb. And, he went on, she would certainly have overset without the securely anchored raft. The holes in her hull were high and dry, and perfectly accessible. The carpenter confirmed Wiki's feeling that only one strake needed to be replaced, as the others could be easily mended in situ.

Lawrence J. Smith was less than impressed. Indeed, he was not even particularly interested, instead taking great pleasure in informing Rochester that Captain Wilkes could well find his unaccountable delay quite unforgivable. Told about the murder of Captain Reed, he expressed the opinion that the authorities in Rio should have handled the case. Notified that Passed Midshipman Kingman had been knifed as well, he became even more contemptuous, declaring that the failure to promptly report the sad loss of an officer—a man of importance to the expedition!—was a particularly grave lapse on Rochester's part.

Rochester listened attentively, blandly, and in silence. Then, having invited Smith to supper on the *Swallow*, he quit the *Flying Fish*, taking the much relieved Wiki with him. "And I hope Festin can rise to the challenge," he said as the boat pulled away. "Much as I'd love to poison the pompous little prawn, it wouldn't look good on my record."

Thirty-one

*N*ext morning when Wiki came out of his state-room, Rochester was sitting at the saloon table already, even though it was not yet dawn. Pouring a mug of coffee, Wiki said, "How did it go?" He had been on watch at suppertime, so had not been one of the party.

"The meal was delicious—Festin excelled himself!"

"I know," said Wiki. He'd watched with interest as Festin made a thick pie crust out of flour, shortening, and the gravy from the meat he'd been stewing. Then, after filling the crust with chunks of tender meat and baking it, the cook had cut it into squares which he steamed before serving so that the pastry puffed up. He had given a square to Wiki to taste, and very good it had been, too.

After it had slid delectably down to his stomach, Wiki had hung around, partly in the hope of another sample, and also because the squat little man was having one of his lucid spells. It had proved worthwhile: not only had he enjoyed a second helping, but they'd had quite an interesting little conversation.

It had started off in unpromising style, with Festin chanting, "Galley, pantry, galley, pantry, galley, pantry," as if it were some weird nursery rhyme; but then the cook had demanded, "What *te reo Maori* call 'pantry'?"

Wiki had hesitated, wondering why he'd asked. Then he'd said, "The word for 'pantry' is *pataka,* only it's not a pantry the way you *pakeha* know it. It's a storehouse for provisions." Using a mixture of English, Maori, and Festin's dialect, he'd tried to portray in words the elaborately carved *pataka* that were built on stilts to preserve their contents from rats, thieves, and damp, and which ranged in size from small boxes to storehouses many feet in length, according to the wealth of the village.

Festin had seemed to find this fascinating, listening raptly with his liquid brown gaze fixed on Wiki's face, and had said with great satisfaction when Wiki had run to a stop, "That is it exactly."

"What?"

"Exactly pantry, aye."

"What do you mean?" Wiki had said, greatly puzzled, but it had been the end of the conversation. Festin had spat over the rail and taken himself back to his stove.

Now, Wiki gulped coffee, looked at George, and said, "Did Smith enjoy Festin's grub?"

"Stuffed himself like a trout, and then demanded that we send over the cook to the *Flying Fish,* his own cook being dead. He changed his mind when I informed him that the cook not only didn't belong to us, being one of the *Annawan* crew, but was suspected of murder in the bargain. Indeed, he studied his empty plate so pensively I wondered if he regretted eating so much—and was emphatic that he didn't want another serving."

"What about Joel Hammond?" said Wiki, because Hammond had been a guest, as well.

"Looked cynical, as well he might. Smith expressed effusive sympathies on the loss of a captain, just like the hypocritical little twit that he is. Then, as the senior navy officer present, he claimed all honor due for the *Annawan*'s reprieve, on behalf of the U.S. Navy."

"What!" Wiki let out a shout of laughter. "How did he manage that?"

"Oh, you know the kind of thing, old chap—how the navy prides itself on being a bastion of support and succor to all its citizens everywhere and in particular those in evil straits on the breast of the stormy wave. Once he'd got all this soft soap off his chest, however," Rochester went on much more darkly, "he ordered Hammond to release the eight sealers who sailed on that *Annawan* discovery expedition and hand 'em over to us, because he reckoned that their testimony's so important they should give it to Wilkes in person."

Wiki frowned. "What did Hammond have to say about that?"

"He was as happy as Old Scratch. In his own words, he agreed that he could dispense with 'em, since he's not going a-sealing any more. Then he launched himself into that ridiculous yarn about the *Mary Dear* and the Lima bullion, but Smith interrupted in his usual style—to order me to take the sealers on board the *Swallow* and carry them to Wilkes *instantum*! I could give him six of my men to fill up the gaps in his crew list, and so—or so he reckoned—I would have plenty of room for the eight."

"*What!* What the devil did you say to that appalling idea?"

"Hammond forestalled me by barking that it seemed god-damned strange to him that someone who'd just been prating on about the goddamned generosity of the U.S. Navy should turn around and propose that we leave before the goddamned job was finished. Then he informed him that insincerity of purpose is an abomination of the Lord. At that moment," George confessed, "I almost found it in my heart to like the man."

"So how did Lieutenant Smith take it?"

"Badly, Wiki, badly. Brushed birdseed off his shoulders and gobbled."

"*Bird*seed?"

"Aye. Stoker, the good fellow he is, seated him directly beneath the parrot cage. Never seen him so wooden-faced as when he did it, neither."

George guffawed, but Wiki's responsive grin was brief. Feeling very disturbed, he said, "I would have thought Lieutenant Smith would want to take the sealers to Captain Wilkes himself, and make sure of all the credit."

"Pointed that out to him myself, old chap! However, he didn't rise to the bait. It's hard to tell what revolves in that nasty little brain, but I suspect he prefers a crew of solid navy lads to a bunch of unknowns."

"So what happened next?"

"Smith informed Hammond that he thought a reasonably competent shipmaster should be able to fix his own ship now that the navy has got her hove down for him, and Hammond informed him that with eight hands gone it couldn't be done. Smith countered that by offering to leave the cutter with Forsythe's men—and I hate to think what Forsythe will say when he hears about *that* little idea." George lifted a wry eyebrow. "Then, when I reminded him that Forsythe doesn't have a second-in-command any more, he had the temerity to say that you could stay behind in that capacity while I sailed off with the sealers."

"Dear God," Wiki prayed. "I hope you put a stop to that."

"I did." Rochester grimaced and added gloomily, "In the meantime."

"What do you mean?"

George sighed. "Hammond made him see sense about the number of men needed to finish the work, but once the *Annawan* is seaworthy again I'll have to do as Smith says."

"*What?*"

"Technically, he outranks me. I have a command, but so does he, at the moment, and he's a lieutenant while I'm only a passed midshipman. If he turns it into an argument, Wilkes will back him up. You know what Wilkes is like about niceties of rank, old fellow."

Wiki silenced, beset by such terrible premonitions that when Forsythe arrived down the companionway in a clatter of urgent boot steps, it didn't seem unexpected.

The southerner was white-lipped and grim-faced, and smelled of sweat and dirt. The instant he saw Wiki, he shouted, "Some goddamned son of a bitch has stolen my knife! My knife's been taken again!"

Thirty-two

*W*iki said quickly, "Where were you when you saw it last?"

"I was on the schooner getting more lines out. It was yesterday afternoon—late."

"You're sure you haven't just mislaid it?"

"Of course I'm bloody sure!"

"My God," said Wiki. "It's our chance to search their chests—and look for a blue and white shirt as well as the knife!" And before Rochester could think to remonstrate, he led the way at a run up to deck.

Ten minutes later the cutter grounded onto the damp, ruffled sand at the edge of the surf. Wiki, Rochester, and Forsythe jumped out and headed for the quartet of tents the *Annawan* crew had set up. As they arrived Joel Hammond emerged from the smallest. He looked surprised, and glanced at the sky to check the sun. As usual, his small eyes passed quickly and dismissively over Wiki's face before he nodded at Forsythe and Rochester, saying, "You're very early."

Rochester said curtly, "There's been a theft. We want to inspect all sea chests before the men start work."

Hammond flushed angrily. Inspecting sea chests was a serious matter, as a seaman's chest was his only private space, jealously protected and cherished. A sailor kept not just his spare clothes in there, but letters and mementos of home, as well. However, he could say nothing to stop them. Theft was a very serious matter as well, particularly with seamen, who traditionally had very few possessions.

He demanded, "What was stolen?"

"If they don't know what we're looking for, we're more likely to find it."

"How do you know it wasn't your own men? Have you searched their chests?"

"Of course," Rochester lied.

There was some angry muttering when the *Annawan* hands understood what was happening. Ignoring this, Rochester, with Wiki and Forsythe, headed determinedly into the first tent, which housed the five ordinary seamen of the crew, including Pedro da Silva—who, it immediately became apparent, did not have a sea chest, his tattered finery being bundled up in a shabby striped poncho. He didn't seem at all embarrassed about it, instead greeting Wiki in a comradely kind of manner, as if they were coconspirators, his chest so puffed out and his manner so self-important that Wiki realized with a sinking heart that what Pedro had witnessed from aloft during the two murders must have been confided to one and all by now.

Keeping his expression noncommittal, he cast an eye over the contents of the poncho, and then passed on to the four American seamen, whose chests were a testament to the high regard in which they were held. A couple were intricatedly carved, while others had been painted inside the lid with lively scenes of ships and seas. The rope becket handles were a credit to the marlinespike craftsmanship of their owners.

Wiki inspected each one carefully, but without touching either chest or contents, getting the owner to turn out the pieces one by one instead. They held all the small necessaries of a shipboard existence—paper, pens and pencils, thread, needles, fishhooks, Bibles, spare clothes. One or two of the men were affluent enough to own a spare pair of shoes. Every seaman had a loaded pistol— for snakes, Joel Hammond snapped when asked. He'd given permission, which was comprehensible, under the circumstances. There was no sign of Forsythe's knife, nor of a blue-striped shirt. Wiki looked at Rochester and nodded, and the five men were dismissed to head out smartly to the beach.

They moved on to the next tent, which held the eight old sealers, including Jack Winter, Folger, and Bill Boyd. Their chests were more battered, which, considering the arduous circumstances in which they lived and worked, was not particularly surprising. Wiki was startled, however, to see how many of these hard-bitten men carried books with them—one even had a full set of Shakespeare. Up until now he'd assumed that sealers, though some of the bravest and most daring seamen afloat, were mostly uneducated. They, too, carried loaded pistols. Otherwise, their chests were innocent of striped shirts and purloined knives.

Rochester and Forsythe left the tent with Joel Hammond, but Wiki lingered. The last chest to be inspected had belonged to Bill Boyd, who was now hunkered down restowing the contents. Wiki said to his bent back, "We need to look in your tool chest, too."

"It's with the other tool chests in the officers' tent."

It had not been Boyd who answered, but Folger. The boatswain's mate, still repacking his chest, had not even looked up. Wiki was silent a long moment, looking from one to the other. Then he said abruptly, "You're close kin."

It was a statement, not a question, but Folger went red and blustered, "We don't even look alike, so how can you say that?"

Wiki shook his head, having known they were kin from the very beginning. That Folger was heavily bearded while Boyd was clean-shaven might have disguised their relationship from their shipmates, but in the Pacific people distinguished each other by attitude, build, mannerism, and movement, not by what they wore or how they were groomed.

But it was hopeless to try to explain that, so instead he remarked, "You do fly to his defense rather readily. He's not your son, but your nephew, I think."

"My sister's son, but I raised him as my son after she died," Folger reluctantly admitted, but then added aggressively, "And it ain't no crime, you know."

"Of course not," agreed Wiki. "But I do wonder if I should believe him when he says there was no one in the pantry the afternoon that Captain Reed was killed."

Jack Winter exclaimed, "Mr. Coffin, if that broken-brained Robert Festin told you at any time that he was in the pantry, he was wrong!"

Wiki said quietly, "On the contrary, I think there's a good possibility that he was there."

"Then you're mistaken, Mr. Coffin!"

With the loud sound of the steward's voice, Bill Boyd had at last looked up. Slowly, sensing something was wrong, he lumbered to his feet and looked questioningly at Folger, his big hands opening and closing at his sides.

Folger said, "It's all right, lad. He's not accusing you of anything." Then he swung round at Wiki and demanded, "You're not, are you?"

Instead of answering, Wiki said, "He's deaf, isn't he?"

"Aye—but it don't make no difference! He's a hard worker, my Bill, and he can understand what is said no problem as long as the other speaks clear and he's watching his face at the time."

"I know he's a hard worker. You told me yourself that he got a marvelous amount done in the bo'sun's locker the afternoon of the murder," Wiki reminded him. "Which means that he could have been too preoccupied to notice Festin in the pantry, particularly since he couldn't hear him. And as for you," he snapped, swinging round at Jack Winter. "You were so busy enjoying yourself with the cutter's men you wouldn't have noticed it if a squad of marines marched down into the pantry!"

"That's a lie! I swear on my mother's grave he wasn't there!" Jack Winter squawked, but Wiki left the tent without bothering to reply.

Thirty-three

*O*nce outside the sealers' tent, Wiki stopped and looked around. One of the *Annawan* boats was heading out to the brig, crewed by the seamen whose chests had been inspected first. Smoke plumed from the distant galley chimney, and Wiki realized that they had gone to collect their breakfast. The sealers, too, had come out onto the beach, and were talking together in a huddle, their attitudes unmistakably angry and hostile. They, too, were staring at the *Swallow*.

There were two tents left to search—Annabelle's, which was closed up tight, and the smallest one, where Joel Hammond and his first mate were housed. When Wiki pulled the flap aside, it was to see Forsythe going through various tool chests as Rochester watched. Joel Hammond and his first officer, their expressions furious, were taking clothes and other possessions out of their own sea chests. Wiki gathered that it had been Forsythe who had demanded that the officers' chests should be inspected, too, a peremptory request that had almost developed into a fight before Rochester had stepped in and quelled it.

Neither sea chest, Wiki noticed from the deliberate distance he kept as they were turned out, held any books. They didn't hold anything of interest to the investigation, either, and the toolboxes, though promising to start with because of the sharp implements they held, yielded no evidence, either.

"Well?" demanded Joel Hammond, still red with affront when they'd finished. "Have you found what you wanted?"

Forsythe, without bothering to look apologetic, shook his head.

"So are you going to tell us what you're searching for now?"

George Rochester said, "Lieutenant Forsythe's knife was stolen."

"For God's sake!" Hammond exploded, and whirled round on Wiki, recognizing his presence at last. "You can't mean you gave him back the same goddamned knife I hauled out of Captain Reed's corpse? What kind of goddamned sheriff's deputy do you think you are? You tamely handed the murder weapon back to the killer!"

Forsythe had gone white, a bleached shade of fury which was almost instantly overtaken by a flood of red. He roared, "That's a lie!"

"Aye? When the captain's widow herself swears that she saw you on the quarterdeck? And when it was *your* goddamned knife I found in her husband's body?"

"It was *not* my bloody knife! She's lying—and so are you, god-damn it!"

"You were there when I handed it over, so you saw the stains of blood." Hammond's mouth pursed righteously, and he said, "That's God's evidence, so far as I'm concerned."

"Oh, for Christ's sake!" Forsythe exclaimed. His fists were

clenched, but to Wiki's relief, instead of attacking Hammond he barged furiously out of the tent.

He had moved so fast that he was out of sight by the time Wiki and Rochester emerged, so instead of going after him they stopped and looked around. Piles of goods littered the strand in every direction. The knife could be anywhere, Wiki thought, and was washed by a wave of depression.

"In another few days," he said moodily, "the *Annawan* will be fixed, and our reprieve will be over. Joel Hammond will insist on sailing away to look for his treasure; you'll be forced to take that sealing gang on board; and I'll have got no further in finding the killer." And it was partly Rochester's fault, by banning him from leaving the brig, he thought, but did not say it. Instead, he added wryly, "We have to face it, George, I'd make a better horse jockey than a sleuth."

"Cheer up," Rochester urged. "We might have to take eight on board—but it's not nearly so bad as the prospect of being lumbered with the *Annawan* people all the way to Rio. Seventeen men! Where the devil would we have put them all?" he rhetorically demanded.

Wiki cast him a sideways glance and then returned to his dark study of the beach. People were working on the *Annawan* already, though the boat with the breakfast was still returning from the brig accompanied by the two boats that belonged to the *Swallow*, both full of men. In the distance the *Flying Fish* floated on her dappled reflection, with no sign of life on board. Lieutenant Smith, he noticed, hadn't offered any of his men to help with the repairs.

He said, "Sixteen."

"What?"

"That's the number of men on the *Annawan*."

George shook his head. "Seventeen."

"You're counting Annabelle."

"No I'm not."

Wiki frowned. He had his notebook in his pocket, and now fetched it out. By sheer coincidence it fell open at the page where he had copied the crew list, and he read it again now, counting down the column. "Hammond, the cook, the steward, the first mate, the bo'sun and the bo'sun's mate, Folger's five sealers, and five more seamen add up to a total of sixteen."

"Have it your own way—but I *can* count, you know."

George sounded unusually irritated. Wiki paused, looking at his notebook as uneasiness riffled the short hairs on his neck. He said uncertainly, "But the list—"

"As I said, have it your own way!"

"*E hoa,* no." Wiki shook his head, beset by an indefinable sense of oncoming crisis. "You must have a good reason to be so definite—so when did you do this counting?"

"That first day on the *Annawan,* the afternoon Reed was murdered. I came on board, and counted sixteen hands as Hammond sent them about their duty. It's something instinctive, in a captain. Then you came on deck with the seventeenth man."

"*What?*"

Wiki remembered it vividly. He had been in the hold, and had come out into the bright sunshine to see Rochester on the quarterdeck talking with Joel Hammond. He remembered how glad he had been to see him. He looked down at the list again, not counting this time, but reading the names he had copied there.

One was missing. There was no Xavier York Zimri Green, or even an X.Y.Z. Green. Alphabet Green's name had not been on the crew list. *Alphabet Green was the seventeenth man.*

Without a word he swerved on his heel and pushed back into the officers' tent. Hammond and Hunt had their heads together in a muttered conference. Ignoring this, Wiki snapped, "Where's seaman Green?"

"*Who?*"

"I don't know what you call him. Xavier?"

"You wouldn't be talking about *Mister* Green, by any chance?"

Wiki blinked with surprise, but said firmly, "That's the man."

Strangely, the atmosphere of barely controlled rage fled, to be replaced by an air of caution. Hammond and Hunt glanced at each other, and then looked around as if Mr. Green might materialize out of the draperies covering the tent frame.

Joel Hammond said, "He sleeps here, but I don't know where he is most times."

"Why isn't he on the crew list?"

"Because he's the goddamned supercargo, why else? He was Captain Reed's agent—the man in charge of trade. As I told you, he's *Mister* Green. He came on board at Rio, and he ain't nothing to do with me."

My God, thought Wiki. Suddenly a great deal was coming clear. He said slowly, "So Captain Reed decided to bring the *Annawan* to Shark Island after he picked up Mr. Green in Rio? After he'd heard what *Green* had to tell him about the wreck of the *Hero*?"

Again, Joel Hammond looked at Hunt, who shrugged and shook his head. "Who knows? Mr. Green was the supercargo of the *Hero*, true. Why don't you ask his widow?"

"Why not?" said Wiki softly, and left the tent.

Then he stood still, his eyes scanning the beach again. There was no sign at all of Alphabet Green—he'd vanished as if he'd never existed. George Rochester was down at the edge of the surf—Wiki could hear him issuing orders. The cutter was still floating close to the beach, but when Wiki looked in the direction of Annabelle's tent, to his alarm Forsythe was there. Annabelle was standing in the opening of the flap, and he was gesticulating angrily.

He crossed the space swiftly and touched Forsythe's shoulder, then danced out of range as the southerner whirled around, his fists up and his face suffused with rage.

"She's sticking to that goddamned story!" he yelled.

Annabelle was on the verge of tears. "I swear I saw someone on the quarterdeck!" she protested. "And it was you, I swear it was you!"

"Do you believe her?" Forsythe demanded.

"She certainly saw *someone*," Wiki said bleakly. He looked at Annabelle and demanded, "Who was in the galley just before Ezekiel was killed?"

"What?" She trembled visibly.

"You called out to *someone*. Tell me the truth! Was it Robert Festin?"

"No! Why would I call out to him?"

"He wasn't in the galley?"

"No! I don't know *where* he was."

Forsythe shouted, "What the *hell* does this mean?"

Wiki said grimly, "It means that there was no one at all in the galley—and that it would be a very good idea to search her tent."

"What?" Annabelle cringed, going white and then red as horrified emotions chased each other across her face. "Search my things? But why? Wiki, how can you do this to me? I've done nothing wrong!"

"One of the murder weapons is lost. It could be hidden here."

"What? *C'est impossible!*"

Wiki wanted to hold her—to shake her. He couldn't, of course, but his voice shook as he demanded, "Do you want to risk the knife being used against *you*?"

Numbly, she shook her head, and shrank away as they both pushed past her into the tent, to be enfolded by her scent of perfume and dusting powder. Clothes were strewn everywhere, piled on the lady chair, the dresser, and the mattress. Forsythe went straight to the barrel of weapons and tipped it over on the one bare patch of floor with a great thump and much crashing. Then he made more noise as he sorted roughly through the pistols, knives, muskets, and clubs, throwing them back one by one.

Annabelle, her face paper white, was no help at all with searching her baskets and trunks, so Wiki went through them himself, feeling extremely uncomfortable about it. As always, he was amazed at the unyielding weight of corset stays, and wondered why women tortured their delicate flesh into strange and difficult shapes. Petticoats and gowns shimmered and rustled and sagged in his hands. One of the boxes was entirely filled with hats, and another with shoes, but there was no sign of the knife. A search of the drawers of the one dressing table was equally fruitless, though it turned up two loaded pistols, plus, very oddly, a leather belt with two attached holsters for the pistols. Obviously, he thought, it had belonged to Ezekiel, but he couldn't imagine why it was stowed with her things.

Then, right at the back of the tent, behind the dresser, he found a large and sturdy trunk. He looked at the folded clothes it held—and froze.

"My God," he whispered.

"What is it?" Forsythe's voice said in his ear, and then whispered harshly, "Wa-al, by all the little gods, look what we've got here."

At the top was a small pile of blue and white shirts in a distinctive style, each with a band at the neck instead of a collar—a band that was secured with a single large deer-horn button.

Thirty-four

*A*s one, Wiki and Forsythe leapt into the cutter, while Forsythe barked at the crew to get back to the brig. Then, when they were under way, he turned to Wiki and said grimly, "You'd better tell me what this is all about."

"It was Alphabet Green."

"Who?"

"Annabelle Reed's cousin."

"Who?"

"The man who escorted Annabelle to the wake. You told me about that yourself."

Forsythe's mouth opened and shut, and then he said thoughtfully, "That man, huh?"

"Aye." Then Wiki frowned, remembering that Alphabet had taken Annabelle back to the after house once the prayers were over—which meant that he hadn't been present when Forsythe's knife had been stolen from his belt at the time of the spree.

Nevertheless, he persevered, saying, "He must have been the one who stole your knife—not once, but twice. Did you notice him getting close to you when you were working on the *Annawan?*"

Forsythe's mouth compressed, and he bit out, "I didn't notice anyone. I put the knife down and plain forgot about it—the same as I did just before the wake, the same night that Zack was killed."

"What!"

"When you asked me today where I was when I saw it last, I not only remembered where I put it down on the *Annawan* yesterday afternoon, but at the same time I damn well remembered that when I lost it on the night of the wake, I'd seen it last in the captain's cabin."

"You *left* it in the captain's cabin before you went off to the prayers?" Wiki echoed incredulously. *My God*, he thought, so *that's* how Alphabet got hold of the knife that night!

"Annabelle Reed asked me to cut a lashing around one of her trunks, and I hauled it out, and put it down, and . . ."

And left without remembering to pick it up again. Wiki finished the sentence in his mind. The confession, he saw, made Forsythe very angry, as if he were looking for someone else to blame for his lapse.

Wiki said grimly, "I wish you'd remembered that earlier."

"Well, I bloody well didn't, did I? I had enough on my mind!"

"I *knew* Alphabet spent the night of the wake in the after house—he told me himself that he slept in Captain Reed's stateroom because Annabelle was scared to be alone. Because he left the deck as soon as the prayers were over, I didn't think he'd had a chance to steal your knife. If I'd known that you'd left it in the cabin, it would've been a different matter."

"It's not my goddamned fault!" Forsythe sounded at the end of his tether. "I've only just remembered, as I said—she's a witch of a bitch, as you should bloody know—she stops a man from thinking straight in his head. And Zack was making sheep's eyes at her, too, which made me wild. Then I found that Zack had been cheating those bloody sheep of seamen, and I had to shake him around to get him to give their money back. Then we got drunk, so I have trouble remembering what happened. So, for God's sake, stop getting at me—I had enough on my mind! And I blame myself worse than you can ever blame me," he muttered.

The cutter arrived at the side of the brig, and Wiki scrambled up to deck with Forsythe close behind. Sua and Tana were there, but otherwise the brig was apparently deserted.

Forsythe shouted, "What are you two black bastards looking at?"

The two Samoans disappeared rapidly into the forecastle. Forsythe swerved round at Wiki, and snapped, "So what next?"

"Festin—I have to talk to Festin." Wiki lifted his voice, and shouted, "Robert!"

"What? But Annabelle Reed said that he wasn't in the galley— so what the hell d'you reckon he could've seen? The only other place he could've been was the pantry—and the pantry is out of sight and sound of the deck, as you keep on pointing out."

"But was the galley empty when he left it? That's what I'd like to know!" And Wiki shouted again, "Robert!" Still, there was no reply. The deck planks echoed as he strode over to the galley and looked in the door, It was empty. Frowning, he looked around, and said, "So where the hell is he?"

"Oh, for God's sake," said Forsythe impatiently, and ran to the companionway door. Wiki could hear his boots thundering down the stairs as he hollered, "Festin! Festin! Come out from wherever you are, you sogerin' bugger!"

The echoes faded into silence. Wiki looked around, beset by the same sense of oncoming calamity he'd felt when his instincts had been trying to warn him that there was a shark in the water. Then he turned into the galley, looking for some hint of where Festin had gone. The fire was still hot, and there were chunks of salt meat simmering in two great caldrons on top of the stove. It was as if the Acadian had just stepped out the door.

Because of that instinctive sense of impending doom, Wiki reached up, plucked his *taiaha* off the two hooks where it rested, and then turned, looking out the doorway. Out of habit, he held the weapon at a slight diagonal across his body, the pointed tongue downward, and the killing blade uppermost. There was a slight sound from behind him—or behind the galley shed. He turned, and something in the grate caught his eye—scorched wood, and the dull gleam of hot metal. He hunkered down, putting his *taiaha* on the floor, and gingerly hauled it out of the embers. It was a skinning knife—and he was almost sure that it was the same long knife that he had plucked out of Kingman's dead thigh.

The memory of that awful moment when he had bent to cut the rope that held Kingman to the bottom of the sea and the shark had bulleted past was so vivid that the rush of brutal movement from behind seemed almost inevitable. A hard arm hooked around his neck, dragging back his chin, and he glimpsed the flash of a knife from the corner of his eye. Wiki felt just a touch of searing pain under his left ear before his knees flexed powerfully, straightening his legs. With one violent movement he threw himself backward on top of his assailant.

As the blade left his neck he rolled over, frantically grabbing about the floor for his *taiaha*. Meantime, his attacker came to his feet faster than seemed possible, both arms wide, one hand holding Forsythe's knife, the other gripping the knife Wiki had plucked from the grate. It was hot—Wiki could see the skin of Alphabet Green's hand whitening and crinkling where he held it, but Alphabet didn't seem to notice the pain. Instead, his glare was fixed on Wiki's face. Not a word was said. He charged at Wiki again, and again Wiki rolled away from the long knife, still groping for his *taiaha* but forced by another attack to roll away from it.

Then he was on his feet, crouched and weaponless. Green was between him and the doorway, his expression set in vicious triumph. He made another lunge with the long skinning knife. Wiki threw himself to one side, crashing against a wall. A huge fry pan fell down, distracting Alphabet for a critical instant, and Wiki flung himself the other way, snatching at his *taiaha*. The power of *Tumatauenga* surged into him with the touch of the wood.

Although he did not know it, Wiki's eyes were bulging from his head with fury, and he was grunting wordlessly, "Ha! Ha! Ha!" His tongue lolled out in contempt and defiance, matching the *arero,* the carved tongue of the *taiaha*. Alphabet's own eyes widened. The long knife slashed down hard. If it lodged in the wood, it could tear the *taiaha* out of Wiki's grip. He parried desperately, forced to hold the pole short. The blade slid down the toughened shaft almost all the way to his hands, then back again as he flipped and whisked it.

He jabbed again with the pointed end, hoping to force Alphabet out into the open air. Instead, Green stayed in front of the doorway, keeping him trapped in the limited space. He was thrusting at Wiki with the long skinning knife, while his other hand brandished Forsythe's blade ready for use. Wiki's only defense was to keep on the move. Dancing back and forth as far as the space would allow, he constantly jabbed with the tongued end of his weapon, hoping to trick Alphabet into the same mistake that Rochester had made the first time they had jousted—the assumption that the point was the lethal part of the weapon. Wiki had the advantage of height already—what he had to do was to fool Green into ducking under the business end.

He jerked the tongue upward, flicking the collar of hair and feathers across Alphabet's face. Green swayed back, and laughed aloud as he lunged forward and up. Wiki skipped back, wincing as he came up hard against the hot stove. To Green, he must have looked trapped. Wiki saw the gleam of satisfaction in his eyes. He jabbed again at Green's face, his movements deliberately desperate. Snarling triumph, Green ducked under the point and lunged forward. Wiki sidestepped smartly, whisked the *taiaha* around, and crashed the *rau*, the striking blade, on Alphabet Green's lowered head.

For a long instant Green teetered. Wiki saw his staring eyes roll up until only the whites showed. Then, as the knives clattered loose, Green crashed to the floor like a poleaxed beast.

Forsythe emerged from the companionway door just as Wiki staggered out onto the deck. "There's no one down there," he said. "Festin and Stoker must have gone on shore." Tana and Sua had come on deck, too, but it was Forsythe who inquired, "What the hell was all that racket?"

"Alphabet—Alphabet Green. He must have come with the boat that fetched the breakfast, and stayed behind when they left," Wiki gasped. He hadn't realized that the deadly battle had taken such a short time, or that he was panting with exertion. Sweat poured off him. He was trembling like a leaf. All at once he was aware of bleeding from his neck, but when he put up a shaking hand it was to find it was nothing life-threatening, just a deep nick.

"What?" Forsythe strode quickly to the galley and went in. After a short moment he came out again without saying a word.

Wiki took three steps to the rail and sucked in three huge breaths of fresh air. Then he turned and said more calmly, "He was lying in wait for me—behind the galley, I think. He'd already found the skinning knife—the one that . . . that was in Zachary Kingman's body—and had thrown it into the galley fire. Then, when I was hunkered down getting it out of the grate, he rushed me from behind, and damn near cut my throat with your knife."

Forsythe scowled. "*My* knife?"

"Aye. If he'd killed me with that—*that* knife, *your* knife, and managed to get to shore before my body was found—with *your* knife, *that* knife—you would have been blamed, for sure."

From Green's point of view it had been a perfect setup, Wiki thought. Forsythe had been shouting obscenities when he'd come on board, and was obviously in a savage mood. At any kind of trial Tana and Sua and the cutter's men would have testified that he'd been in the throes of one of his rages. His derisive opinion of Wiki was known throughout the fleet. Forsythe could have swung for his murder, and probably the other killings as well.

Wiki said grimly, "He was the unlisted seventeenth member of the complement of the *Annawan*—the unknown fifth man who was still on board the schooner when Captain Reed was knifed. I'd believed all along that Alphabet Green had been one of those who came to the *Swallow* when we first arrived in the bay—that he was just an ordinary member of the crew. Once I knew that he wasn't, it was obvious he was the killer."

"But how the devil did he do it?"

"He was the man in the galley. I think we'll find when we ask Annabelle that that's why she went to the galley so often—it was their private meeting place. He was probably there when she left to take the bottle of brandy to her husband—but we'll have to ask her to make sure of that, too. Then, when Captain Reed threw her out of the cabin, she ran back to the galley because she expected him to be there still—but he was gone. He'd dropped through the hatchway to the steerage, and had made his way between decks to the after hatch. *He* was the man Annabelle and Pedro da Silva glimpsed on the quarterdeck, broad enough in the shoulders to be mistaken for you."

"But what about Festin?" Forsythe demanded. "Where the hell was he? According to him, *he* was the one in the goddamned galley."

"He was in the pantry. Boyd said he wasn't there, but it turns out that Boyd is very deaf. Alphabet Green forced Festin to say he was in the galley to give himself an alibi, and put me off the track." Alphabet had browbeaten Festin right before his very own eyes, Wiki thought ruefully, and yet he hadn't noticed.

"And poor Zack?" Forsythe's voice rose. His eyes had gone flat and blank, just the way they had when he'd first heard that Zachary Kingman was dead. "Green killed Zack too?"

"Aye. Zachary Kingman made a fatal mistake by staggering to the after house, and Green grabbed his opportunity. He had your knife ready to hand, so it was a perfect chance to eliminate your alibi for Captain Reed's murder, and at the same time lay the blame for both killings on you. He was wearing one of Reed's shirts already, so his own clothes were saved from being spattered. When he put the bloodied shirt in the galley fire, he also went to the bo'sun's locker and exchanged your knife—the one he'd used to kill Zachary Kingman—for the knife that Joel Hammond had left there. At the same time, he took one of the grindstones and a length of rope, then carried them to the after house, tied the stone to Zachary Kingman's ankles, and dropped him overboard."

Forsythe demanded, "But why did he kill Captain Reed in the first place?"

"You'll have to ask him that when he comes to," Wiki said tiredly, and was startled to hear Forsythe's sardonic guffaw.

"You must be joking," the big Virginian said.

"What do you mean?"

"That's quite a weapon of yours, Mr. Deputy Coffin. You should be proud of it. This bastard who killed Zack and done his best to kill you, too, is as dead as last week's mutton."

Thirty-five

*A*nother day, another burial, and another argument about who should conduct the service. Joel Hammond reckoned that Rochester should do it. Not only had he taken the service before, but he was the highest-ranking American there, he figured, and a representative of the U.S. Navy to boot. George pointed out that not only did he not feel like lauding a man who had murdered a brother navy officer, but this time Lieutenant Forsythe was in attendance, and it was a well-known fact that Lieutenant Forsythe outranked him when they were not on board the brig *Swallow*. Forsythe, for his part, delivered the information that there was no point in asking him, as he was only there for the satisfaction of seeing the dirt stamped down over the body of the man who had killed his best friend.

Then Lawrence J. Smith arrived and the fuss came to a sudden stop as he immediately claimed the right to conduct the service, being the most important person around. Then there was a long pause as he ruffled through a Bible for the most portentous passage possible, while the coffin lay in the open hole that had been dug next to Captain Reed's grave, under the same dusty tree.

For Wiki, the scene was startlingly reminiscent of the day of Ezekiel Reed's burial. The grave-digging party leaned on their shovels; the seamen who had come to witness the burial shuffled about in the hot sun; and Annabelle Reed wept into a handkerchief. He himself was keeping a tactful distance from the mourners, lingering about the fringes of the cemetery and contemplating headstones. Vaguely recollecting the crypt that had looked as if it had often been lifted to receive more coffins before being closed again, he hunted about until he found it. It had sunk even further, he noticed—it was even less level with the sward. When he put his weight on the big rectangular stone, it tipped so that he could see recently disturbed dirt where it had been lifted and then carefully set back in place. Then he saw scrapes in the pathway nearby which matched the ruts in the track up the cliff, and indentations where hoisting equipment had been lodged.

So this was where the crew of the sloop *Hero* had hidden the bullion, he thought in a strangely remote kind of way. He wondered rather ghoulishly how many skeletons they had uncovered while they were enlarging the hole beneath the slab, but otherwise he felt an almost complete lack of interest, because his mind was mostly taken up with wondering whether it was right that he should be there. After all, it was the funeral of a man he'd killed himself, something about which his feelings were muddled.

The killing had been in self-defense, but he had to keep on reassuring himself about that—which was crazy, because he realized now how close Alphabet had come to killing him that first day, when he had been testing the timbers in the hold. He remembered the strong smell of onions on the Cajun's breath; he remembered that he had felt threatened, even then. Then, Alphabet had relaxed, and stepped away—because he, Wiki, had confessed that when he was sixteen years old he'd been madly in love with Annabelle Green.

Wiki turned to another worry—Annabelle herself. She now behaved as if she hated him—as if she felt he had betrayed her. For hours she'd refused to speak to him, taking refuge in hysterics instead. Finally, however, she'd admitted that her cousin had indeed been in the galley when she had taken the bottle of brandy to the cabin. And Festin? Robert Festin made even less sense than usual when questioned, but that didn't matter, because it was so obvious now that he had been in the pantry all the time. Forsythe, at last, was entirely in the clear. The man Annabelle had glimpsed on the quarterdeck had been her own cousin, though she had refused to confirm it, weeping wildly instead.

Wiki left the unstable stone slab, with its mute evidence of where Alphabet Green had hidden the bullion, to stand by one of the tallest upright headstones. Lieutenant Smith found his place in the book, and then droned on and on while insects whined, birds chirped, and the sun beat down. At long last he ran to a stop, and the grave-digging party was at work again, tossing dirt into the hole. The thudding as clods hit the coffin lid and then the shovels smacked them down seemed unnaturally loud.

To get away from the unsettling noise Wiki left the burial ground altogether, heading down the track to where some men were wrenching a plank from the wreck of the *Hero*. As he neared, Wiki could hear them drilling out treenails. The *Hero*'s running aground had probably happened at night, he thought, and definitely during a gale, because she'd been run up so hard that the bowsprit was lost in the scrub. It had been an act of great courage and desperation on the part of her master—whoever that brave captain had been.

Annabelle had confirmed, too, that her cousin had been the super-cargo of the *Hero*, and that he'd fled to Pernambuco in the sloop's boat with the others. Wiki remembered how weather-beaten Alphabet had looked, undoubtedly a heritage of that passage, and wondered what had happened to the other seven men in the boat, along with their knowledge of where the bullion had been hidden. Had Green bought them off, or had he got rid of them by some other means? Wiki remembered the savage look on his face as he'd attacked, and grimly thought that the second was the more likely option.

As he arrived on the beach he heard a cheer as the plank came free from the sloop. Borne by willing shoulders onto a flat patch of grass, it was energetically attacked by the boatswain and carpenter, who strove with their adzes to turn it into a match for the gap in the *Annawan* hull—wider at the bow end, and narrowing amidships. The funeral party was straggling down the trail now. Hearing the commotion on the beach, the seamen broke away from the pro-cession, running eagerly to join in the work.

The day progressed with the crashing of sledgehammers as the replacement plank was slammed into place. By evening a caulking gang was dangling over the side of the schooner on lines, working with their wedges, caulking stuff, and tar. The work on the schooner was very obviously coming to a culmination—so Lawrence J. Smith called for a conference.

It should be obvious to everyone, he declared when they were all assembled, that nailing a few sheets of copper over the replace-ment plank and then letting out the cable so the schooner could tip back to her rightful level could be managed with ease by the *An-nawan* men who were left, plus the cutter's men under the supervi-sion of Lieutenant Forsythe, with Wiki Coffin to assist. The murderer had been uncovered, executed, and properly put to rest—or so he pointed out—and there was no reason whatsoever for the two navy vessels to linger here. They could rest the night, and then they must weigh anchor.

As the early sun rose Wiki stood glumly on the quarterdeck of the *Swallow*, watching the eight sealers come on board with their sea chests on their shoulders. Folger and Bill Boyd, he noted, were bringing their tool chests, as well—it was the first time he realized that they owned their own tools. He wondered how they felt about their abrupt transition to the navy. The previous day he had noticed the sealing gang conferring in a huddled group at least twice, just as they had after their sea chests had been searched. There was the same surly, hostile air about them, and he had felt a touch of the foreboding that had assailed him every time he had pictured the entire complement of the *Annawan* boarding the *Swallow* for the passage to Rio. But there were only eight of them, he emphatically thought—and it shouldn't take many days for George to rendezvous with Captain Wilkes.

Nevertheless, he said to George, "You'll take care?"

"I won't have the chance to do anything else, with that panicky little prawn in command of the other ship."

Rochester was standing in his favorite pose with his hands lightly clasped behind his back, but his expression, as he watched Smith take on six of the brig's men, was not benign at all. One of them was the *Swallow*'s cook, which meant that Stoker would have to be cook as well as steward. George, though he had simmered on the verge of open rage, hadn't dared argue, knowing that a highly biased version of the events at Shark Island was going to be poured into Captain Wilkes's ears whatever happened, and rebellion would only make it worse.

He turned his glare to the *Annawan* and said, "I wish the poisonous little bastard had seen reason and given us one more day— just to make sure that she doesn't go back to leaking the instant she's on even keel again."

Wiki said, "She won't."

"Nevertheless," said George, but didn't finish the sentence. Instead, he looked at Wiki and then away, saying again, "I'll try to make sure that we don't get more than a day's sail ahead of you. You have the course I gave you?"

"Aye," said Wiki.

"You don't have to stay, you know. Forsythe wouldn't care if you didn't."

"I know that," Wiki said wryly. But he didn't want to leave until he'd somehow got Annabelle to forgive him—and he thought he knew the way to do it.

Forsythe was conning the *Flying Fish* out to the open sea. Lawrence J. Smith had weighed his certain knowledge of the southerner's terrifying seamanship against his fears of unknown reefs and shoals, and had opted for the devil he knew best. Accordingly, the cutter followed, and so Wiki was able to stay on the *Swallow* until the two vessels had made the other side of the shark-fin-shaped headland.

Then it was time to leave. *"E hoa,"* he said. He and George shook hands in their special way, forearms linked, and then hit each other hard many times on the shoulder, as *pakeha* men who are great friends do when meeting or parting. Wiki dropped a canvas bag with a few possessions into the cutter, where his *taiaha* was already carefully stowed, and then picked up the parrot cage. Stoker had been almost as tragic at being parted from the parrot as he was at being relegated to the position of cook-cum-steward, but Wiki was determined to give the bird to Annabelle and watch her joy and relief as she released it. In his mind, he could see the smile in her eyes. That, he thought, was when she'd relent and forgive him.

"You're set?" said Forsythe, at the tiller. Wiki nodded, remembering belatedly that he had forgotten to tell George where the bullion was hidden but not really caring, and they were off. Within instants, it seemed, the *Swallow* and the *Flying Fish* were out of sight.

In a remarkably short time they were back in the cove, where Festin was eagerly waiting. "Ho, ho," he said when Wiki waded onto the beach with the parrot cage in one hand. "*Pâté à la râpure* tonight, no?" he joked. "Bloody good." Being such an admirer of Forsythe's style, he had opted to join the cutter's camp rather than stay with the *Annawan* men where he properly belonged, and *pâté à la râpure* was the name in his language for what Constant Keith referred to as chicken stew pie.

"He's not for eating," Wiki said firmly, and hung the cage from a branch of a nearby tree. The parrot, he noticed, seemed to like it. The bird looked almost as good as new, though its beak was peeling in bits like the skin of a rotten orange. As Stoker had predicted, the scales over its eyes were coming loose. Then Wiki turned and stretched, looking at the curling lace of the surf on the damp gold sand and the turquoise of the lagoon beyond. It was an idyllic spot, but he couldn't wait to leave. When the cutter's men were ready for the afternoon's work, Wiki went with them to the schooner to help the remaining crew, who were in the hold shoveling the ballast from one side to the other.

Already, the hull was beginning to creak as the *Annawan* tried to set herself back on an even keel, so Wiki and the cutter's men boarded the raft and started letting out the cable. With more cracking noises the schooner began to roll. More shoveling, more slacking of the hawser, and her masts began to revolve against the sky. Then evening came, and the masts were upright—and in the morning her holds were still dry.

"Goddamn it," observed Forsythe in disgust. "If that pompous little bugger had waited just twelve more hours, we could've sailed with the *Swallow*."

Thirty-six

*W*hile the cutter's men were getting the boat ready for departure in the morning, Wiki scrambled over the rockfall, finding Hammond and the remaining *Annawan* crew assembled on the beach. All the tents save Annabelle's had vanished, their contents removed to the brig, and hers was being taken down. Hammond was talking to Annabelle, but as Wiki came up he turned and walked away. It was Wiki, then, who helped her into the boat, though her hand was stiff and unwelcoming, and he was the one who helped her back on board the schooner.

Then she and Wiki were alone on the deck, and the beach was quite empty. Hammond and the *Annawan* crew had trailed up the cliff, disappearing from sight at the first steep bend. Were they going to the graveyard to check the whereabouts of the bullion, ready to retrieve it when the cutter had gone? Perhaps.

Annabelle said matter-of-factly, "So again we part."

"Aye," said Wiki, hunting for a note of sadness in her voice but not finding it. She was wearing a plain blue cotton dress with big front pockets in the skirt, a workaday outfit cinched at her waist with a leather belt, but looked breathtakingly lovely. Wiki wondered what would happen if he held out his arms to her, but didn't quite dare do it, so instead he looked at the sky on the eastern horizon. It threatened a storm, but Forsythe was determined to sail.

He saw Forsythe clambering over the rockfall, his rifle over one shoulder and a sack of flour in the other hand. Then the big Virginian was striding along the beach. Behind him came Robert Festin, carrying the parrot cage in one hand and a molasses keg on his shoulder.

Wiki heard Annabelle's sucked-in breath. When he looked at her, she was dead white, and was beginning to tremble. Thinking he understood her distress, he said softly, "Don't be afraid. When you release the bird, Ezekiel's spirit will fly away, too."

She made a strange noise, halfway between a sob and a laugh, but said nothing. Taking a boat to the raft, Festin and Forsythe clambered across it and then on board, and Wiki went to meet them as they climbed over the rail.

Robert Festin put down the birdcage, carried the molasses keg to the hatchway by the forward house, and jumped down the ladder to the between-decks space. After he'd stowed the keg Forsythe handed down the sack of flour, and then, as Wiki watched through the aperture of the hatch, Festin stacked it by the bags of stores that had already been loaded.

Looking up at Wiki and beaming broadly, he said, "*Pataka,* ha?"

Wiki frowned. For some reason the fine hairs on his neck were bristling.

He said, "What do you mean?"

Festin, below him, waved an arm around the between-decks steerage area, and said, "*Pataka*. Pantry." Then, still grinning smugly, he mounted the ladder to arrive onto the deck the way Wiki had seen him emerge before, his head first, then his broad shoulders, and his spindly little legs last of all.

Wiki said numbly, "*That's* what you call the pantry? The between-decks storage?"

"*Pataka* pantry, exactly."

"You were *there*—between decks—when Captain Reed was killed?"

"Aye. Not the goddamned galley, no."

"But Alphabet Green . . . ?"

"Ah." Festin grinned. "In goddamned galley, he."

"Jesus Christ," Wiki whispered. "*It was you!*"

Forsythe said alertly, "What the hell is this?"

"*Robert Festin was the man on the quarterdeck!*"

"Just quick look," Festin protested. "To see what crash meant, crash on cabin floor."

Wiki echoed blankly, "You heard a crash in the cabin?"

"Aye, big bump in the cabin. Me jump up after hatch, have quick look, see Mrs. Reed running, she get to galley, she turn round, I quick back down hatch. Back to *pataka*, aye."

"And what did she say before she turned round?"

"To Alphabet Green?"

"Aye."

In his antique French, Festin said, "*Je l'occist!*"

Wiki shut his eyes, translating Festin's sixteenth-century language into Annabelle's more modern tongue, saying to himself, "*Je l'ai tué!*" He opened them and stated tightly, " '*Je l'ai tué*' is what she really said, isn't it."

His face round with surprise, Festin nodded.

Forsythe said, "How the hell do you know that?"

Because, Wiki thought, da Silva had laughed that what she had said had sounded like *tu-whit-tu-woo,* the call of an owl. *Je l'ai tué—I have killed him!* That was what Annabelle had gasped to Alphabet Green as she'd run up to the galley door.

Then she had spun around and run back—why?

Something—a sound—warned him, sent the hairs lifting on the back of his neck. Wiki whirled. Annabelle was holding the birdcage over the rail, and shaking it so violently that the parrot fell off its perch. Wiki heard it squawk, and saw it beat its wings in fright.

Forsythe's voice said again, "What the *hell* is going on?"

Wiki said numbly, "She did it. She killed her husband. She murdered Ezekiel Reed."

"*She?* But that ain't possible! She's only a weak woman, goddamn it! The knife went all the way through his chest, you were with me when we saw it!"

"She grabbed the skinning knife and stabbed it into her husband's back. It didn't kill him—instead he ran toward the weapons that were hung on the wall, and . . ." Wiki took a shaking breath, the murder scene vividly in his mind's eye. Then he said, "She pulled the rug from under his feet."

"The mat?"

"Aye." The blood-soaked mat Hammond had used as a winding sheet.

"That was the crash Festin heard," Wiki shakily went on. "When she pulled the rug from under his feet he fell backward onto the knife, driving it all the way through his chest. Annabelle ran out of the cabin to the galley, calling out to her cousin that she had killed him—and then she realized that she had to roll Reed's body over so that the knife handle was upward, and so she ran back."

No wonder, he thought grimly, that she had been breathless when she'd come to the rail when he had arrived at the side of the schooner—or that her hands had been covered in blood. She had heaved the corpse over by gripping the edge of the mat, which was why they had found it alongside the body.

Forsythe scowled deeply, and then he said, "But after she left the cabin I heard the old man's voice shouting—"

He silenced. Annabelle, her expression utterly panic-stricken, dropped the cage over the rail—and as it fell the door swung open and the parrot tumbled out with a squawk and a few flying feathers.

The bird plunged like a stone, recovered an inch from the surface, and then soared up, screaming. It screamed, "Goddamned bitch!" in such a human voice that Wiki flinched. Then it was off, flapping across the beach and into the scrub, croaking obscenities as it went.

"*Jesus Christ!*" shouted Forsythe. "That's the sound I heard! It wasn't the old man—it was the bird! That's why she covered the cage, to stop it talking again!" Then he yelled, "Look out!"

Annabelle had hauled two pistols out of the holsters in her pockets. "*Jesus,*" cried Forsythe. He swung his rifle off his shoulder. Wiki shouted, "No!" and threw himself to the deck, diving toward Annabelle as one gun fired. He felt the wind of a pistol ball as it whined across his back. Then another shot crashed out, and another. He frantically crawled, trying to get to Annabelle to save her without being killed himself. Abruptly the shooting stopped.

"Jesus," said Forsythe as Wiki scrambled to his feet. Most unusually, the Virginian's voice was shaking. "My God, she was determined to put you away—she could have got all of us if she wasn't so determined to get you first. Are you hurt?"

Wiki was unscathed. Instead, it was Annabelle who was slumped to the planks. Forsythe might have been uncharacteristically slow, but his aim had been as unerring as ever. Wiki desperately wanted to run to her, but was shaking too much to move.

Forsythe demanded angrily, "Did she really think she'd get away with it?"

The *Annawan* seamen were bursting out onto the beach. A boat was pushed out and then Joel Hammond ran across the raft and up onto deck. With an incoherent cry he ran over to Annabelle's body, and scooped her up to his chest. "Oh no," he said, rocking her body in his arms. *"No."* And Wiki thought, yes, Annabelle had believed with good reason that she'd get away with killing the three of them, because this man would have covered it up—just as her cousin had tried to cover up her murder of Ezekiel Reed.

Forsythe said aggressively to Hammond, "How long have you been making a cuckold of old man Reed—while all the time you and his woman was pretendin' that you hated each other, huh? But you wanted his fortune as well as his wife—so you planned to kill him off! So she would inherit his fortune and you could share it!"

"Fortune?" Hammond let out a harsh travesty of a laugh. "What goddamned fortune? Annabelle wasn't his goddamned heir! When he died she got nothing!"

"So you were going to steal his bullion," Forsythe exclaimed, enlightened. "That's why you were prating on about that mythical Lima silver! You was going to collect the hundred thousand dollars in bullion, take it on board, and then pretend it was treasure trove so that Reed's real heirs couldn't claim it!"

Joel Hammond said sullenly, "That's a very neat theory. The problem is that once her cousin Green was dead we didn't have any goddamned idea of where it was buried. He was the one who hid the silver, and he showed Ezekiel Reed where he put it, but no one else knew."

When you put Annabelle to rest in the burial ground up there, maybe you will notice the lid of a crypt has sunk a bit and find you have a good idea, after all, of where it was buried, Wiki coldly meditated, but didn't open his mouth. Instead of saying anything he thought of all the people who had died because of that silver bullion.

"Wa-al, ain't that a pity—and after we was kind enough to fix your schooner, too," drawled Forsythe, sounding a lot more like his cynical self. "It must've been a nasty moment when you holed the poor old box—but then we come along with the *Swallow*. What would you have done if we hadn't been so handy with our carpentry, huh? My God, I think Hudson of the *Peacock* was right, after all—you was set to seize the *Swallow* like the goddamned pirates that you are!"

"Don't be so sure that it hasn't happened!" Joel Hammond flashed from where he crouched with Annabelle's corpse in his arms. "Those bloody sealers are determined to get a ship of their own, and I think they'll find Rochester an easier target than Nat Palmer!"

My God, thought Wiki. It was a confirmation of all his misgivings about taking the *Annawan* crew on board. There might be just eight in the sealing gang—but because Smith had taken six hands and he himself had stayed behind there were only nine *Swallow* men left. He turned round to Forsythe and said urgently, "George can't be more than a day's sail away."

He saw Forsythe cast a glance at the sky. The day was growing to a close and the storm was threatening on the horizon, but the southerner nodded and lifted his voice to hail his men. The cutter arrived, and he jumped down into it.

Wiki looked at Robert Festin, and said, "You'd better come with us." His life wasn't worth much if he remained, he thought. Obviously, Festin agreed. The cutter danced on the water a long way below, but without a word he took a deep breath and jumped.

Within an hour they were through the shoals and reefs. The forbidding silhouette of the fort was on the sternward horizon, along with the reassuring flicker of the U.S. flag that they'd left behind, and then they were out in the open sea. As dusk fell Forsythe moved, breaking a long, long silence.

"Goddamn it," he said. "She was such a good-looking woman."

"Aye," said Wiki. His cheeks were wet.

"So they plan to seize the *Swallow*, eh?" Forsythe said broodingly. "Wa'al, we'll soon put a stop to that," he said, and the cutter raced on through the night toward the threatening storm.

Epilogue

ive days later the cutter finally raised the expedition fleet. They had been the longest and worst days of the whole of Wiki's seafaring career. The northeast wind had blown hard, and the seas had risen high while the rain streamed down. With nine of them in the thirty-foot boat, life had been cramped in the extreme, with just about as much daily exercise as taken by a chicken in a shell. The cutter had jinked and bounced so unevenly that they had been forced to relieve themselves in a bucket and then tip it over the side, and with the sternward half of the boat open to the elements all the time they were under sail, not only had the men been constantly drenched, but the provisions were soaking wet, as well.

There were two berths tucked under the decking that had been built up to the foremost of the two masts, but after Wiki had tried one out he had known exactly why Forsythe and Kingman had come on board the brig *Swallow* each night of the passage out to Shark Island. They were six feet long and just twenty inches at the widest part, but the worst was the utter lack of headroom; because the decking was so close to his nose he was forced to lie on his back, as there was not enough space to accommodate his shoulders if he lay on his side. After half an hour of jouncing painfully on his backbone, Wiki had gladly given the berth over to one of the others, and wished him better luck with snatching a little slumber.

Worst of all was his state of mind, swinging from ominous thoughts of the *Swallow* at the mercy of the sealers, to the dismal notion that the expedition fleet had finished the charting job and was on the way to Rio, which would mean that they were steering in the wrong direction. However, on the fifth day, that particular fear was put to rest with the sight of towering canvas on the horizon.

As if the spirits were amusing themselves at the cutter's men's expense, the weather was fair, with a steady breeze to fill the sails, and the sea as smooth as any sailor could wish. Being so low in the water, they were almost upon the fleet by the time they spied the *Vincennes,* so that within minutes they could count the ships—six of them, six! Wiki could hardly believe it—both the *Swallow* and the *Flying Fish* were there!

Forsythe, characteristically, ordered one of the swivel guns manned, and so the cutter joined the fleet in a thunder of noise and smoke as all the ships returned the rolling salute. The brig *Swallow* was tucked close to the stern of the flagship *Vincennes,* as dashing and pretty as if she had never left her post, rising high above the cutter as Forsythe, at the tiller, rounded up to her stern to a chorus of hip-hurrahs. A rope immediately dropped. Wiki jumped, grabbed it, and was hauled up and over the rail by Sua, his brown face broader than ever with his welcoming grin.

Wiki couldn't believe that the brig could look so wonderfully natural. George Rochester was there, shaking his hand and hitting him on the shoulder as if he wanted to dislocate his arm, while Midshipman Keith gleefully hovered about. Forsythe arrived over the gangway then, followed by the cutter's men, with Robert Festin bashfully bringing up the rear. Everyone was shouting deliriously at once, and no one was making sense. After five days spent bouncing about in the cutter, to Wiki the *Swallow* looked and felt *huge*— the two masts rose higher than he remembered, the rigging was a loftier web, and the deck was so stable and *safe*. The sense of reprieve and celebration was overwhelming—and then a horribly familiar voice echoed from the deck of the *Vincennes*.

It was Captain Wilkes, a glittering figure on the poop, with his speaking trumpet to his lips, and his first lieutenant and his purser beside him. "Lieutenant Forsythe, at long last I see you—and you, too, Mr. Coffin!" he bawled, and his first lieutenant howled through another trumpet, "Toe the line for inspection!"

Wiki, with Forsythe and the cutter's men, shuffled along the line that had been painted on the deck of the *Swallow* for the random inspections that Captain Wilkes loved to carry out in the name of discipline. As the distant spyglass scanned the parlous state of the cutter's crew in merciless detail, and the man who wielded it ranted on at length about their horrible appearance, Wiki became acutely aware that he, like his eight companions, stank to high heaven. His clothes, like theirs, were filthy, and had dried in untidy creases. Because of his mother's heritage Wiki scarcely ever needed to shave, but the rest had grown wild salt-stiffened stubble that stuck out like porcupine quills.

"And what the hell have you been doing, Mr. Coffin?" Wilkes demanded, turning his attention from the cutter's men. "Your duty was to report back from your mission without a moment's delay—and yet

I had to send Lieutenant Smith in the *Flying Fish* to remind you of your obligations! Lieutenant Forsythe—what is your excuse for your late arrival, sir? Both the *Swallow* and the *Flying Fish* rejoined us more than forty-eight hours ago! Have you been vacationing? Using the cutter as your personal yacht? Cruising the coast as your fancy commands? Smarten yourselves up, both of you, and report to the *Vincennes* on the instant!"

Then, at long last, the speaking trumpet was lowered, the tall, hectoring figure disappeared into the after house on the flagship, and Rochester's remarkably kindly voice ordered the victims of the verbal assault to stand down. Forsythe, his expression wearily sardonic, took himself off to his stateroom to clean up. The cutter's men, too, disappeared in the direction of food, coffee, and fresh water, taking Robert Festin with them. Wiki, however, stopped firmly on deck, being too riven with curiosity to contemplate anything else. Rochester was full of questions, but he didn't pay attention to any of them yet, being too full of urgent queries himself.

"The sealers," he demanded. "Where are they?"

"Gone," said Midshipman Keith, grinning widely. "Departed, sir, departed."

"But where?"

"Lawrence J. Smith came on board, gathered them up, and took them on board the *Vincennes*, intent on claiming all the credit," said George. "I tagged along as a kind of Greek chorus."

"So how did Captain Wilkes take the news that they had been to the Antarctic continent already?"

"Badly, judging by his expression, but he didn't have a chance to speak for quite a long while—that pompous little prawn belongs on the stage of a lecture theater, not the quarterdeck of a ship. By the time Smith had run to a stop, Wilkes had recovered his composure.

He greeted them with remarkably professional courtesy—and then he assigned them all about the fleet."

"They're to join the expedition?" Wiki exclaimed.

"Exactly," George returned. "That is what Wilkes, in his wisdom, has decreed. Three of 'em are on the *Vincennes*, three on the *Peacock*, and two on the *Porpoise*—and they have strict orders to share their knowledge of sailing in iceberg-ridden seas with as many of the expedition hands as possible."

"My God," said Wiki. This boded badly for the future, he mused.

"Appalling thought, ain't it, considering their record of inciting desertion. All we can do is thank Old Scratch that the *Swallow* wasn't considered grand enough to be favored with their presence."

Wiki shook his head wonderingly. "And I had such terrible prognostications about them seizing the *Swallow*. Thank God I was wrong."

"Oh, but I am quite certain that you were right," Rochester assured him.

"Their insistence on keeping their tool chests with them in the fo'c'sle was particularly ominous," said Midshipman Keith gravely.

"Jack Winter had the absolute sauce to reassign poor Stoker to the position of cook, so he could take over the pantry," said George. "I soon put a stop to that! I didn't relish that troublemaker being so close to my quarters. I couldn't have slept at night, knowing he was lurking about the after accommodations."

"And they had a nasty habit of muttering together while they looked around the brig," Constant Keith said darkly.

"Arrogant lot," said George, and nodded. "That bo'sun, Folger, is a particularly dangerous-looking cove, and that lad of his, Boyd, has a most suspicious look."

"We held particular fears about their actions at night, the *Swallow* folks in the fo'c'sle being so outnumbered," contributed Midshipman Keith. "However," he said smugly, "we foiled 'em, Mr. Coffin, we foiled 'em magnificently. Mind you," he added, "they made it easy."

"And how was that?" said Wiki bemusedly.

"They sent a deputation to the cabin saying they refused to berth in the same fo'c'sle as godless Indians!"

Wiki said incredulously, "They objected to living in the same fo'c'sle as Sua and Tana?"

"Aye. Then Sua and Tana got into a huff and informed me they would rather sleep in the boats in the davits than live in the same quarters as ignorant *papalagi*," said George. "Which was followed by a deputation from the *Swallow* hands declaring that they would refuse duty if Tana and Sua were forced to leave their rightful berths, and a dreadful ruckus commenced."

"And you said that made it *easy* for you?"

"We took all the *Swallow* men out of the fo'c'sle and made them look for berths elsewhere, which left the sealers in full possession," quoth George, his expression complacent.

"You gave way to the sealers' demands?" Wiki incredulously demanded.

"That's how we forestalled their foul design."

Said Midshipman Keith smugly, "It was my plan—though it was our carpenter who did the work. During all the fuss he quietly bolted a cleat on each side of the fo'c'sle door, and fashioned a bar to fit in the cleats. Then we gave the sealers a watch below in the fo'c'sle, seeing as it was now their private room—and barred the door as soon as they was all inside. They made a bit of a racket at first, but when we didn't pay any attention they soon quieted down."

Wiki's face was creasing up with an incredulous grin. "You *imprisoned* them—until Lieutenant Smith arrived on board to carry them to Captain Wilkes?"

"Exactly," George agreed. "And warned 'em before we let them out that we would tell Captain Wilkes the entire story if they made any complaint."

Forsythe arrived back on deck at that moment, obviously ready to head over to the *Vincennes* and face the worst, but Wiki was laughing too much to notice. "Well done, Midshipman," he said, sobering at last. "What made you think of it?"

"Aha, Mr. Coffin, you taught me yourself, sir, that improvisation is the soul of seamanship."

Suggested Reading

Erskine, Charles. *Twenty Years Before the Mast: with the more thrilling scenes and incidents while circumnavigating the globe under the command of the late Admiral Charles Wilkes 1838–1842.* Washington, D.C.: Smithsonian Institution, 1985.

Philbrick, Nathaniel. *Sea of Glory: America's Voyage of Discovery, the U.S. Exploring Expedition 1838–1842.* New York: Viking, 2003.

Reynolds, William. *The Private Journal of William Reynolds: United States Exploring Expedition, 1838–1842.* Edited by Nathaniel Philbrick and Thomas Philbrick. New York: Penguin, 2004.

Reynolds, William. *Voyage to the Southern Ocean: The Letters of Lieutenant William Reynolds from the U.S. Exploring Expedition, 1838–1842.* Edited by Anne Hoffman Cleaver and E. Jeffrey Stann (and with an excellent introduction and epilogue by Herman J. Viola). Annapolis, Md.: Naval Institute Press, 1988.

Stanton, William. *The Great United States Exploring Expedition of 1838–1842.* Berkeley, Calif.: University of California Press, 1975.

Viola, Herman J., and Carolyn Margolis, eds. *Magnificent Voyagers: The U.S. Exploring Expedition, 1838–1842.* Washington, D.C.: Smithsonian Institution, 1985.

Wilkes, Charles. *Narrative of the United States Exploring Expedition.* 5 vols. 1844. Reprint, Upper Saddle River, N.J.: Gregg Press, 1970.

As Wiki sails toward Brazil, he has no idea of the amazing adventure fate and the winds have conjured up....

In Joan Druett's third seafaring mystery, Wiki meets his father by a stroke of fate. The chance encounter sets in motion a series of events that leave two men dead and his father the prime suspect. Wiki must clear his name and unmask the real killers, before the expedition sails on—leaving his father at the mercy of an unforgiving Brazilian court.

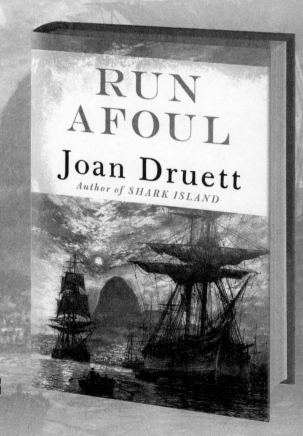

RUN AFOUL

Joan Druett

Author of SHARK ISLAND

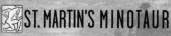

ST. MARTIN'S MINOTAUR

www.joan.druett.gen.nz
www.minotaurbooks.com